1

The
DEAD
PASS

The
DEAD
PASS

Colin
Bateman

headline

First published in Great Britain in 2014 by
HEADLINE PUBLISHING GROUP

1

Cataloguing in Publication Data is available from the British Library

Hardback ISBN 978 1 4722 0123 2
Trade paperback ISBN 978 1 4722 0124 9

Typeset in Meridien by Palimpsest Book Production Limited, Falkirk, Stirlingshire

Printed and bound in Great Britain by
CPI Group (UK) Ltd, Croydon, CR0 4YY

HEADLINE PUBLISHING GROUP
An Hachette UK Company
338 Euston Road
London NW1 3BH

www.headline.co.uk
www.hachette.co.uk

For Isaac

Prologue

Nothing worse than a muscle-bound guy gone to seed, big still but flabby, labouring for breath at the slightest exertion. And this isn't the slightest exertion: it's Billy the Bear running full pelt across the sand, the endless sand, in the dark, hardly even a star in the sky. He keeps looking back, and there's pinpricks of light behind him; they're holding up their mobile phones, either to see better or the bastards are trying to film the chase, the hunt, the execution.

Billy knows his number is up, but he's not going to give in, not till there's nothing left. He needs the cavalry, he needs a tidal wave. He needs divine intervention, but that's unlikely, not after what he's done, seen, aided and abetted and commissioned; there's blood on his hands. So much blood. There's salt in the air, the freezing bite of autumn wind, a howl that will cover up his screams. As he pads slower, and slower, he feels twin ruts in the sand; he knows what they are, he watches them some weekends, cutting up the smooth expanse of the beach here at Benown, kite-surfing capital of the north-west. If he'd one of *them* now, he'd outpace them for sure, but not like this, not like this. He barely had thirty metres on them at the start; now he can almost feel their feet thumping into the sand, feel the vibrations. They're close enough to shoot him, but they don't want that, they want the pleasure of the capture, the begging, the muzzle to the side of the head, the pull of the trigger, the ecstasy of the explosion.

How did it come to this? That it all ends here?

Less than an hour ago he was dancing, dancing in Derry. Big man dancing. And loving it. Crushed up, with a poppers chaser, then taking it hard upstairs in the dark room. But it's never enough, never a-fucking-nuff. He let himself be talked into going outside, promise of a proper shag in a hotel room, shoulda guessed something was up when the guy tells him they're driving to the hotel when he knows it's just around the corner. But there's a bottle of whiskey in the back, so he takes a swig, takes another, and is just enjoying the heat when the doors open and fellas get in either side of him and put metal to his head, and they fucking have him. Nothing said beyond 'All right, Billy,' and then they were off and driving and Billy knew it wasn't going to end well but he couldn't focus, couldn't work out if the driver was the honeytrap, offering up his arse, or if he was doing someone else in the dark and the driver just pulled him out of there on the promise of more, better, harder, longer, the fucking usual. Someone said to him once, 'Ah, Billy, always thinkin' with your dick,' and that was before they knew he was gay or whatever the hell he was. They were right, of course. Billy the Bear let his dick take him all roads: any port in a storm.

With all the drink and the shit and all the corners and maybe even the fear he threw up over himself. They all swore and the windows came down on both sides of him and it was exactly what he needed, the upchuck and the cold night air, and by the time they were skirting the beach his head was pretty clear. But he kept it down and bowed and groaned and moaned so when they got there and hauled him out they didn't even have their fucking weapons up, thought he was some fucking pansy ripe for the slaughter, but he surprised them all right; you didn't get to live this long in his world without being able to pull one out of the fire, and he did surely, bringing his fist up on one, near breaking his neck his head snapped back so fast, and then he was out and running, up on to a low wall and thump down on to the sand and just fucking charging.

But now they're getting closer, closer. He can hear them laughing above the wind, egging each other on, and then there's a crack and something whistles past him. He knows there's not much more strength in him. He's been zigzagging all over but now his legs are so heavy they're hardly moving. He can hardly catch a breath. There's only the sea in front of him, only the sea.

3

1

It was one of those days, one of those days when it's near dark by lunchtime, the rain teeming out of the heavens, traffic backed up and pumping all along the Lisburn Road, a pain in my head from the air pressure, stagnation and Jameson's, two cases to be working on and none of them as interesting as the cobweb on the high ceiling and the bluebottle helplessly caught in it; I was thinking about age, love, sex, sex, food and the health benefits that come with drinking seven cans of Diet Coke a day when the phone rang and a voice I recognised said: 'Well, you're a grandad.'

It was a lie, a damn lie, but I knew it meant I had to drag myself over to the hospital to make smiley at a barely sixteen-year-old Lolita with a bouncing babe, and her proud ex-druggie one-legged teenage lover, and the ex-Mrs S. with her worried-happy-beaming-lovely eyes, and wonder how the hell I'd ended up outside of but eternally connected to any of them. The only thing they had in common, apart from a weird mathematical sense that they belonged together, was that they all found me despicable or annoying or embarrassing or tragic, except when they required money, when I suddenly became their best chum, their rock, an inspiration, and now a fucking grandad to be sucked dry. I had to go pretend that I had the slightest interest, and pick up a book token or a pot plant or gold or Frankenstein or mare on the way, or maybe I'd just take the IKEA cot I'd lovingly assembled over the past week in my office but which I now realised was too fucking wide to get out of the door. Physics really fucks me off. If it was small enough to get in then it should be small enough to get out. Maybe life doesn't work like that, but it fucking should because I was stuck, stuck, stuck and my cot, which might once have caused my triangle of grief to look at me in a more favourable light, was not for moving. I would have to take it apart, but then reassembling it would be all but impossible because not only had it proved fiendishly complicated to put the bastard together in the first place, but immediately following my triumph I had torn the instructions into a thousand pieces and flushed them down the toilet and said ha! So I was nodding down at the cot, swearing and thinking that it would actually be simpler and quicker to get the builders in to widen the doorway, when a woman's voice said from down the hall, 'Are you the private detective?'

And I said, 'Well I'm not the fucking furniture remover, that's for sure,' before I even looked at her, but then followed it up with: 'There's a buzzer at the bottom of the stairs you're supposed to press.'

'The door was open,' she said, and with that my security was breached again and my fate sealed, etc. etc. It was hard to tell how old she was, what with the energy-saving bulb halfway down the hall that seemed to hurl out dark matter, but first impressions had her south of ninety and north of sixty. She was a little old woman, with a sad face that got sadder as she got closer. She was wearing a trouser suit that might have been fashionable in the seventies, or at least for sale. She said, 'I'm looking for Dan Starkey.'

I said, 'He's just popped out, he'll be back in an hour.'

'Oh,' she said. 'Maybe I'll wait.'

I said, 'Sorry. An hour, possibly two.'

'But I've come all the way from Derry, on the bus.'

I said, 'Do you have an appointment?'

She shook her head. I put my hands on the cot and gave it a shake. I said, 'What brings you all the way from Londonderry?'

'My son,' she said. 'I'm looking for my son.'

I said, 'I'm not sure he's much good on missing persons. He prefers the higher-profile cases. International intrigue, religious cults, fate of nations, shit like that.'

'I don't mean that kind of missing,' the old woman said. 'I don't think he's run away or lost his mind or anything like that. I think he's been murdered.'

I gave her another look. I said, 'And why would you think that?'

'Because,' she said right back, 'he's in the murder business.'

2

I make a habit of grabbing any and every excuse not to do the right thing, which in this case was going to see what was likely to become my step-grandchild, helpless and gurgling in hospital, instead of wasting my time with a rain-damp old woman who'd taken an eighty-mile bus ride to see me. It's the nature of me. And I don't mean in a good way. But I am a helpless slave to avoidance. So I said to the woman that I'd try and track Dan Starkey down and if she wanted to pop into the café across the road I was pretty sure he'd be down shortly.

'Order a pot of tea for yourself,' I said, 'and a Diet Coke and two German biscuits.'

'I don't like German biscuits.'

'They're not for you,' I said. But I gave her the wiseacre smile I had perfected over the years, calculated to charm and defuse any situation; you would have thought that over those years I might have realised that actually it doesn't have that effect, that usually it makes matters worse. But no, only in retrospect. But I'm a great one for perseverance, as bad guys usually discover, so I kept at the smiling even though she wasn't getting it at all. Maybe she had her mind on other things. She nodded at me, then trundled off.

I stared at the cot some more. Then I gave it a bloody good kick. This didn't make it any smaller, though it did cause two wooden bars to splinter; if ever I did get to hand it over to the youngsters, they would presume I'd rescued it from a skip. Even though they didn't have a penny to their name and were largely dependent on Starkey charity, they would look at me with disdain and moan about what a cheapskate I was.

So I gave it another kick.

Then I grabbed up the screwdriver and took the rest of it apart. It took ten minutes. I walked down the hall to the storeroom and rescued the original packaging I'd stuffed there and put the components back in their box, then struggled down the stairs with it and outside into the rain. It felt heavier than it had when I'd brought it up to the office. Maybe disappointment, frustration and embarrassment were adding a few pounds. From his doorway, my friendly neighbourhood butcher Joe said, 'Can I give you a hand?' and then pre-empted my response by giving me a slow handclap. I would have told him where to go, but he had access to a large range of carving knives and cleavers and a criminal record as long as his heavily tattooed arms, so I gave him a 'Ha!'

and struggled on to the car. I set the box down and opened the boot. I loaded it in.

I sauntered back down the alley. Joe was still in position. He said, 'I hear you're a grandad.'

'You're very well informed,' I said.

'Twitter,' he replied.

'Fuck sake,' I said.

'Aye.'

He turned back inside. I crossed the road. The café was bare-bones basic, which was fine by me. It had become my home from broken home. They were used to me bringing my clients in. They'd whine, I'd dine. It was the business I was in.

As I sat at the table, Diet Coke and German biscuits in place, I put my hand out to the woman and said, 'Sorry, I'm Dan Starkey.'

'But you . . .'

'I usually refuse to recognise myself, it's a defence mechanism.'

'A . . .?'

'In case you're Rosa Klebb, sent to assassinate me. Not that you look like Rosa Klebb.'

Though she did.

'Rosa . . .?'

By way of distraction I lifted a biscuit and bit into it. I have a sweet tooth. Just one, thanks to having a sweet tooth. I now boast a rather fetching set of slightly too white top-row crowns. I bought them with some of the fee I received for my last case, which involved a teenage Messiah and a religious cult called the New Seekers, who were still growing apace. The waitress behind the counter had lately taken to sporting the NS emblem and now rarely laughed at my jokes.

'And you are?'

'Moira, Moira Doherty.' She put her hand out. Liver spots. 'And I have no intention of assassinating you.'

'That's what they all say.' She took a sip of her tea. I said, 'You came all the way from Londonderry just to see me?'

'No. I mean, not exactly. I came to see a woman, a journalist, at the *Belfast Telegraph*, and she suggested I talk to you.'

'Ah,' I said. 'Would this woman happen to be called Sara – Sara Patterson?'

'Yes . . . how did you . . .?'

'We're old frenemies. And did she speak fondly of me?'

'She said you were tricky . . .'

'Tricky . . .?'

'. . . and expensive, but if I offered you half as much as you wanted you would probably do it.'

'Well you've shot yourself in the foot there.'

'How do you mean?'

'Well, knowing that, I'll double my price and then make it look like I'm being nice and end up doing it for what I would normally get.'

'And what do you normally get?'

'Three hundred a day plus expenses.'

'Well then I'll offer you one hundred and fifty a day and half of your expenses.'

'Dammit, you have outfoxed me.'

'Or you may have outfoxed me, Mr Starkey.'

'And you'll never know.'

I lifted the side plate and offered her the remaining German biscuit.

She hesitated, then took it. 'I really don't like them, but I did pay for it after all.' She fixed me with a look. 'I imagine you *are* tricky, Mr Starkey . . .'

'Dan, please . . .'

'But I think tricky is exactly what I need.'

She set the biscuit down beside her. 'I will keep it for the bus home.'

'Sounds like a plan,' I said. When she did not immediately speak I showed her my palms and said, 'Fire away.'

This, finally, and unexpectedly, produced a smile. It made her look less like Rosa Klebb and more like Judi Dench. I said, 'What?'

She said, 'Shot yourself in the foot, fire away – your language is grounded in violence. It's quite appropriate, actually. My son is Billy Doherty.'

'The drummer with the Undertones?'

'No, different Billy Doherty. Billy the Bear.'

'Billy the Bear,' I said. 'Right. Though I can think of many reasons to murder a drummer, I'm afraid I haven't heard of Billy the Bear.'

I was thinking that Sara Patterson might have fobbed a nut off on me.

'Billy is my son. He was a big kid, and just kept getting bigger. They called him Billy the Bear when he was in prison and it kind of stuck.'

'Prison,' I said.

'Off and on. Last time he was six weeks on remand in Magilligan.'

A low- to medium-security prison outside of Londonderry. I knew the government had been promising to shut it down for years, mostly because it was old and decrepit and laid out in politically uncomfortable H-blocks, but somehow it endured.

'Might I ask what he was in for?'

'Drugs.'

'Taking, stealing, dealing, manufacturing?'

'Yes,' she said. 'And a gun.'

'Okay. Is he or has he ever been part of an illegal organisation?'

'Yes, the IRA, the original version, not those . . . *boys* who call themselves the Ra these days.'

'Okay,' I said. 'And nowadays? Gangster, community worker or politician?'

'The former.'

'Okay. And now you suspect he has been murdered.'

'I know he has been murdered.'

'And how do you . . .?'

'Because he hasn't been seen for two weeks, and that's not my boy. And there's this . . .' She lifted her handbag up on to the table, unknowingly setting it on top of the German biscuit. She produced an iPhone. She pressed a couple of buttons and turned the screen to show me a photo: I saw what had once been the end of a street of terraced houses, but the houses themselves were no more, leaving just a lovingly preserved gable end. I recognised it instantly, because it was famous, infamous, a symbol of everything that had been and perhaps still was. Huge letters were plastered across it:

YOU ARE NOW ENTERING FREE DERRY.

It had been a rallying point, a symbol of defiance, an inspiration or an antagonism. And now it was a tourist attraction, first stop on a Bogside terror tour of legenDerry.

'Sweet,' I said, 'but I don't see what . . .?'

'Oh, sorry,' said Mrs Doherty, 'I just need to . . .'

She turned the screen towards her and then used two fingers to enlarge part of the photo. She nodded again, satisfied, and turned the screen back to me.

It was the bottom left corner of the wall. Someone had spray-painted:

BILLY THE BEAR, RIP.

She said, 'That's why I'm sure.'

'But it might only be graf—'

'No. Do you know Derry at all?'

'Not—'

'It's like posting a royal birth outside Buckingham Palace; no one puts anything on there without it being ratified. It's the gospel truth.'

'Okay,' I said, 'if you insist. And what exactly is it that you want me to do?'

She sat back. She sighed. 'Do you know something, Mr Starkey? I wasn't exactly sure what I wanted when I got on the bus this morning. Just someone to do something. I've tried the Ra themselves, new and old,

I've tried the police, the local papers, and I've trekked all the way down here to talk to the *Telegraph*, but nobody seems particularly interested. It was only when I was standing in your hall across the way, when I saw what you were doing, that I realised what I really need.'

'What was I doing apart from swearing?'

'You were standing over a cot and looking very, very sad.'

'Angry,' I said.

'No. You were sad. I know that look, that feeling. I knew then what I wanted, and it's very simple. I just want my baby back.'

3

Maybe I should have heard of Billy the Bear, but I had a hard enough time keeping up with what was going on in Belfast without having to keep tabs on our second city, our Maiden City. I knew the streets of Belfast like the back of my hand, and the streets of Londonderry like the sole of my foot. That is, I was aware that it was there, had seen it a few times, but wasn't overly familiar with it. All I really knew was that it had once been subject to a siege and stood firm against King James, it had a wall around its old city, and it had been the cradle, or crucible, of our Troubles. More recently it had been declared UK City of Culture, which had proved as divisive as thirty years of internecine warfare, if not quite as bloody. I would hesitate to ever describe Belfast as my comfort zone, but if I was forced into it, then Londonderry was definitely outside of it.

So I said no.

Made an excuse, too busy.

And gave her a lift to the bus station on Great Victoria Street because I felt a bit sorry for her and it was miserable outside.

Except by the time we got there I'd talked myself into a maybe, and she was so grateful I graduated to a probably. She said she didn't have much in the way of money, but she could possibly afford a week of my time if I charged her half my normal rate. She said it with a smile and I laughed. I said I wouldn't charge until I'd established what was involved. She had her handbag in her lap, and was peering inside it. Then she checked her pockets.

She said, 'Did I not pick up that biscuit?'

I said nothing, though I could see it was still stuck to the bottom of her bag. She delved inside the bag and this time produced a photo and handed it across. 'This is Billy,' she said.

It was her son, sitting on a stool in a bar. He was in a vest top that emphasised his gut; his arms were sunburned up to where the arms of a T-shirt would have started, and there was a similar V around his neck; there was a sombrero on the wall behind him and assorted optics; also, an Irish flag. Billy was indeed a bear of a man. He was holding a pint up and grinning. He had his free arm draped around the shoulders of a younger man, topless, tanned, muscled and grinning.

Mrs Doherty said, 'We were in Portugal. We loved that holiday. He was so good to me.'

'Who's this?' I asked, finger on the other guy.

'He worked in the bar. Billy was larger than life. He

made friends everywhere he went.' She pursed her lips. She closed her handbag. It was still raining and for several moments her eyes followed the shift of the wipers. Then she turned to me. She said, 'Mr Starkey, don't get me wrong, I know my son did many bad things, and I probably don't know a tenth of them, but all I can do, all I can keep in my heart are the many good things he did, for me, for his friends. He is my son. He was my son. The very least a mother can expect is to be able to think fondly of her son. She should die before her son does. And if that isn't to be, then she should be able to mourn him properly. Have you ever lost anyone very close to you?'

'Yes, I have.'

'Then you will know.' She put a hand on mine, where it was resting on the steering wheel. 'And I know you'll do your best.'

Her eyes were wet. She climbed out of the car, bag over her arm, German biscuit still clinging on, and moved towards the station, passing without a glance the statues standing resolute outside: grandly called *Monument to the Unknown Woman Worker*, they were two beefy Belfast girls who didn't look like they'd take many prisoners. Mrs Doherty paused just before she entered the station, looked back at me, and raised her hand in a little wave. I waved back. I had a sudden thought that maybe I had just been expertly worked, but then I dismissed it. When did I get so cynical? I smiled to myself: Trish would say I was born that way. I would have said it was the day I met her.

*   *   *

I drove across town, up the Newtownards Road and out to the Ulster Hospital at Dundonald. I parked and stood staring at the boot, regretting that I hadn't taken a photo of the cot when it was up, and briefly debating whether I should take up the box with its component parts to prove that I had been thinking about the baby. And then I decided no: Trish would shake her head and say, 'You know as well as I do it will stay in the box. Like the Scalextric, always on a promise.'

The maternity wing was in a high-tech new build off to the left of the main hospital. When I reached the first floor there was a nurse on the desk with a smile that was not welcoming. She wanted to know if I was immediate family and I said, 'Well that's the sixty-four-thousand-dollar question.' She looked at me like I was mental and asked point blank if I was family again and it was on the tip of my tongue to say I was the grandad but I couldn't quite, so we looked at each other for what seemed like a long time, at least until the door opened behind her and Trish was standing there saying, 'Well?' So I made eyes at the nurse and she said, 'Only two visitors at a time.' I said, 'What difference does three make?' and she said they were the rules. Trish said for me to go on in, she needed some fresh air. I said, 'How did it go?' and she said, 'Bloody.' I said, 'How are the foundlings?' and she rolled her eyes. 'Just be nice,' she said. 'I'm always nice,' I said and she rolled them again. I looked at the nurse and she said, 'Third room on the left.'

Third room on the left, the door was open. Lolita

was breastfeeding. Bobby was reading an Xbox maga-
zine. His eyes flitted up and he grunted. Lolita smiled
and said, 'Hello you.'

She was sixteen, and not a blood relative, and breastfeeding was the most natural thing in the world, but
also she was sixteen, not a blood relative, and she was
called Lolita, so I didn't quite know where to look.

I said, 'Hi. Hello. How're you doing?' while gazing
at her forehead.

She said, 'Well my crack's up like a bap, but otherwise
pretty good. Do you want to hold him?'

I swallowed and said, 'He appears to be busy.'

'Oh, he's been off and on all morning. A bit like
his da.'

Bobby snorted, I reddened.

'In a minute, maybe,' I said. 'Does your mum know
the good news?'

Lol shrugged. The baby released the nipple. I studied
the car park outside. Lol's mum had joined the New
Seekers and did not approve of her situation. Lol and
Bobby both lived with Trish. And with the birth I now
realised that the triangle had become a square. Or a
rectangle. Or a rhombus. It was difficult to say which,
but I knew it would change things. It would either
squeeze me out further or suck me right in.

I said, 'Someone should tell her. She'll come round.'

'Yes, and Jesus will come somersaulting through the
door after her.'

'I'm not sure it's Jesus that's the problem,' I said.

'How do you mean?'

'Nothing.' The whole thing about the teenage Messiah wasn't fully out there yet, and it wasn't the time or the place. When I looked back down at Lol, she had made herself decent and was holding the baby up to me. 'Take him,' she said.

I was all butterfingers, but I cradled him in my arms and said, 'Hello, wee man.'

Lol said, 'I was thinking about calling him Dan.'

Bobby said, 'Over my dead body.'

I said, 'There's no need for that' to Lol, while beaming.

'Fucking right,' said Bobby.

'Joe the Butcher sends his best,' I said.

'Maybe we'll call him Joe,' said Bobby.

'Or Butch,' said Lol, and they both giggled.

I handed him back.

He wasn't my flesh, or blood. He was the unplanned offspring of a teenage Lolita called Lolita, and a screwed-up druggie whose mum had been murdered and whose leg had been lost, and they were probably planning to bleed me dry for the next twenty years.

But I felt a little moist in the eye.

I said, 'Someone once named a horse after me.'

Lol said, 'Was it a good horse?'

'It won a few races, then got put out to stud.'

'Story of your life,' said Bobby.

Trish was waiting in the hall outside.

She said, 'Cute, huh?'

I said, 'Yup, the baby's nice too.'

She said, 'Ha.'

I said, 'You're going to have your hands full.'

'Sure what else would I be doing?'

'How about your job?'

'The hours are harder to come by, and I'm bored with it.'

'Are you also bored with earning money?'

'No, but I have you for that.'

'In case you'd forgotten, hon, we're decree absolute.'

She nodded at me. 'Is that the way you're going to play it?'

'It's the way I could play it.'

'You're the one who brought Bobby into our family.'

'Our family. Right.'

'You know what I mean.'

I folded my arms. I said, 'The baby is cute. They seem very comfortable with him. Do you have a master plan?'

She shook her head.

'Somewhere down the line they're just going to get up and walk out, get their own place, take little Dan with them.'

'Little Dan?'

'Wasn't my suggestion. Lol's. But I've heard worse.' I gave her a smile. 'I know, she's playing me like a fucking drum.'

'Maybe we're both being played.'

'Maybe we are.'

'But I can't help myself,' said Trish.

'I know that,' I said.

4

Soon as I was back out on the road, I put the phone on speaker and poked Sara Patterson.

She answered with 'Hey, Grandad!'

I responded with 'Jesus fucking Christ.' She cackled. There was a hum in the background, quieter than in my day but still unmistakably the sound of a newspaper office in motion. Questions being fired, keyboards being caressed, and laughter. Always laughter. I said, 'Twitter has a lot to answer for and I'm not even fucking on it.'

'You should think about it, it's great. But that's not how I know. There's a photo up on Instagram.'

'Brilliant,' I said.

'And it is. He looks just like you.'

'That's impossible.'

'No it's not, you hear about it all the time, dogs looking like their master.'

'I'm not even going there.'

She laughed again. She said, 'So, what do you want? Hectic here.'

'Why, what's up?'

'Nothing, but you know how it is, in the old days everything would crank up towards deadline; now it's a rolling deadline so it's always cranked up. Does my head in.'

'Like you'd know about the old days.'

'All right, Grandad, have it your way.'

'I was just calling to thank you.'

'For . . .?'

'Sending an old biddy my way.'

'An old . . .'

'Billy the Bear.'

'Ah, right. Yes, the formidable Mrs Doherty.'

'Formidable why so?'

'Because back in your day she was a . . . well, what we call these days an activist, but back then, trouble-maker. Civil rights, nationalism, republicanism, all-round mouthpiece and agitator. Do you remember Bernadette Devlin?'

'Of course, but I'd be surprised if you do.'

'I studied her at school.'

'Christ.'

Bernadette Devlin was a firebrand who was once the youngest Member of Parliament and remembered fondly in certain circles for slapping Home Secretary Reginald Maudling in the face after his comments on Bloody Sunday.

'Well,' said Sara, 'Moira Doherty was like Bernadette's little sister; not quite as well known on the national scene and more of a back-room operator, but everyone in Derry knows her. She's been involved in everything and pretty much everyone thinks she knows where, as they say, all the bodies are buried.'

'Except for that of her son.'

'Except for that of her son. Exactly.'

'Brilliant,' I said. 'And here's me thinking she was just some sweet old dear.'

'She comes across that way. But she was definitely a bit of a tornado in her day. She's just mellowed with age.'

'So why'd you pass her along to me? Why didn't you run with it?'

'I tried to, took it upstairs, but they're not really interested. Starting a campaign to look for the body of an ex-IRA man at the behest of his Republican mother when there are still innocent bodies buried out there they're refusing to give up? They wouldn't touch it with a bargepole.'

'Then why should I?'

'I thought you might need the work.'

'I'm coming down with work, as it happens.'

'Then blow her off. I was just thinking of you.'

'If only I could believe that.'

I drummed my fingers on the steering wheel. I was a turn away from the office.

I said, 'Why wouldn't she say anything about her background? Didn't she think I'd find out?'

'Maybe she presumed you knew and were being diplomatic. Though it wouldn't be like you. Or maybe she wanted to suck you into it first. I told her you were a good man with a good heart.'

'You told her I was tricky.'

'And so you are, but that doesn't mean your heart isn't in the right place. Sometimes.'

I said, 'If it smells like trouble, it probably is trouble. I don't need trouble. Not at my time of life, not with my new responsibilities.'

'No, you don't, Grandad. Maybe it's time to sit back, take the easy ones, look after your family. There's no need to rage against the dying of the light, Starkey, no need at all.'

I gave that due consideration.

Then I said, 'You bitch.'

Sara cackled again and hung up.

5

The apartment was scrupulously clean. Dishes done, carpet vacuumed, every glass in its place. It smelled of Pine Fresh. I listened to the silence.

It wasn't that I craved company, but its absence was starting to gnaw at me.

My apartment at St Anne's Court, in the heart of the Cathedral Quarter, overlooks a lovely square and the Mac, a theatre that competes with the Lyric on the other side of town for the hearts and minds of Belfast's culture vultures. It was one of the selling points the estate agent was particularly big on when I was looking at the place. My response was along the lines of a silent 'Could I give a fuck?' I just wanted somewhere to put my head down at the end of the working day, somewhere to retreat to after a night in the Bob Shaw around the corner, somewhere to entice a string of incredibly gorgeous lovers, somewhere I could leave crisp bags lying around without someone harping at me to pick them up, some-where I could use one finger to swing my underpants round my head and fire them off in any damn direction I liked before I went to bed so that they would still be there in the morning, or in a month, and it would make not a damn bit of difference to anyone. I could watch football until the early hours, and if I chose to do a sit-up, there wouldn't be anyone snorting in derision in the background.

These were all the things I started out doing.

Trish had said I was living a bachelor life with her anyway, so I was bound to be better off on my own. Except the longer it went on, the more I realised that it wasn't temporary, that she wasn't going to cave in and beg me to come home, the less comfortable I became. I missed her. I missed our laughs and our sex and even our bantering arguments. I wasn't lonely, exactly. I didn't stay awake nights pining after her, but I was aware that somehow my life was off kilter. I was starting to feel uncomfortable by myself, unsettled, anxious. I was spending less time in the pub, more drinking at home. I didn't have friends. Mouse had been my bestie, but he was eight years dead. I had acquaintances I could joke with in the pub. But they were all younger. And after a while, they didn't seem to want to spend as much time in my company. They had heard my stories once too often. They didn't get the references. The last time I'd been in there I sat on a stool at the bar, my phone dead, and out of despera-tion I picked up a programme for the Mac I despised and flicked through it. I realised that I'd been to see every single production, one of them twice. In fact I had a drink-hazy recollection of a member of staff asking me if I wanted to become a 'friend' of the Mac because I was there so often. I could sponsor a seat or volunteer to work as an usher. I declined with a not so silent *fuck off*.

I made a sandwich and opened a Harp. I sat at the kitchen table. The absence of anyone chipped at me some more. I would have been happy for *someone* just to visit or squat. Even if they just sat in the spare bedroom and never came out, the very knowledge that they were there might have settled me. But there was no one, just that cool, ominous silence.

Patricia might have said, 'Well have you invited anyone?'

And no, of course not.

I texted my unlikely friend and said I was lonely.

She texted back, *Likewise*.

I poured a drink, just a little one, and opened up the laptop.

She texted, *Maybe you need a dog*.

I texted back, *Pets aren't allowed*.

Tell them it's not a pet, it's a working dog. It helps you sniff out clues.

Lol, I texted.

But not lol.

I turned to my laptop and Wikipedia for Moira Doherty. There was an image of her with flowing red hair, talking through a megaphone during the Battle of the Bogside, three days of rioting between nationalists and loyalists in 1969. She was arrested and later served a short jail term for incitement to riot. There was a photograph of her helping the wounded on Bloody Sunday, and again at the barricades as they were swept away by the British Army during Operation Motorman. She was a prominent figure in the campaign in support of the hunger strikers in the early eighties, and set up or joined what read like an endless succession of socialist-themed political movements throughout the next decade, none of which seemed to last very long. At the start of the nineties, not long after she'd given birth to Billy the Bear, she had been shot three times by a loyalist death squad that had not lived up to its name. Her wounds were relatively minor, but the incident appeared to cause her to withdraw from her life of protest and public activism. Wikipedia didn't have much to say about what she'd been up to over the past twenty years beyond a vague reference to working with community groups in Londonderry.

My unlikely friend texted: *Or a hamster. They couldn't complain about a hamster.*

Oh yes they could. They have hamster detector vans.

Billy Doherty didn't warrant an entry in Wikipedia. But there were many, many references to him on Google. He was in prison for extortion, demanding money with menaces; he was hardly out before he was back in on a two-year sentence for possessing ammunition. He was later caught with a boot full of Ecstasy tablets – his left cowboy boot – but charges were dropped on a technicality. He was questioned about an attempted murder. He was hauled in for the shooting-up of a bookmaker's office. His name was repeatedly linked to dissident Republican groups, in particular the Continuity Irish Republican Army and then its splinter group Oglaigh na hEireann. He was a Republican, a nationalist, a freedom fighter, a drug dealer, an enforcer and perhaps not very proficient at any of them, judging by the number of times he had been arrested and the years he had spent in prison. He seemed like the kind of man who would be feared, but also have very many enemies. He was a big guy with a bald head and a black beard. You couldn't miss Billy the Bear.

My unlikely friend said, *You should come and see me.*

I said, *You're far away and it's miserable out there.*

What else are you doing?

Working.

Drinking?

Barely started.

Then pour it back in and drive down.

You're not the boss of me.

Really?

6

Ballyferris Park is halfway down the Ards Peninsula, a forty-minute drive on a good day. This wasn't such a good day; it was late-afternoon dark and the winding coast road was slick with rain and little flurries of November sleet; I took my life in my hands and continued texting. Christine had picked up on the Twitter feed about little Dan; she was bored; there was more paper-work in planning for world domination than she had imagined; she was stir crazy; it was getting to the point where she could hardly walk around without getting hassled; there were a lot of crazies out there, and not just in her own organisation.

Every time I approached the gates at Ballyferris I got the willies, and I suspected the guards got them every time they were forced to nod me through; not just the guards, but every New Seeker who encountered me along the crumbling, discoloured corridors of the rambling old house or saw me out walking with Christine on some of the thousand acres they had under cereal or livestock. I felt gloriously out of place. Her right-hand man, her Rasputin, former Stormont minister and now Rev. Pike, had the biggest willy of them all, seeing as how I'd caused his original downfall, had a knack for stirring up trouble and appeared to be becoming a rival confidante of the Messiah-in-waiting. He glared and stared and fidgeted every time I crossed his eyeline, and I never seemed to be very far from it.

There was nothing pre-planned about it, my growing habit of going down to see her. It just kind of developed. My relationship with Christine went back more than a decade. I'd helped her to flee with her mum from Wrathlin Island, off our north-west coast. A rogue priest had proclaimed the little girl the new Messiah, and it had all gotten messy, then violent. Trish and I had just about escaped with our lives. Christine had dropped out of sight after that, and I'd barely thought of her for years. Then the New Seekers began to appear. At first I'd thought it was the deposed politician Pike who'd set up the church, mostly to celebrate his own wonderfulness. But then I'd discovered that it was built around the very same Christine: people were flocking to the now teenager. I hadn't yet worked out if Pike was a genuine convert or was using her the way Colonel Parker used Elvis. And I hadn't decided if Christine's talents were God-given like Elvis's clearly were, or if she was all smoke and mirrors, more like some poor Irish Liberace. But at least she had something the rest

33

of her church didn't: a sense of humour about it all, a cynicism, and a lively spark. I still didn't know if she truly believed she was the Messiah, and we got around talking about it by not really talking about it. She was a curious combination – sometimes an old head on young shoulders, other times a wide-eyed jejune caught up in something outside of her control. The fact was that I just liked talking to her. She was the only person I could discuss things with who didn't seem to have an agenda. That is, an agenda that concerned me. Her other agenda was pretty big.

There was designated parking outside the main building. There was a space with Pike's name on it and a shiny BMW with this year's registration; about a dozen other cars were parked in assigned spaces and none of them looked like they would have to be worried about facing an MOT any time soon. Christine was still too young to drive, but I was kind of intrigued as to what she would choose when the time came. If her popularity continued to grow exponentially, the manufacturers would be lining up to name a model in her honour. She'd make the Vauxhall Messiah *the* car to seen in.

I hurried through the growing sleet into the foyer. There was a reception desk these days instead of the old telephone stand, and a scanner to check for weapons. IDs had to be scrutinised, appointments verified. The happy-clappiness I'd observed during my first visit had been slowly eroded. There were a lot more heavies about. Maybe there'd been as many before but they'd been less obvious, their threat nullified by the ridiculousness of their robes; but designers had been called in, the robes were being phased out and what was very definitely a uniform had taken their place. It made the Salvation Army look like the Salvation Army.

I mentioned this to Christine and she said, 'Yeah, and we're thinking about a modern slant on the swastika.'

'You can say that to me. Say it to Pike and he'll have them stitched on by sunset.' She laughed her splendid girlie laugh, lifted her can of full-fat Coke. 'I'm serious,' I said.

'I know you are. But the robes were ridiculous.'

'That may be, it doesn't mean you have to go all Imperial Stormtrooper.'

'I think they're quite cute.'

We were in her apartment at the top of the house. A lounge, a bedroom, a study, a bathroom. Sweeping views across the fields to the sea, although most of it now obscured by a curtain of sleet. The lounge where we were sitting was austere, two sofas, a sideboard, a coffee table, some old photos of the family who'd once owned the place. Christine sat opposite me, her legs tucked under her. She looked a little sad. Her eyes were dull, her face pale and pinched.

'Are you not bored here?'

'Frequently.'

'You should get a place in Belfast. More to do.'

'Plenty to do here, my friend. Anyway, Pike doesn't like me going to town.'

'So he's calling the shots.'

'He's looking after me.'

'I should report him to social services. You're still a minor, you know.'

'With your record of looking after minors, I'm not sure they'd take you seriously.'

I gave her the fake smile.

'How is the baby?' she asked. 'A little boy.'

'All parts seem to be in working order.'

'Did you hold him?'

'I did.'

'And how did that feel?'

'Okay.'

'Okay?'

'It felt . . . grand. I don't know. What do you want me to say?'

'That you were overwhelmed with love, maybe.'

'I was overwhelmed with love. Maybe.'

'You don't ever really let yourself go, do you, Dan?'

'Yes, I do. And generally it gets me into trouble, so I try to keep it in check.'

'Well maybe you should try to loosen up a bit, enjoy the moment.'

'Says the girl locked up in her remote castle.'

'I'm not locked up anywhere.'

'Really?'

'And it's for my own protection anyway.'

'According to the Prince of Darkness.'

'Don't call him that.'

'Why, is he listening?'

'Probably.'

And he probably was.

She said, 'So tell me – what's this new case?'

'What new case?'

'You may not be aware of this, Dan, but every time you're offered a new case, a case you're not sure about, you're suddenly available to come down here, because you want to talk to me about it. I'm like your spiritual adviser.'

'I thought maybe it was the other way round.'

'I'm going to take life advice from you, Dan?'

'Why not? I'm the wee devil on your shoulder.'

'Sure I have Pike for that.' She cupped her hands over her mouth and called out: 'Only joking!'

We pretended to listen for a response.

Then we sat quietly. It was not uncomfortable. There was a lot of activity in the house and around the estate – at any one time there were hundreds of converts at work – but her little apartment was well insulated from the grind of productivity and the preparations for power. Her followers were deluded, undoubtedly, but to judge from overheard conversations, general snooping and plain-to-bloody-behold observation, they were utterly convinced of their own fabulous destiny. It was fascinating, and in equal parts frightening and funny.

She said, 'Go on, tell me about the case.'

I said, 'A woman wants me to find her son. She thinks he's been murdered up in Londonderry.'

'And?'

'She has history of being involved in stuff, and he has history, and they're altogether quite the family. I'm not sure I want to put myself through all that nonsense again.'

'All what nonsense?'

'Ah, you know, where I get excited about something but end up getting threatened, beaten up, tortured and shot at . . .'

'Especially now that you're a grandad.'

'Especially now that . . . tell me this, do you all communicate with each other behind my back, just to wind me up?'

'Yes, absolutely.'

'*Really?*'

'You'll never quite know.' Christine unfolded her legs and stood up. She took her Coke with her to the window. 'It's miserable out there,' she said.

'Doesn't seem like a barrel of laughs in here either,' I said.

She ignored that and said, 'I don't really know Derry. I, we, have not made many inroads up there. I'm told they're set in their ways, insular.'

'I don't think that's exclusive to Londonderry.'

'Case in point.'

'I'm sorry?'

'Londonderry.'

'Londonderry?'

'Dan, these days, everyone just says Derry.'

'Not everyone.'

'But you're deliberately making a point. It winds people up.'

'That's my job.'

She shook her head. 'It's little wonder people beat you up. Do you know what you really need? A guardian angel of your own. Someone to shush you when you open your stupid mouth.'

'And yet here I am, still living and breathing.' I touched my head and smiled. 'Touch wood.'

'Eventually, you know, your luck will run out.'

'Eventually. Although I'm sure God will continue to look out for me.'

'He may be busy elsewhere.'

'Well you'd know that better than me. Just – maybe this isn't the time to be disappearing to Londonderry.'

'With your new family commitments.'

'Something like that.'

'Or it's exactly the time. You'll be needing the money.'

'There's that. Though she's not offering much.'

'Well maybe I could add something to it.'

'How do you mean?'

'I told you, we haven't made many inroads up there. There's one small church that's converted, but there's a lot of local resistance, some threats, nothing too serious. Perhaps if you were up there anyway, you could look into it, see what the problems are? Maybe see what we're up against?'

'You mean like a paid ambassador of the church?'

'Something like that.'

'Like a missionary?'

'If you like. Are you interested in a missionary position, Dan?'

There was a glint in her eye that was decidedly

inappropriate, given that she was sixteen, and the daughter of God, but it was Christine all over. I said, 'I'm not working for the New Seekers.'

'I'm just trying to help.'

'And I appreciate it, but no. Once you start paying me . . .'

'What's the difference? It's a job. You work for other big concerns. Who was it last summer, the Wolff media empire, they're hardly paragons of—'

'That was different.'

'How?'

I shrugged. 'It just was. Anyway, usually I end up pissing my employers off, and I wouldn't want to get in your bad books.'

'That's . . . sweet?'

'I didn't mean it to be.'

'Well. Okay. Up to you. So what're you going to do about your case?'

'Sleep on it. I just don't know if I can summon the energy. You know, maybe I'm like a boxer who doesn't know when to hang up his gloves.'

'Or a novelist who just gets better the older he gets.'

'Name me one.'

'Look – what if God gave you a unique set of gifts that aren't that obvious to the casual observer? You agitate, Dan, and things happen. Maybe that's what your Mrs Doherty needs. Maybe she came to you because there's no one else can do what you do. You are the plumber who unblocks the system.'

'You mean I stir the shit.'

'Meaning she came to you for a reason that is not yet clear.'

'Or because I'm cheap, and she's desperate.'

'She's desperate, Dan.'

I smiled at her. But it wasn't returned. She was too young to get it.

I got up from the sofa and joined her at the window. The sleet was thickening up into snow and starting to lie. I zipped up my jacket and raised an eyebrow.

'Quite right,' said Christine. 'You wouldn't want to get marooned down here. We might convert you.'

'No,' I said, 'you wouldn't.'

The snow was already building up on the windscreen. When I got in, the car wouldn't start. I'd replaced the old one when money from the Wolff case came in. But it hadn't been a huge improvement, though part of that might have been because I hadn't had it serviced or oiled or watered since. It had been getting more temperamental as the autumn progressed, but this was the first time it had actually failed me. I got out and went back to reception and told them I needed a push.

'Don't tempt me.'

I turned to find Pike standing at the bottom of the stairs. He was wearing one of the crisp new uniforms. It didn't look different from anyone else's, which surprised me. I expected epaulettes, quite possibly medals, but no. His face was ruddy, his hair cropped short, his eyes as cold and superior as they always were.

'Rev. Pike,' I said. 'Was that a joke?'

'No,' he said.

'Was *that* a joke too?'

He ignored that and moved up beside me at the reception desk. He reached across and turned the visitors' book. He studied it for a moment, then said, 'Twenty minutes? It hardly seems worth the effort.'

'Well we do most of the personal stuff on FaceTime.'

He gave a slight, dismissive shake of his head. 'I don't like you coming down here, Starkey,' he said. 'You unsettle her.'

'I doubt that.'

'She's actually quite fragile – she's young, this is a big thing.'

'Really? Is it?'

'And I don't appreciate sarcasm.'

'Really?'

'In future, if you want to come down, you run it past my office first. Otherwise you won't get through the gates.'

'Is that so? You've checked that with her, have you?'

'It's my responsibility to look after her, Starkey, and that means shielding her from inappropriate contacts. She's a sixteen-year-old girl, and you're a middle-aged man with an alcohol problem.'

'Is that so? Is that worse than a middle-aged man with a corruption problem who keeps a sixteen-year-old girl locked up in his attic?'

Pike's eyes flitted to the receptionist, a young man doing his best to look like he was studying his computer screen, but there was a new flush to his cheeks that suggested otherwise.

'Why don't you go and wait in your vehicle, Starkey? I'll send some of my people out to see if they can get you started.'

He spun away and began to hurry down the corridor to the left of the desk.

'Thanks,' I called after him, 'appreciate it.'

He didn't respond.

7

It was gone eleven when I drove out of the underground car park at St Anne's Court; the slush had frozen up overnight, and with the sun barely making any impression it showed little sign of melting; traffic wasn't heavy, but it was slow; if it hadn't been slow I might not have glanced across at St Anne's Cathedral, or the steps leading up to it; I probably wouldn't have seen the girl in the combat jacket and the fur hat pulled down low, the girl with the rucksack hanging off one shoulder; the girl waving in my direction. I gave an embarrassed wave back, presuming she'd mistaken me for someone else, or was waving at a friend on the other side of the street; but then she jumped up and came running over and around to the passenger side, and before I could reach across and lock it against the intrusion of a nut, the door was open and she'd jumped in. She beamed at me and said, 'I've been freezing my butt off since nine, did you sleep in or something?'

I said, 'Christine – what the . . .'

She nodded ahead and said, 'Go!'

The traffic had freed up ahead of me on Donegall Street. I moved the car forward, but slowly, looking for somewhere to pull in.

'Christine – I'm on my way to Londonderry.'

'Yup, so am I!'

'What're you . . .?'

'Well you weren't keen to sort out our problems up there, so I thought I'd take a look myself.' Someone honked behind us. She glanced back, gave a little wave. 'Any objections?'

I moved the car forward, at least as far as the lights at the turn on to York Street. I stopped on red, looked at her, shook my head and said, 'You can't just—'

'Yes I can. But if you'd rather I get the bus, then I can do that, though you'll have to lend me the money. Just thought you'd like the company, seeing as how we're best buddies and all that.'

'Christine . . . no harm to you, but it's just not . . .'

'. . . appropriate for you to be taking a ride with a sixteen-year-old virgin?'

I cleared my throat. 'Yes,' I said. 'And please don't say that.'

'What, virgin?'

'Yes! Christ!'

She giggled. She pulled off her hat and shook her hair out.

'I told you I was going crazy down there. And I just want to go and help my people. I want a lift, Dan; as soon as we get there I'll go on my merry way. Okay?' We locked eyes. After about ten seconds, and without breaking contact, she said, 'The lights have changed.'

A moment later, there was a sustained blast of a horn from behind.

The road ahead was merging on to the M2; there was traffic on both sides of us now, and no easy option to immediately pull off.

I said, 'Bloody hell.'

'What's wrong with you? Am I cramping your style or something?'

'No . . . it's . . . what does Pike think about this?' She snorted. 'He doesn't know?'

'We had words.'

'Great.'

'About you. He doesn't like you coming down. I stuck up for you.'

'I don't need you to stick up for me.'

'Well I did anyway. And then I snuck out. I tell ya, it's bloody Baltic down the Peninsula at five in the morning. But I stuck my thumb out and someone stopped almost immediately. Amazing.'

'Right. But you've let him know what you're doing?'

'Nope.'

'You should let him know. You're his prize asset, he'll be going mental.'

'Good. And I'm not anyone's asset.'

'You should still let someone know.'

'Someone does. You do. Now do you think you could stick the fricken heating on?'

I supposed there wasn't any harm in giving her a lift.

I suppose a lot of things and I'm right some of the time, and catastrophically wrong a lot of the rest of the time. However, she was in the car already, she was heading my way, so it wasn't that much to ask.

I'd phoned Moira Doherty an hour before: told her I was taking the job for sure, that I'd appreciate it if she gave me a tour of the city, of the places her son knew, briefed me on their shared history and the history that wasn't shared. Then she could leave me to do my thing. She was grateful that I was committing but some-what reluctant to take on the tour. She was no longer living in the city, hadn't been back for a while, and gave me a rather weak 'It's changed so much, I'm not sure I know it very well now.' I insisted. It was a way to get to know her as much as anything. She agreed eventually: we were to meet at two p.m. at Badgers, a bar in the city centre.

It's roughly a ninety-minute journey to Londonderry; the M2 gets you about a third of the way there, then it switches to the single-lane A6, which is as slow as begot. We skirted Toomebridge, Castledawson, Maghera, chatting freely at the start but then slowly running out of conversation. We were indeed friends, but mainly by text, when you can dip in and out of it; together, in a car, with nothing but the open road, it became increasingly awkward. Our chats together at Ballyferris, our walks through the grounds, were almost under controlled conditions, never unobserved, always finite, almost like visiting a patient in a hospital – this, with no rules, no boundaries, felt strange, unusual, somehow wrong.

As we climbed towards the Glenshane Pass, the clouds above began to release fresh flurries of snow.

The Glenshane is, without doubt, the most miserable stretch of road on the entire island of Ireland. Cutting through the Sperrin Mountains, it rises to over a thousand ridiculously exposed feet and attracts the worst weather you could wish for; when the rest of the country is sweltering you can be sure that the Glenshane is fog-bound, or the rain is sliding off the mountains; crossing the Glenshane at any time is at the very least a dare and very occasionally a death sentence. You don't want to break down on the Glenshane, and certainly not in winter. It's just an endless undulating blanket bog. People use it because it's direct and somehow thrillingly beautiful in its pure barrenness, but you really don't want to spend any more time there than you have to. You climb, you climb, you climb and then you dip and dip and twist. You get the hell out of there as quickly as you can. There's nowhere to hide on the Glenshane. Just when you're reaching the highest point, with the snow coming down in sheets and the road getting thick and slippy, with visibility decreasing with every foot you ascend, the last thing you want is for someone to clutch your arm and say, 'Stop the car . . .'

'Aye, right . . .'

'Stop it! Please!'

We were already going scarcely faster than a milk float, but I slowed it a little more. I glanced across and saw that her face had drained of colour; there was a thin coating of sweat on her brow; she was nodding her head frantically at me and then clutched her hand to her mouth as her eyes widened in desperation. I pulled the car quickly to the side of the road and felt it sink into soft snow. Christine threw the door open and tried to hurl herself out, but her seat belt kept her just inside. She threw up, a projectile vomit on to the pristine snow. I looked away and swore. When I looked back, she was half hanging out, with one hand fumbling for the seat-belt release.

I took hold of her arm to stop her catapulting forward, then pushed the button. She groaned, shrugged me off, and rolled out of the door and on to her knees. She threw up again. Behind us a lorry went roaring past, giving us a blast of its horn for good luck. Christine threw up again. The snow was coming down even harder, visibility was down to virtually nothing, and with the height the temperature had dropped exponentially.

I got out and, keeping one hand on the car for support against the elements, hurried round beside her and crouched down. She was trying to catch her breath.

I gave her an utterly useless 'Are you okay?'

'Yes . . . yes . . .'

And then she threw up again.

Another lorry came past, this time sending a spray

of snow up and over the car to land on us. Christine remained on her knees, retching now, nothing more to come up. I took off my jacket and put it over her. I squeezed her against me and said, 'C'mon – let's get you back inside.'

She shook her head. 'No . . . no . . . please . . .'

'You have to . . .'

'No!'

She tried to pull away from me, but I held on to her. She was staring out into the snow, her eyes wide, drool freezing to her raw cheeks.

I dragged her up. She fought against me as I opened the back door and pushed her inside. She landed face down on the back seat, groaned again and retched. I shut the door and stepped back around to the driver's side. I climbed in and revved the engine, but when I tried to pull out, the back wheels spun and stuck, spun and stuck. 'For Jesus' sake!' I gave it one more go and we came free, shooting back on to the road just in time to nearly get crushed by another lorry emerging from the freezing curtain. I braked hard and we slid along, missing its tail end by about a foot. I swore again.

From the back, Christine said, weak and raspy, 'Are we . . .?'

'We're fine.'

I started forward again. But the snow was now coming in huge sheets, obliterating the road ahead. Five hundred feet further down and we'd probably be fine, but it might as well have been five million. There was nothing but a white curtain – until the briefest shift in the wind gave me a jagged view of something blinking on and off ahead of us. It was impossible to say how far away it was, but it was definitely a red light, a beacon, literally a sign. I eased the car forward, scared that at any moment it would tip over the edge of something and plunge us somersaulting into a void. My eyes strained for another glimpse. It might only have been the brake lights of another vehicle, but they would at least be something to follow, something that might lead us out of this nightmare if we could just get close enough.

We inched ahead.

In the back, Christine struggled up to a sitting position.

She said, *'Dan . . .'*

I said, 'It's okay, it's okay . . . shit!'

The lights had disappeared again. I didn't know whether to stop and run the risk of some other vehicle ploughing into us, or press on into the unknown.

Christine pulled herself forward. She pointed. She said, 'There . . .'

I looked to my left. A red glow. Nowhere near where I expected it to be. In less than a minute we had drifted ridiculously off course. I eased the car towards it, and gradually, gradually the redness came into focus – neon in the whiteout. Reading:

The High Chaparral.

8

We stumbled through the swing doors of the High Chaparral and almost fell on our faces. We were plastered in snow from the short charge across the car park into the welcoming glow of the second highest pub in Ireland. I knew it was the second highest pub because there was a big sign above the bar that said so. I had my arm tight around Christine, trying to keep her upright. We stood, breathing hard, relieved and astonished to be there, to find such unexpected relief. There were about six other customers, none of them paying much attention to us, and a burly fella with a short beard behind the bar who nodded at us and said, 'Are you in for something to eat?'

I said, 'I think we need an ambulance . . .'

But Christine straightened beside me. She gently patted my arm. 'I'm okay . . . I'm all right . . .'

'No, you—'

'I'm fine, honestly . . .'

I looked at the barman and said, 'We nearly got bloody killed out there, couldn't see six inches in front of us.'

'Aye, looks bad,' he said. 'These are our specials.' He thumbed behind him at a blackboard. 'Though we're out of lamb. Had a busload in. Why don't you take a wee seat and I'll bring the menus over? Can I get youse a drink?'

I stared at him, surprised and a little appalled by his indifference. Christine nudged me and said, 'Have one.'

I blew air out of my cheeks and said, 'Sure, right, hot whiskey for me . . .' I looked at Christine, pallid still, shaken. 'And hot whiskey for her.'

'Right you be,' said the barman.

I guided Christine across to a table with a tattered-looking banquette on one side and a chair on the other. I settled her on to the banquette and she immediately lay down, folding her elbow under her head for a pillow. But her eyes were brighter, and the colour was seeping back into her cheeks.

'Are you sure you don't want me to . . .?' I asked. She shook her head. 'Was that like . . . carsick?'

'No . . .'

'Morning sickness?'

'*What?*'

'Because I've experience in this area. If you're preg—'

'I'm not pregnant!'

Other customers looked round.

I said, 'I'm only ask— I mean, you were so sick . . . it was fucking green . . .'

'I know what it was.'

'But you're feeling better?'

'Yes.'

'Do you want something to eat?'

'No!' She pushed herself up on to her elbow. 'No . . . I mean, thanks, but—'

'Is there something you're not telling me, like leukaemia or—'

'Leukaemia! Dan, please, I was just a bit sick . . .'

'A bit sick, it was shooting out of you like—'

'I would recommend the lasagne,' the barman said as he appeared beside us, drinks on a tray. 'The wife makes it herself.'

'No,' I said, 'no thanks.' He handed the menus over. 'How long do you think we're going to be stuck here?'

'Till all the lasagne is gone. Nah – maybe a couple of hours. It's really changeable, one minute it's arctic, the next the sky's as blue as anything. It won't be so bad down below, so if the rain doesn't come on and clear most of it they'll send a snowplough up and push through.' He looked at Christine. 'You okay, love? You do look a bit peaky.'

'I'm fine. Honestly.' She sat up properly and lifted her hot whiskey and took a sip. She nodded appreciatively. 'Thanks, though. Never been so glad to see somewhere warm and welcoming.'

The barman beamed. 'Well, we do our best.'

Actually, judging from the state of the place, his best wasn't that great. The bar was warm and welcoming only in comparison to the blizzard outside. One might have expected a roaring fire or pumping central heating, but the only heat appeared to be coming from a three-bar electric fire. There was a stiff breeze blowing in through the shaky-looking window frames. The decor was strictly 1970s and the carpet underfoot was sticky and stank of cigarettes and beer. But it was a port in a storm, and we had to be grateful.

Ever the journalist, I said to him, 'You must hear plenty of tales of woe up here.'

'Aye, well, I expect I will – but we've only been open a month.'

'Really? I mean . . .' I nodded around the place.

'Well, by that I mean we bought it literally lock, stock and barrel a few weeks ago. We were just driving past, spotted this place, called in for lunch, we got talking to the owners, found out it was up for sale, must have been something about the view, it was a gorgeous view, and maybe the lack of oxygen at this height, but by the time we walked out we'd made an offer. You see, it may not look like much, but we see the potential. Thought it was better to keep it open for passing trade rather than shut down and remodel. But once we see in the new year we'll close up for a couple of months, give the place a lick of paint.'

I nodded, smiled. 'Well, good luck with it,' I said.

He thanked us and left us with our menus.

I looked at Christine and said, 'Lick of paint? He'll need more than luck.'

Christine said, 'The . . . High Chaparral. Is it like Gaelic or something?'

'Youngsters,' I said.

'What?'

'It's named after a Western TV series.'

'Western? Like Western hemisphere or . . .? I don't get what . . .'

'No, I mean . . . cowboys and Indians? Westerns?' She nodded vaguely at me. 'The High Chaparral is the name of the ranch in . . . *The High Chaparral*. It was huge in its day.'

'It's like you're speaking in tongues. When exactly are we talking about?'

'The seventies,' I said. 'Okay, so maybe you weren't born.'

'Maybe? My *mum* wasn't even born in the seventies.'

'Christ,' I said, and downed my whiskey.

The snow was not letting up. The lights flickered several times and the owner – Gerry Breslin – reassured us that there was a back-up generator if required. There was no phone signal, the TV went down, there was just easy country and western playing through some crackling speakers. Eventually his wife brought out plates of her lasagne free of charge and we all tucked in, apart from Christine. She stood by the window, looking out, watching the snow. Our fellow guests comprised four members of a German family, one doctor heading to Belfast for a conference, and a young mother with a teething toddler who'd been going to visit a relative in Londonderry from Maghera. She said, 'I should have known better, first bit of snow and this place goes nuts.' The Germans looked bemused as much by the lasagne as by the weather. I could sympathise. It was like eating a damp microwaved carpet.

Gerry's wife, Margaret, a buxom woman with grey brushed-back hair and a ponytail, offered me seconds and I said no. She said please and I reluctantly took more on board. She nodded at the window and said, 'Is your daughter okay?'

I said, 'Yeah, I think so. She just took a funny turn earlier.'

She gave a sympathetic smile and moved on. I lifted my plate and joined Christine at the window. I said, 'First you were stuck on the Peninsula, now you're stuck in the middle of nowhere. Maybe your destiny is just to be stuck.'

She didn't respond. She didn't react. She just kept looking out.

I said, 'Maybe it's an inner-ear problem. Maybe we're at too high an altitude for you and it makes you feel seasick. Sure you don't want some lasagne? It'll line your stomach, and quite possibly the floor of any church you care to hijack.' Still nothing. I put a hand on her arm and gave it a little squeeze. 'You okay?'

The slightest nod. 'I saw something.'

'Something? Where?'

'Back there. Where we were. I saw something.'

Her eyes flitted to me: wide and scared.

'Something like . . . what?'

'I don't know.'

'Do you mean you saw someone, someone out in the snow?'

'No. Not exactly.'

'You probably saw a sheep, they're out there, yer man at the bar told me, there are raggedy sheep all over the place, and some of them probably in the lasagne.' I showed her my plate. 'And there's plenty left.'

She shook her head. Her eyes returned to the window. 'No,' she said, 'it wasn't a person. Or a sheep. I don't know.'

'O-kay,' I said.

I returned to the bar and ordered another couple of hot whiskeys. I stood sipping them and chatting to the doctor. I started telling him about Christine's symptoms but he stopped me and told me he was a doctor of philosophy. The whiskey was in so I asked him what the hell use that was in a snowstorm with a sickly child and he said, well, he was sorry for her situation and the best we could do was to be philosophical about it. He was smug and I didn't like him very much but it was better than trying to infiltrate the Germans or the single girl sitting in a darkened corner breastfeeding her child at least a year after she should have stopped.

Instead I said to Gerry, the owner, 'It's an interesting business model. Customers who can't escape and then you offer them free lasagne.'

'There's no such thing as a free lasagne,' said the doctor of philosophy.

It grew dark outside. There was a strong wind and

the lights were flickering on and off. We got a game of cards going and I lost some money to the cheating Germans. The woman with the suckling child walked the floor with him because he was teething. She kept looking out of the window to see if the snow had stopped and complaining about her family being worried. The doctor of philosophy said, 'We all have families,' and I said up to a point. After several more whiskeys I found that I could hardly walk, so I curled up on the banquette. Before I nodded off I heard the mother say she was going for a pee and could someone hold the baby. Everyone else being drunk, including the Germans, she gave it to Christine. As soon as she handed him over, the baby stopped crying. She had a way with her, our Christine, I thought, and succumbed to the darkness.

9

And then someone was shaking me, and my head was busting, but I rolled over on the banquette and Gerry was there, his face full of concern and saying, 'Mister – your daughter, we're not sure where she is.'

I tried to force the fug from my head. I blinked around me, at the Germans pulling their coats back on and the mother zipping the crying toddler into a fleece and the doctor of philosophy nodding at the snow-spattered window with darkness beyond. 'Wah?'

Gerry gave me another shake. 'There's a snowplough coming up the hill, youse'll be able to leave in a minute, but we can't find your daughter . . .'

'Whaddya mean you can't . . . she must be . . .'

'She's not here! We went to bed, everyone else camped out down here; snow's stopped, clouds lifted, phones are back on, they called to say a plough's coming through, but there's no sign of her. We've searched everywhere.'

Then Margaret was at his shoulder. 'She's gone out, she must have gone out.'

I was up then and fully awake, zipping my jacket. It was three in the morning. 'Do you have a torch or something?' I said, already moving towards the door.

'You won't need it,' said Gerry.

'What do you mean I won't . . . it's the middle of the fucking—'

'Just take a look.'

He indicated the door. I shook my head and yanked it open. I stepped out. Gerry came out behind me, with Margaret, the Germans and the mother all following.

And we stood there for a moment, Christine forgotten, all *oohs* and *aaahs*.

Because it was, simply, thrilling. The sky was clear, there was a full moon, and a billion, billion stars, all reflecting off the pure white brilliance of the pass, of the Sperrins; absolutely fucking stunning.

The doctor of philosophy was at my shoulder. He said, 'Fan-dabby-dozy.'

And I had to agree.

'This,' Gerry said, 'is what makes it all worth it.'

'Look,' said Margaret.

I followed where she was pointing and saw twin beams of light further down the pass. It was hard to say exactly how far away they were – at least a mile, maybe two.

'That'll be the plough,' said Gerry.

The Germans were standing with their necks cricked back, staring into space. The doctor of philosophy said, 'I'm buying shares in this place. This is epic.'

Gerry snagged my arm and pointed down. There were footprints in the snow, leading away. I nodded. We set off. He was in hiking boots. I was in Oxford brogues that had me slipping all over the place as I struggled on the sharp incline of the field we were crossing. It was lovely and crisp underneath, and would have been a joy to walk on if the wind hadn't been slicing across us, stinging like salt in a paper cut.

I said, 'How long do you think she's been gone?'

'An hour, maybe. I didn't go up till late but she was still standing there.'

'Did she say anything?'

'No, just staring out of the window.'

I nearly went flying; Gerry grabbed me, steadied me. Christine's footsteps were clear in the snow, and the light was so good we could see them clearly ahead of us for several hundred metres – until they suddenly disappeared. We hurried forward, me with one hand on the back of Gerry's jacket to help keep me upright. As we approached the end of the tracks, Gerry stopped. 'Careful,' he said, 'it drops here to the road . . .'

We helped each other down and picked up her tracks again as they followed the rough outline of the road. But as I looked ahead I saw something about two hundred metres ahead of us – the outline of someone sitting in the snow and partially covered in it, like a statue.

'It's her,' I said. 'It's her.'

Gerry just shook his head.

'Christine!' I shouted. 'Christine!'

There was no response. I looked at Gerry. He was thinking what I was: she was dead, frozen. As we began to move towards her, Gerry stumbled suddenly, his arms flailed and then he let out a shout as he tumbled away. He let out a winded *whumf* as he hit the ground, and then a 'Fuck!'

I peered over what must have been the edge of the road and down a short incline to where he was lying flat on his back.

'You okay?'

He clutched at his ankle and yelled, 'No I'm not fucking okay!'

I looked towards Christine again, kneeling there so gloriously framed by the heavens, so still, and began to gingerly ease my feet over the edge, but I'd barely any grip. Then I just thought, *Fuck it*, and leapt out into the air. I landed on my feet, on the road, perfectly, for all of a millisecond, before my shoes flew out from under me and my arse hit the ground with a crack. I sat where I was for a moment, bum bone in agony.

Gerry said, 'You okay, you fucking eejit?'

'I'm used to it,' I said. But I only had eyes for the girl. 'Christine!'

Still nothing.

I gingerly pulled myself to my feet, nothing obviously broken, then put a hand out for Gerry. I got him half up, but when he tried to put weight on his ankle he let out a cry, screwed his face up and then lowered himself back on to the snow. 'I can't walk on this,' he said.

'I can give you a . . .'

'No . . . I'll be fine – look . . .' He nodded down the road. The snowplough was already a lot closer and would probably reach the High Chaparral in a few minutes. 'They'll be able to see us by now. Just . . . go to her.'

I looked towards Christine. Part of me didn't want to go anywhere near her. Perhaps most of me. I had form with dead children. And that was what she was, a child masquerading as a Messiah. I had no idea what had dragged her out into the cold – whether the sickness that had suddenly come upon her earlier had unhinged her, or maybe she'd just cracked under the pressure of her bizarre life – and it didn't really matter. She'd been out in the freezer for hours with only the thinnest of jackets for protection. It hadn't exactly been my job to look after her, but we were friends, and she'd gotten sick, and I knew that if I'd stayed with her rather than getting pissed at the bar she might still be alive. She was a vulnerable teenager, on the run, with obvious issues, and I'd preferred Jameson's company to hers.

But it had to be done.

I gave Gerry a nod and then began to slip and slide towards her, my arse sore, my skin red and raw, wind chill Christ knows what, but the lot of it dwarfed by the dread of what I would find.

I was up behind her then, could see ice in her dank hair, the nape of her neck bone white.

'Christine,' I said quietly.

I put a hand on her shoulder.

And her tiny pink hand clamped straight on to it.

I jumped and said, 'Fuck – Christine! Are you . . .?'

But she didn't seem to hear me. I kept her hand in mine but moved round to face her and crouched down. Her eyes were open, but staring straight through me.

'Christine . . .'

Her voice came, small but determined: 'I believe in God, the Father almighty, maker of heaven and earth . . .'

I said, 'Let's get you out of here.'

'And in Jesus his only son Our Lord, who was conceived by the Holy Spirit, born of the Virgin Mary . . .'

'Yes, that's all well and good, but let's get you—'

'Suffered under Pontius Pilate! Was crucified dead and buried!'

'C'mon now . . .'

I moved behind her, placed my hands under her arms, and began to drag her up. As I did, her head twisted round and she cried: 'He descended into hell! The third day he rose again from the dead! He ascended into heaven, and sitteth on the right hand of God the Father almighty . . .'

'Christine! Please . . .'

'From thence he shall come to judge the quick and the dead!'

From way back, Gerry shouted: 'Is she okay?'

'Grand!' I called.

I finally had her on her feet. She was shaking. I tried to hug her to me. She resisted at first, but then her legs gave way and she collapsed into me. But she wasn't finished:

'I believe in the Holy Spirit, the holy catholic Church, the communion of saints, the forgiveness of sins . . . the resurrection of the body, and the life everlasting.' She finally pressed her head into my chest, let out a massive sigh and whispered, 'Amen.'

10

It's a city built on hills, and on either side of the Foyle river. The west bank is known as Cityside and features the original walls, most of the touristy bits and the Bogside, which is a largely Catholic and nationalist neighbourhood, and home to various dissident Republican groups; it borders a smallish Protestant enclave called Fountainside. The east bank is known as the Waterside, and is home to mostly Protestants and Unionists. The two banks are connected by three bridges: the Craigavon Bridge, the Foyle Bridge and the pedestrian Peace Bridge. That's where Christine wanted dropped, on an icy morning, nine a.m. I told her I admired the symbolism of it and she said, nah, it was just quicker.

We'd eaten a large Ulster fry in the High Chaparral, with Gerry and Margaret fussing around us, apologetic for our enforced stay, as if they were responsible for the sudden blizzard. We were the only remaining customers: the Germans, the mother and toddler and the doctor of philosophy had shipped out as soon as the snowplough cleared the way and were gone by the time I carried Christine back into the bar. I'd wanted to take her to hospital, but she refused; she said she'd been sleepwalking, it happened a lot, and she was now just cold and exhausted and embarrassed and full of apologies. So she was bundled off to a spare room upstairs while I made do with the banquette. When she came down for breakfast, she seemed like her old self – happy, chatty, cheeky and appreciative of her huge plate of food; she was literally and metaphorically full of beans. If there were any ill effects from her trauma she did not display them. After we ate, she helped me shovel snow off the car. It started first time. She didn't say much on the drive in. I kept it light and casual: I'm a bit worried about the throwing up and the sleepwalking and you maybe want to get it checked out and she said sure she would, and we both knew she wouldn't.

I didn't quite know where I was going, but I managed to find a car park connected to the Foyleside shopping centre. Then I walked her to the Peace Bridge. Four metres wide, one hundred and one metres long, and temporarily closed because someone had been shot halfway across it in the early hours of the morning and then thrown over the security rails into the freezing water below. There were forensic teams on the bridge, and police divers in inflatables below. We stood and watched the activity for a little bit. Nobody else seemed much interested, apart from the tourists, who were put out that they couldn't get across to Ebrington Barracks, the old army fort and parade ground that had lately been redeveloped as a concert venue, as easily as they wished.

I said to Christine, 'Looks like you're going to have to take the long way round. Will I give you a lift?'

'No, I'll be fine, honestly.'

'Sure?'

'Sure.'

We looked some more at the bridge.

I said, 'Irony, eh?'

She nodded. She said, 'Unless of course calling it the Peace Bridge was just sarcastic, in which case . . .'

'Inevitable,' I agreed. She thumbed behind her in the direction of the Foyle Bridge. I said, 'You have my number.'

She said, 'I had your number a long time ago.'

Which seemed very profound for a sixteen-year-old. But maybe she was only sixteen in earth years. She was a smart cookie, for sure, but odd as begot, and as she walked off I felt a tinge of concern for her, for what she might find out there, away from Pike's prison on the Peninsula, away from the cosseting and the worship.

I've never been the world's greatest timekeeper, but I was coming up on being eighteen hours late for my appointment with Mrs Doherty in the Badger Bar. With the phone signal suddenly lost over Glenshane and then not restored until the early hours, I hadn't been able to cancel; I'd left a voicemail for her first thing, but as yet no response. I tried again as I walked through the shopping centre, but it went the same way. I emerged from the centre with the Badger straight in front of me and only a little bit beyond it the Millennium Forum, which was advertising a tedious-looking punk musical. The bar wasn't open yet, but it was still a useful place to get my bearings; when I was trying to familiarise myself with somewhere new, I usually started by going to the place I was supposed to be, and then gradually worked my way outwards.

I'm not a great one for history, but it was interesting enough walking around, if punishing on the calf muscles. I'd sung 'Derry's Walls' about a thousand times as a youngster, because everyone I knew did. It was a loyalist song and I lived in a loyalist area and you learned it by rote without ever thinking about what you were yelling out. I'd pretty quickly shed my loyalist skin when I entered my teenage years, but the old tunes still lingered. Now I was walking those very walls with their ancient cannons and uncomfortable cobbles, enjoying the view over the Bogside. So much of the Troubles emanated from Londonderry; a beaten-down people had risen up and probably caused a lot more havoc than they initially intended; they had played host to urban warfare, and if the shooting on the Peace Bridge was anything to go by, it probably wasn't done yet. I strained to see if the graffiti about Billy the Bear was still visible on the Free Derry wall, but it was just too far.

By the time I came back round to the Badger, it was open and I went in for a pint. There was a copy of the *Derry Journal* on the bar and I read that as I supped. There wasn't anything overly dramatic on the front page: a new superstore on the Waterside winning planning permission, a light show to mark the first anniversary of the City of Culture, a favourite son who was now a minister at Stormont had met the Japanese prime minister to discuss jobs. Londonderry isn't that big – maybe a quarter of a million in the hinterland, but the city itself only boasts seventy-five thousand souls, most of them divided into two uneven camps; small enough for everyone to know everyone. I tested the theory on the barman and asked him if he knew Mrs Doherty, who I was supposed to meet in this very bar, and he said no. I asked him if he knew the legendary Billy the Bear and he said no. I said maybe it would be easier to tell me who he did know and he said he knew no one because he was from Poland. I told him his accent was very good and he said he worked at it. I checked my phone. Still nothing. I didn't have an address for her. I tried checking online and then by thumbing a crumbling telephone directory; there were a lot of Dohertys. I gave up after the first half-dozen – no, they didn't know her; no, they weren't related.

Billy the Bear's address I already had. According to the most recent of the articles I'd read online, his last court appearance had been in June. Police acting on a tip-off had raided his apartment on Shipquay Street looking for weapons. He'd been charged with possession

71

of a model 17 Glock pistol and was remanded in custody to Magilligan prison. He'd been released in September, charges dropped on a technicality, although it didn't mention what that technicality was. Shipquay Street was a three or four minute stroll around the outside of the Richmond Centre, the smaller of the two shopping centres on either side of the Forum; it was another cobbled road, half given over to small shops, a variety of offices and mainly first- and second-floor apartments. Billy's was towards the top end of a steep hill; there was a Mace on the ground floor. There was a doorway to the side of the shop with two buzzers; neither of them had names or numbers where they were supposed to be. I pressed the top one. A man answered with a gruff: 'What?'

I said, 'Hi, hello, I'm looking for Billy Doherty.'

'Join the club, pal.'

'I was wondering if I could come up and have a word with you about—'

'No, fuck off.'

But actually, he fucked off.

I pressed the lower buzzer. A woman answered hello, and I told her I was looking for Billy Doherty. She told me to hold on for a moment, and a moment later the same guy came back on and told me to fuck off again. I pondered that for a little bit, and then pressed the top buzzer again. He came back on and I said, 'Hello again, you sound a little out of breath.'

He said, 'Do you want me to come down there and break your legs?'

I said, 'Why would I want that?'

'Fuck off!'

Sensing that I wasn't going to get much further with him, I stepped away from the buzzer and into the grocery shop. I bought a Twix. As the portly middle-aged guy behind the counter was giving me my change, I said, 'Sorry to trouble you, but I'm just wondering who owns the flats upstairs? I'm interested in renting.'

'Don't know.'

'They're just upstairs – they must come in here, or you see them going in and out?'

'No.'

'You've never seen them?'

'No.'

I nodded. It was hard to believe. I said, 'I'm not the police or anything. Tell you the truth, I work for Billy Doherty's mother. I'm looking for her son, you know, Billy the Bear? He lived upstairs, I'm just wondering who took over his apartment or who's living there now.'

He just looked at me.

And I looked at him.

Eventually I said, 'It's little wonder small businesses like yours are going under.'

'I'm not going under,' he said.

'You will. It's inevitable, with your customer relations.'

'My what?'

'Exactly. I just bought a Twix and asked a polite question and all I get is attitude.'

'You think buying a Twix gives you the right to ask nosy questions?'

'It was a polite enquiry.'

'You lied. You said you wanted to rent the place, and only when I didn't tell you anything you said you were working for his mother.'

'So you do know him?'

'Whether I know him is neither here nor there. It's none of your business.'

'Is that what you say when someone comes in and asks for directions?'

'That's different.'

'How?'

'They're not asking for information relating to where I live and work. I can't give out that kind of information. It's Data Protection.'

'That's fucking rubbish.'

'There's no need to swear.'

'There's every need! Data Protection your old fucking arse. And you know something? I've changed my mind. I don't want your fucking Twix.' I put it back on the counter. 'And I want a refund.'

'I can't give you a refund, you've handled it now.'

'I picked it up and put it down and picked it up. It's in a fucking wrapper.'

'Nevertheless.'

'I want my money.'

'You can want all you like.'

'I'm entitled to a refund.'

'I'd beg to differ.'

I nodded. He nodded. I lifted the Twix again and turned. I stopped short of the door, beside a display of fruit. All kinds of fruit. Apples and pears and melons and grapes and some I didn't recognise. I had little experience of any of them in their natural form. I looked back up the shop. He was still watching me. I picked up an apple. I took a bite. I replaced it. I picked up another. Took a bite. Put it back down. Then a third. He was coming out from behind the counter. I bit into a fourth. He was hurrying towards me. I lifted another apple and stepped outside of the shop with it. I raised it to my mouth, pretended to pull a pin out of it, and rolled it down the aisle towards him. And mimed an explosion. He actually hesitated. I laughed and hurried away.

He swore down the hill after me.

I was a middle-aged man, ffs, and yet – very satisfying.

11

I lingered at the bottom of Shipquay Street until the Mace man retreated inside his shop. I called Mrs Doherty but again got her voicemail. I thought maybe she had changed her mind about me taking on the case and was screening her calls. I texted Sara Patterson and asked if she by chance had an address for her and she came back with a curt *I'm driving*. I texted back: *Then concentrate and stop texting!* I was wondering what the hell I was still actually doing in Londonderry if Mrs D was playing so hard to get, but I was also peeved at being told to fuck off at Billy the Bear's apartment and annoyed by the Mace man and wasn't about to go quietly into the early afternoon. Plus I had nothing better to do with my time.

I crossed to the other side and wandered back up Shipquay Street. There was a café just at the entrance to the Richmond Centre that afforded me a reasonable view of the apartments. So I took a seat at the window and ordered a hot chocolate and looked across. It seemed logical to assume that the man who'd responded to the buzzers was either the landlord or owned or rented both properties. He had said he was also looking for Billy the Bear, although that could have been in jest.

I was just debating ordering another cup when I saw movement across the road. The front door opened and a young woman with shoulder-length dark hair and wearing black jeans, trainers and a puffa jacket came out. She stopped, lit a cigarette and stood facing the door. It opened again and three more young women emerged, two blondes and a brunette. They also lit up as soon as they reached the footpath. They stood in a little group, chatting and joking for a bit, before turning as one and walking off down the street together, arms hooked. I was still following their progress when my eye was drawn back to the apartments. My friend from the Mace had appeared in the doorway of his shop and was talking to a young woman in blue jeans, green jacket, and with her hair tied in a ponytail. They both laughed at something, and then the young woman turned and pressed the lower buzzer. She spoke briefly into the intercom and was admitted. The door had barely closed when two other women approached, pressed the buzzer and entered. A couple of minutes later another turned up.

I ordered a second hot chocolate at the counter. The waitress said she'd bring it over. I was intrigued by the comings and goings. Four in, four out. A change of shifts. When the waitress arrived I said, 'Don't suppose you've any idea what sort of a business they're running across the road? Above the Mace?'

The waitress looked where I was looking, and then smirked. 'Tell you the truth, love, we were wondering that ourselves, see them going in and out all the time. Delores in the back there thought it was a hoor-house, but then there's never any fellas going in. You from the dole or something?'

'Nope, just curious.'

'Aye well, one of the girls was in the other day buying coffees, and Delores, she's a brass neck on her, she says to her, what is it youse are doing over there, all you pretty girls, and the poor wee thing did a reddener and mumbled something about a film company and skedaddled quick as she could. So now Delores thinks they're making, you know, blue movies.'

I smiled. Blue movies. No one had called blue movies blue movies in years.

'But then she said there's still no fellas going in so maybe they're making – you know, lizzy movies . . . you know – girls doing it to each other . . .'

'Right. Could be. Never know.'

She nodded at my hot chocolate and said, 'Do you want a Flake in that?' Then she gave me a broad wink and said, 'More than those girls are getting anyway!' and cackled off to get me one before I'd had the chance to say no.

When she brought it back and slipped it gracefully

into the cup, I said, 'Is that what you think too, lizzy movies?'

The waitress looked across at the apartment. She pursed her lips. 'Mmmm, no, I don't think so. It's probably telly-marketing. Or like a call centre. They're everywhere these days. I mean, imagine making a blue movie in Derry! You'd never be able to show your face round here again. Or your fanny, for that matter.' She gave me another wink and was just turning away when she stopped and came back to me with her hand raised to her mouth. 'I'm sorry,' she said. 'I shouldn't be talking like that. I don't know you from Adam and those girls are lucky to be doing whatever it is they're doing, we all are. I mean, we're all but one step away from that poor woman they dragged out of the river this morning, aren't we? There but for the grace of God . . .'

She shook her head, crossed herself, and turned back to the counter.

I watched her go.

I looked at my choco, the flake melting into the froth.

I picked up my phone, and sighed and put it down again.

Knowing.

I'd been in the business of asking and poking for too long not to be surprised by it. But it was still a surprise every time.

The waitress was right. We are all but a couple of missteps away from a bullet, from being dumped off the Peace Bridge in the early-morning murk, from frogmen plunging into the icy depths to recover a corpse, dragging a pallid, bloated, misshapen shell with its exploded head straggling brain matter and pondweed into an inflatable. One wrong word, one crossed line, one ancient enmity and any one of us could end up like that poor woman, on a slab, in a morgue, several times removed from answering her phone, picking up her messages and keeping some idiot in underpaid and insecure employment.

12

There was nothing official yet, but it had leaked out, a slip of the tongue, a careless whisper, and in a few moments it was out in the Twitterverse, and that was good enough for the TV crews on the city side of the river to be saying the dead woman had been named locally as Moira Doherty, the well-known former nationalist, Republican and civil rights activist. They said she had taken a back seat since the Good Friday Agreement and that she'd lately been working as a community worker. These experts, half of whom probably had no useful memory of the Troubles, were blaming dissident Republicans, a catch-all for anyone running around with a gun and a grievance. They were making much of her getting killed on the Peace Bridge, and what it meant.

There were plenty of reporters down there, and I mingled. Most were from the local radio stations and papers, but word had been out there for long enough for some others to have driven up from Belfast. I should not have been surprised then to see Sara Patterson amongst them, but I was.

I said, 'When did you find out?'

She said, 'Nice to see you too.'

I said, 'You could have told me.'

'I thought you knew, I thought you had the finger on the pulse. Soon as I heard, I jumped in the car.' Sara was wearing a smooth black leather jacket, a tartan skirt with black leggings and short leather boots. Her hair was shoulder length now, dirty blonde, and it suited her. She was young enough to be my protégée, and old enough to not take me seriously. We had a flirtatious relationship. Mostly I flirted and she rolled her eyes. I couldn't quite tell whether she enjoyed the mild suggestiveness of it or found it slightly creepy. 'I thought that's why you were looking for her address.'

'Nope. Just trying to track her down. Was supposed to meet her yesterday but got waylaid.'

Sara nodded and we both looked back out across the bridge. It remained cordoned off, with a forensics team still visible and tourists on both banks snapping away. The Terror Tours were big business, and now they'd turned interactive.

'When did you last speak to her?' Sara asked.

'Yesterday morning. You?'

'She called me from the bus to thank me for putting her in touch with you but asking if there was anyone else I could recommend. Did youse not hit it off?'

'She seemed sweet when I left her.'

'Well she thought you were fobbing her off. I told her you'd a funny way with you and to give you a chance.'

'Give *me* a chance?'

'What've you heard?' Sara asked.

'In the twenty minutes I've been here? Not much beyond someone phoned it in.'

'Claiming responsibility?'

'Not so I've heard. A witness.'

'Out there? In the middle of the night?' Sara asked. 'With the snow coming down?'

'I don't know.'

'There's bound to be security cameras.'

'Aye. If they're working.'

We both looked for them.

Couldn't see them.

'Why would she go out there in the middle of the night, it Baltic out?' I asked.

'Maybe she was doing a bit of soul-searching. She'd lost her son. Maybe she was meeting someone. Maybe it's a robbery gone tragically wrong. Maybe,' Sara said, with a somewhat mischievous twinkle, 'you want to drive out to her home with me, take a look around?'

'You know where she lives?'

'Lived. And yes. More or less.'

'How so?'

''Cos when she came to the office, I told her I was from up this neck of the woods . . .'

'Londonderry?'

'Not quite – Castlerock? It's—'

'I know where it is.'

Village, thirty miles away along the coast.

'And she said she was living there at the moment, just moved in, and because I know the town I asked whereabouts and she told me. But I'm thinking, if she's just moved in, probably there's not many people who know that, if she had ID on her it'll probably be for an old address, so we might get a chance to check it out before the police or the rest of the press pack get there.'

'Sounds like a plan,' I said. 'And why exactly are you asking me?'

'Because we work well as a team.' I raised my eyebrows. 'And because if there's any trouble, you'll be there to defend me.'

She smiled and turned away.

'Why would there be any trouble?' I called after her.

'Because it goes with the territory!'

I nodded.

She had a good point.

We took her car. It had smelled of dog last time I was in it.

It still smelled of dog.

She apologised and said she'd bought a puppy and it wasn't trained properly yet. 'Shits in the house, shits in the car. I rub his nose in it, doesn't make a blind bit of difference. Reminds me of you, actually.'

'Cheers,' I said.

We crossed the bridge and then began the climb up

towards the small airport at Eglinton and from there on
to Limavady and the coast road. We had the radio on to
BBC Radio Foyle listening for updates

'I didn't realise you were from up this direction.'

'Uhuh.'

'You've lost the accent.'

'I'll soon slip back into it.'

'Deliberate decision?'

'Yup. Hard to make your way in the big smoke if
you sound like you've just stepped off a tractor.'

'Yup,' I said, 'you'd soon hit the grass ceiling. You
still have people up here?'

'Mum, dad, three sisters, two brothers, many, many
nieces and nephews.'

'Excellent. Glad I asked. I'll wait in the car.'

'Excuse me?'

'Well you'll be wanting to see them. I don't want to
get in the way.'

'Starkey, I'm here for work, not a gathering of the
clan.'

'Disowned you, have they?'

'Why would you say that?'

'You're so reluctant to see them. What'd they do that
was so wrong?'

'Starkey? Why don't you just concentrate on the
scenery?'

'God,' I said, 'it must be something terrible.'

I concentrated on the scenery of the coast road and
the fabulous might of the Atlantic in winter. I'd been
to Castlerock before. When I was a kid. Before foreign

holidays became the norm. Half the population decamped to the north-west coast for the first two weeks of July. If you were of vaguely nationalist pedigree you crossed the border to vacation in Donegal; everyone else ended up in the caravan sites and guest houses, amusement arcades and chip shops of Portrush or Portstewart, or if they were booked out, or your parents had an aversion to candyfloss and slot machines, in Castlerock, which was much quieter, slightly more upmarket. A population of not much more than a thousand swelled to many times that during the summer, and it probably still did. What it had over its two local rivals, which had their own fabulous beaches, was Benone Strand, seven miles of sand and dunes between the village and Magilligan peninsula. One of those vast, epic stretches of beach that seemed to go on for ever, or at least as far as the British Army firing range and Magilligan prison at its northern end.

Sara asked me what I was smiling at and I said nothing. Then: 'I was here on holidays. Twice.'

'Enjoy?'

'I'd take myself off all day. I played soldiers in those dunes. Lawrence of Arabia.'

'The mind boggles.'

We drove into the village.

I said, 'So what're we looking for?'

'The Twelve Apostles,' said Sara.

13

Mrs Harbinson, the manager, stood in the doorway of the first of a terrace of twelve labourers' cottages. She peered at Sara's card and said, 'You're not anything to the Freehall Road Pattersons?'

'That would be my mum and dad,' said Sara.

'I thought I recognised your face! You're Betty's girl? Och, why didn't you say? Come on in.'

She stepped out of the way. Sara smiled and entered. As I followed her in I said, 'And I'm her spiritual adviser.'

Sara said, 'Don't listen to him, he's working with me – we're trying to get older journalists back into employment.'

I gave her a face and she gave it back.

Everything I knew about the cottages came from Wikipedia, which was very handy, although there was a reasonable chance it was also wrong. They were built in the nineteenth century and had somehow acquired the nickname of the Twelve Apostles and some measure of fame only because they had been designed by the architect Edward Godwin. They'd fallen into disrepair over the years but relatively recently had been given a new lease of life as holiday cottages and short-term rentals.

Mrs Harbinson ushered us on to a small sofa in the lounge-cum-office. Hardwood floor, smell of polish, TV fixed to QVC; a small desk with a computer and various leaflets for local attractions.

'And how are they keeping?' she asked. 'Haven't seen them in ages.'

'They're fine,' said Sara.

'Which is more than we can say for one of your tenants,' I said.

Mrs Harbinson's brow furrowed.

Sara quickly said, 'Yes, that's why we're here.'

Mrs Harbinson looked suitably horrified as Sara told her about Moira Doherty.

'But I was only talking to her yesterday . . .'

She'd heard the name on the radio half an hour before but didn't in a million years think there was any connection with her tenant, who'd only moved in three weeks previously on a six-month lease.

'I mean, the woman on the radio . . . wasn't she some sort of . . . troublemaker up in Derry?'

'Years ago,' said Sara.

'And she's the same woman as my . . .? But Moira seemed so nice . . .'

I said, 'Someone didn't think so.'

Mrs Harbinson sighed. 'That's just terrible. Terrible.'

She was a rotund woman in a plaid skirt. Her hair was tied back in a bun and she wore thick black glasses of the type that had once been for necessity but which were now increasingly for show.

Sara said, 'We don't know exactly what happened or why, but we are trying to find out a little bit more about her . . . I mean, did you talk to her much?'

'Not really, no, we would pass ourselves, if you know what I mean?'

'Of course. And she lived alone?'

'Yes she did, though she had visitors. Quite a lot of visitors, in fact.'

'What kind of visitors?' I asked.

'I couldn't really say – I mean, they're short-term rentals so quite often you get families taking a block of time and then spreading it out between them. They come and go. Used to be I'd try and keep track of it all, but people want to let their hair down when they're on holiday so I eventually decided just to let them enjoy themselves. Last thing they need is an old biddy like me spoiling their fun.'

'This is even in winter?'

'Sure it is. The beach is a big attraction. Kite-surfers, surfers, trainspotters, we get all sorts. And it can get pretty rowdy. So I lock my door, turn the telly up and mind my own. Moira seemed to have quite the extended family; there were always cousins and nieces turning up all hours of the day or night. In fact now that I think of it, there were some here this morning – I'm up early to walk the dogs, so I saw . . . well, two young fellas coming out of number six.' She paused then. 'You don't think . . .?'

'Probably not,' said Sara, 'if the murder happened in town, but would you be able to describe them anyway?'

'Not really, it was dark still and I wasn't paying attention.'

'But they were young men, you said; you mean like teenagers, or older?'

'I really couldn't say.'

'What were they wearing?' I asked.

'I don't know. Anoraks? Their hoods were up.'

'Did you speak to them? Or was there any contact?'

'Not really. I said, *That's a cold one*. But it was kind of one of those things you say and you don't really expect a response. I mean, there was nothing odd about them, though one of them had like . . . you know, a birthmark on his face that was quite pronounced, but there was no reason for me to be suspicious . . . I didn't know she was . . . and it doesn't mean they had anything to do with . . .' She let out a loud sigh. 'Do you think they were . . .?'

'They could just as easily be friends or relatives visiting,' said Sara. 'Did they just look like they were going for a walk or something? Was there a car?'

'Yes. They drove off.'

'What sort of a car?'

'I don't know. A silver one.'

'Large, small, like an estate car or . . .?'

'I don't know. It had one brake light out, I remember that, I remember thinking should I say something because the police are always sitting just down the road a bit checking for speeders and tax discs and all that, would likely pull them over if they saw a brake light out.'

'But you didn't,' I said.

'No, they were too quick, and you know . . . none of my business really.'

'So did they look like they were leaving for good, or just out for a quick drive or?' Sara asked.

'How do you mean?'

'If they were just popping out to the shop or something they wouldn't have had bags or suitcases with them? But if they'd been staying they might?'

'I don't know. Let me think. Yes, maybe – I mean, the reason I saw the brake light was out was because one of them was putting something in the boot while the other one started the engine. So yes, maybe they had suitcases. I didn't really see.'

'Okay, that's understandable.'

Mrs Harbinson put her hand to her chest. 'My heart is just racing. I mean, if they were . . . you know . . . connected to . . . and they think I might recognise them . . . what if they come back and . . .? And shouldn't the police be here? I'm like a witness to . . . do you think I'll need a bodyguard or . . . or . . . my goodness, isn't this just terrible?'

'I'll tell you what you need,' said Sara, 'you need a nice cup of tea.' She got up from the sofa. 'Is the kitchen . . .?'

'Oh dear, that's very kind of you, but let me . . . I know where everything is.'

Mrs Harbinson moved towards the kitchen, which was in the next room.

'Well I'll give you a hand,' said Sara, and moved to follow. 'Oh . . .' She stopped and looked back at me. 'Dan – do you want to maybe go out to the car, phone the story in?'

'Me? What?' I said.

Sara gave me an exasperated shake of her head. She glanced towards the kitchen, then nodded at the small desk.

'Number six,' she whispered.

Behind the desk there was a series of hooks on the wall with keys hanging on them. Most of them had two keys, but there was just one for number six. Sara raised an eyebrow.

'Ah,' I said quietly, 'the penny drops. Someone to do your dirty work.'

'Well I can't do it,' said Sara. 'We have a strict code of ethics. While you have none.' She turned to the kitchen. 'In fact,' she said, louder, 'I might have coffee if that's okay?'

She stood in the doorway, effectively blocking the manager's view of the lounge.

'Not sure my heart could take coffee,' Mrs Harbinson said.

I stepped around the desk and lifted the key.

For sure the police would be arriving soon and I would not want them to find me poking around in Mrs Doherty's drawers. She had been a public figure, particularly in Londonderry, so it would be different to a common or garden murder; and so the press would arrive in force, to report, to analyse, to pontificate. Sara had a reputation for getting exclusives for her paper, and she was already one step ahead of the pack. It was addictive. I'd been there. In my day you could cut a few corners if it was perceived to be in the greater public interest. It wasn't so easy now. Yet I hardly gave it a second thought. I was going to be implicated anyway because I'd left half a dozen increasingly anxious messages for Moira Doherty and travelled all the way from Belfast to meet her. That alone would warrant eight hours in an interview room.

The cottages on either side of number six were vacant. Moira's lights were all on. I let myself in. As at Mrs Harbinson's, the door led directly into the lounge. The decor and furnishings were the same; all the cottages were probably identical. I stood for a moment taking it in, listening, smelling – a coal-effect gas fire burning in the hearth; three photos of Billy the Bear in cardboard frames above it, two in school uniform, and a third that looked like it had been taken in the same Portuguese bar as the one Moira had showed me a couple of days before. There was a table with a half-drunk cup of tea. A faint odour of toast. The television was on but turned down. A landline phone. I moved into the kitchen. Clean and tidy, with a single plate and a knife sitting in the sink. I used just my wrist to try the back door. It was locked from the inside. I returned to the lounge and then moved up the stairs. Three bedrooms. The first was Moira's. The bed covers hadn't been turned back, but there was an impression on them where presumably she had lain down; there was an ashtray with a half-smoked cigarette put out in it. A small desk stood in the corner, identical to the one Mrs Harbinson used in her cottage. There was a computer monitor lying on its side, a mouse, mouse pad, but no hard drive. The en suite bathroom had lotions, potions and a pair of black lace knickers with a small pink bow on the floor. They could surprise you, old folks. I carefully opened the cupboards and drawers – several changes of clothes, but not much for someone who'd taken a six-month lease. Apart from the photos of her son, there was a definite lack of personal effects. Maybe she just didn't have much stuff. The next bedroom was perfectly made up. The single wardrobe was empty but for a couple of hangers. But when I opened the bedside locker I found an ashtray, a Rampant Rabbit vibrator, three dildos in what might loosely be described as small, medium and fucking massive, plus a half-used tube of lubricant.

Okay, I thought. One of the nieces is going to be missing those.

I moved to the third bedroom. Again the bed was made and the wardrobe was empty. I opened the bedside locker: an ashtray, a Rampant Rabbit, three dildos and some lube.

I pondered on the chances of two nieces not only possessing the same sex toys, but actually forgetting to take them when they left, and concluded that to forget one huge dildo was unfortunate, but to forget two was beyond coincidence.

Outside, car doors slammed.

I moved to the window and peered down at a police car. Two uniformed officers were standing beside it; one was on his radio. They were probably the advance party of what was sure to be quite a wagon train. I moved out of the bedroom, along the hall and back down the stairs. As I reached the bottom, there was a heavy knock on the front door. It was solid wood, so there was no chance of them seeing me; I supposed that when they didn't get a response, their next step would be to peer through the front window, so I waited, giving them time to look into the empty room. There was some indistinct talk between them, then they moved away. I hurried through the lounge to the kitchen and then the back door. I noticed a small spiral-bound notebook and pen sitting on the counter by the door just beneath a second house phone attached to the wall. The notebook was open and there were three telephone numbers written on the first page – the first I recognised immediately as Sara's direct line at the *Telegraph*; the second was my mobile number; the third was unfamiliar. I quickly flicked through the rest of the notebook, but it was otherwise empty. I took out my phone and photographed the page, then slipped out of the back door and worked my way along the open-plan back yards of the other cottages to Mrs Harbinson's kitchen door. I tried the handle but it was locked. I peered through the glass and saw Sara standing with her back to me in the lounge doorway. I tapped the glass gently and she turned. She quickly stepped across and let me in.

'Police at the door,' she said.

I showed her the key to six. She nodded and moved to stand immediately behind Mrs Harbinson, who was on the front step talking to the police. I followed her through and stepped behind the desk; I gave the key a quick wipe and replaced it on the hook.

Mrs Harbinson was just saying, 'Sure, wait there and I'll get the key.'

When she came in, I was just sitting on the edge of her desk.

'Oh, you're back,' she said.

'Aye – came round behind, saw you were busy.'

'I'm just going to show them Mrs Doherty's cottage.'

She moved round to get the key.

'Wish I'd thought of that,' I said.

Sara gave me a look and said, 'We should probably be going anyway. Thanks so much for your help.'

'I'm sure I'll only be a minute, I'd love to catch up with—'

'And so would I. But this is a big story and we really need to get on.'

They said their goodbyes and Mrs Harbinson hurried away with the key. We waited until she'd let the police into the cottage before we slipped out. Just as we drove up to the front gates, three other police cars arrived. Sara flashed her lights to allow them to enter first. The driver of the first car waved a hand in appreciation.

'That's what I like to see,' I said, 'courteous behaviour on the roads, and the police and the press in perfect harmony.'

'Right,' said Sara. 'And . . . anything useful in there?'

It was a question really of defining 'useful'. I was aware that Moira Doherty's computer hard drive might have been stolen. I suspected that she had agreed to a late-night meeting, because she'd gone for a lie-down on her bed but not succumbed to the temptation of getting in. I was puzzled by the fact that she had so few clothes with her for her six-month stay. And discombobulated by the drawers full of sex toys. But was any of this information actually *useful* to Sara Patterson in her job of reporting a murder for the *Belfast Telegraph*? Could she use any of it when none of it was certain or substantive or anything other than conjecture? Probably not. But she was looking at me, all wide-eyed and hungry for facts, ravenous for something that would give her an exclusive, an inside scoop that would leave her rivals floundering in her wake, keep her name on the front page where it belonged, and I realised that I had to give her something.

'Well,' I began, 'there were these sexy little knickers . . .'

14

Sara was less than impressed with the knickers and suspected that I was holding back, but there was nothing she could do apart from pout and huff and look disappointed. I'd lived with Patricia for many years, so it was like water off a duck's back. She asked me where I wanted dropped and I said, 'So is that it? You just use me and abuse me and then toss me out like a used and abused person?'

'Yes,' said Sara.

'Well, what's your plan? Going back to Belfast to write up your story?'

'No, of course not. I'm going to stay up here for a few days, see what happens. You?'

'Yes, me too, absolutely.'

'Why?'

'Why not?'

'I mean, she hadn't quite hired you to find her son, and now she's dead. What's the point?'

'No point. But nothing better to be doing.'

'Starkey.'

'Starkey what?'

'What're you up to?'

'Nothing.'

'Haven't you a grandson to be seeing to, and work and stuff?'

'Yes, and yes.'

'So?'

'So I haven't had a holiday in years, so why not spend a couple of days here? Poke around the City of Culture, take in a few art exhibitions, get up to speed on modern dance.'

Sara sighed. 'Your problem, Starkey, is you take everything personally.'

'I do not. And I'm quite offended that you could—'

'You really do. Moira Doherty's murder wasn't an attack on you. Whoever did it didn't shoot her to annoy you. Whoever killed Billy the Bear didn't kill him just to piss you off. They're not laying bait for you, Starkey, you have nothing to do with any of this.'

'And yet . . .'

'And yet nothing. You don't work for a paper. You met Moira Doherty once. She certainly isn't paying you. Go home.'

I pondered this. We were already most of the way back to Londonderry. Skies were grey and ominous-looking.

As we passed a country cottage, I saw my first Christmas tree and swore.

Sara smiled and said, 'Getting earlier every year.'

'I hate Christmas,' I said.

'I love it!'

'See, that's why we're never going to get together. Unless of course opposites attract.'

'Starkey. We were *never* going to get together.'

'You've just been playing hard to get.'

'No, we were never and are never going to get together.'

'Does being so negative not get you down? You should be open to things.'

'I'm open to many things. Just not you.'

'Yet you keep hanging around with me.'

'Only because you keep turning up and I feel sorry for you.'

'Ah, you'll weaken eventually. Everyone does.'

'Starkey, you're old enough to be my father.'

'I sincerely doubt that. Big brother maybe.'

'And also you're a liability, a shit magnet and you drink too much.'

'You mean I'm like a lovable rogue.'

'No.'

I said, 'So what if her murder is connected to her son's?'

'That's putting two and two together and getting six.'

'Big coincidence, though.'

'We don't even know that Billy the Bear has been murdered.'

'Or that he hasn't. She was convinced. And he's a big man to have disappeared without trace.'

'It happens. He's in the drugs business; sometimes you have to lie low, get out of town, go abroad, make a deal.'

'He was a mummy's boy, he would have been in touch somehow. Maybe they killed Moira to force him out into the open. Or revenge for a deal gone wrong. Or maybe she was working with him. Maybe she was the drug queen of Londonderry. Maybe Billy was just a big plump eejit and she was the real power.'

'That little old woman.'

'Maybe. Maybe she knew every dealer, every deal, or she did the books, she knew where the millions were deposited, all the secret bank accounts. Maybe that's why they stole her hard drive.'

'They stole her hard drive?'

'Did I not mention that?'

'Starkey!'

'Concentrate on the road,' I said.

She besieged me for more, but there was nothing more to give. Apart from the third phone number on the note in Moira's kitchen, and the sex toys, but I was holding them back for now. Sara asked again where I wanted dropped and I told her just wherever she was going.

She said, 'I'm going to the hotel to check in.'

'So am I,' I said.

'Which hotel and I'll drop you there.'

'Which one are you?'

She sighed. 'I'm at the City, Starkey, if it's any of your business.'

'So am I.'

'Starkey, this isn't funny.'

'Indeed not.'

'You're not staying at my hotel.'

'No, I'm staying at my hotel. Maybe it's just a co-incidence, like Moira and Billy the Bear getting murdered.'

'Starkey.'

'That's your problem.'

'What's my problem?'

'You think it's all about you. Attractive as you are, it might surprise you to know that I'm not following you about like a dog in heat, that in fact you invited me to go to the Twelve Apostles and that actually the City Hotel is about the only hotel in the city centre so where the hell else am I going to stay if I want to poke around into this? And actually I was already booked into it long before I knew you were driving up. So put that in your crack pipe and smoke it.'

After a bit, and on the outskirts of Londonderry, she said, 'You know, you're really very annoying.'

'I've been told that,' I said.

Sara parked in the smallish underground car park next to the hotel. She walked ahead of me up to reception while I scoped out the bar to the left and the restaurant to the right. When I joined her at the desk she said, 'Don't let me keep you.' I smiled as if she didn't mean it and said to the receptionist, 'Starting to snow again.'

She nodded and said, 'It's supposed to get heavy.' Then she said to Sara, 'Yes, that's all fine, single room, charged to the *Belfast Telegraph* account.' She pushed a key towards her. 'Third floor, room 311, the elevators are just to your left.'

I said to the receptionist, 'Do many of you read the *Telegraph* up here, or is it mostly the *Derry Journal*?'

She looked a little bashful and said, 'Mostly the *Journal*, I'm afraid. And the *Sentinel*.'

'No worries. It's probably because there's Belfast in the title. They should think about changing that.'

Sara was shaking her head at me. She picked up her key and turned for the elevators. When we got there, she pushed the button and looked straight ahead. It arrived and we stepped in. She pushed three. I pushed eight.

As the doors closed, I said, 'Who's going to feed it?'

'Feed what?'

'Your puppy. If you're staying here, who's going to feed your puppy?'

'None of your business.'

'Husband, boyfriend, girlfriend?'

'None of your business.'

'Want to meet for dinner after?'

'No.'

We arrived at three. She stepped out.

I said, 'I found something else in there too.'

Sara stopped. The doors closed. She had a glimpse of my smiling face.

I travelled on up to eight. Then I came right back

down. I walked up to the reception desk and said hello to the same girl.

She said, 'Oh – is everything okay?'

'Yes, of course, her room's lovely, but slight change of plan. We're covering the murder – you heard about that?'

'Yes, of course, everyone's talking about it.'

'Yep, big story and we're going to go large on it. I wasn't originally going to stay but I think it's important, so we'll be needing a second room.'

'Shouldn't be a problem. Just let me check what we have free.'

'Something on the eighth would be good – it's my lucky number.'

She gave me a smile, checked her computer, and said, 'And that'll be to the same account?'

'Absolutely,' I said.

She nodded, clicked a couple of boxes, and then passed a key card for 811 to me. I thanked her. As I was turning away she said, 'Oh – just one thing, sir?'

I stopped.

'Uhuh?'

'Will you be requiring a newspaper in the morning?'

'Well, I'd like the *Guardian*, but I suppose loyalty to my employers requires me to take the *Telegraph*.'

She gave me a sympathetic look and said, 'Why don't I send both up? After all, you're not paying for them.'

'Good point,' I said.

15

I was lying back on my king-sized. I'd stuffed my face with three courses off the room service menu while steadily working my way through two bottles of their most expensive white wine. I wasn't really one for the grape, but it was free, and it came with an ice bucket, which was about as decadent as I got. My bed had a close-up view of the Foyle, which I might have enjoyed on another night, but that enjoyment was diminished by the fact that front and centre was the Peace Bridge, where my client had been shot and then dumped in the river. There was yellow police tape at the nearest end; it was probably on the far side as well, but there was too much snow falling to see much beyond the CSI marquee that sat halfway along. I supposed they had finished for the night, but for all I knew they were still in there discussing clues and shit.

I FaceTimed Trish and asked after my faux grandkid

and if they were all home yet. She said everyone was fine but they were keeping them in for an extra night. She asked why I hadn't been back to visit and I explained about the Messiah in a snowstorm and the dead woman on the Peace Bridge and she sniffed and said, 'Same old, same old,' and I said, 'Aye.' She said, 'I want you to be part of this,' and I said, 'Part of what?' and she said, 'This,' which cleared everything up. She asked if the hotel was nice and I said, 'Cheap.' She asked if I was drinking and I said, 'Everything in moderation,' and she said, 'Sorry, the picture froze there, did you say *nothing* in moderation?' and we both laughed. We could afford to laugh, we were on opposite sides of the country with no danger of getting into an actual physical scrap. I said, 'Unless of course you want to jump in the car, race up here, tear your clothes off and jump into my bed.' She said, 'Feeling horny, are we?' and I said, 'Always.' 'Looks like you're on the pay-per-view,' she said, and I said, 'How much do you want?' She snorted. Which wasn't very sexy, but I was prepared to overlook it. I said, 'You do know that every single technological innovation has been fuelled by sex? That's why there's a movie business, DVDs, video cameras, computers . . .' 'Nuclear missiles? Toasters?' 'You know what I mean. It's all sex-driven.' 'Good to know you're still having big thoughts, Dan, and they get even bigger the more the wine goes down.' I said, 'I'm not drinking wine,' and she said, 'I can see it in the background, you have an ice bucket with a bottle sticking out of it,' and I said it wasn't mine but my lover's. She said, 'Who? Pamela Hand?' and cut the line.

I lay there smiling to myself for a while. I went looking for pictures of her on my phone and then remembered I'd deleted them in one of those *never-again* moments. I remembered that even as I did it I was aware that I would regret it but blinded by determination and Harp I had persevered. In looking for her I found the photo I'd taken of the notebook in Moira Doherty's kitchen.

I looked at the mysterious third number. It was only mysterious because I didn't know whose it was. But taken in conjunction with mine and Sara Patterson's, and that they were listed one after the other, on the same page and in the same handwriting and via the same pen, it seemed likely that there was a connection. So I called it. It was a landline number, and was answered straight away by a woman who was already in conversation with someone else, something about cigarettes, and it was a voice I thought I recognised. She said, 'Hello,' and I said, 'So how is Shipquay Street at this time of night?' and she said, 'What?' and I said, 'With the snow am I going to be able to get the car up the hill?' and she said, 'It's not that bad,' and then, 'Sorry, who is this?' and I said, 'Can I have a word with the boss?' She put the phone down and the guy came back on. He didn't sound any less grumpy than before. He snapped: 'What? Who is this?' I said, 'You seem to be working there twenty-four/seven, no wonder you're in a bad mood all the time.' He said, 'What do you want?' 'Ah now,' I said, 'that's the fifty-four-thousand-dollar question. I'm just curious as to what you're doing in there; jury's out, you know? Hoor-house or blue movie productions?' 'What the fuck are you—' 'And while you're on, how's Billy the Bear keeping these days?' He swore again. I hung up.

I called Sara's room and asked her if she fancied a walk in the snow.

She told me to catch myself on.

I asked about a drink in the bar and she said it sounded like I'd had enough already. Before I could deny it, she said she was working on her story still and was tired anyway and maybe we could meet for breakfast if my hangover wasn't too bad. I said I didn't suffer hangovers and asked if she wanted me to catch the lift down to her room to help her work on her story and she told me I would regret asking that in the morning. I said I never regretted anything, apart from flares in the early seventies, and she said she had no idea what I was talking about. I asked her if she was sure she didn't fancy a snowball fight and she hung up.

I went downstairs. It was getting on for eleven but the bar was mostly empty. I ordered a hot whiskey. I downed the whiskey and walked outside. The snow was already sitting thick on the pavement, crunchy underfoot, barely another footprint. I started walking, hands jammed into jacket pockets. I was dressed for spring. It was five minutes to Shipquay Street. When I got there, I stood at the bottom and looked up the hill. The snow was uniformly undisturbed on the road and footpaths. There was a bar called the Pub to my left. I thought it was a good name for a pub. It suggested what the place was about. There was traditional music from within, without. I resisted the temptation and walked up to the long-closed café opposite. I leaned in the doorway and looked across at the shuttered Mace and the apartments above. The curtains were drawn on all of the windows on the first and second floors, but the lights were on. Occasionally I saw a shape move against them. I stood for ten minutes, not sure what I was watching for. I tried to convince myself that the Pub would give me as good a view, and failed. I took out my phone and called the number again. I thought, with no traffic and nobody about, I might actually hear it ring across the way, but no; the only sound was of a faint, distant reel from the bar. It rang six times and then the voicemail kicked in.

You're through to Billy and Jacko, leave us a message why don't ya?

I didn't. I called back and listened to it again. If I'd already spoken to Jacko, and knew what he sounded like, then this Billy was Billy the Bear. His voice was deep, sonorous. Maybe Moira Doherty had called the number just to hear her son's voice again.

I decided to save my toes from frostbite and adjourn to the Pub. But before I could step away from the café, the door opposite opened and the first of half a dozen girls came out. I couldn't tell if they were the same girls I'd observed earlier. Too dark, too drunk. Two turned to the right and quickly disappeared over the brow of the hill. The others headed down towards the Guild Hall, stopped briefly at the bottom corner, and then two turned into the Pub. As they disappeared, a minivan with a taxi sign turned on to Shipquay and began to labour up the incline. It stopped outside the apartments and doors opened on both sides. I counted eight girls getting out, and they all disappeared inside. Four more arrived on foot in the next ten minutes. Whatever went on in there, it got busier late at night.

I walked down the hill. A bouncer was standing just inside the Pub door as I entered. He gave me the once-over, a swift nod, and said, 'You're just in time.' He locked and bolted the door behind me. 'There's a pint glass on the bar, stick a fiver in then you're free to travel back in time.' I smiled and nodded like I knew what he was talking about. I put a fiver in the glass. It was pretty stuffed, just like the bar. I ordered a pint. As I waited for it to come, I looked about me, wondering what exactly I'd paid for: the music had stopped, there was nothing but bar chatter, no obvious signs of entertainment pending. The two girls from the apartment were sitting together on one side of a table, each drinking red wine and smoking. I continued to scan around, but nothing jumped out, just a regular pub crowd. And then as I took my first sip, it gradually dawned on me: first the smell, then the hand movements, then the ashtrays; half the patrons were smoking inside. A few were smoking joints, but most were on regular cigarettes. They all appeared very, very happy to be doing it. I had never been a smoker, but I'd never particularly noticed or objected to it. I am all for anarchy and the freedom to kill yourself.

I lifted my pint and walked across to the girls' table.

I said, 'Could you give us a light?'

One of them, short dark hair, designer glasses, held up her lighter.

'And a cigarette?' I added.

She hesitated, then reluctantly offered a box of Embassy Regal. Her make-up was thick, her lipstick scarlet.

I took one and she flicked the lighter. I inhaled. I coughed. I said, 'Is anyone sitting here . . .?' and indicated the two free chairs at their table.

The other girl, mousy brown hair, heavy dark eyeliner said, 'No, and no.'

'I won't say a word, I'll just . . .'

I started to pull one of the chairs out. Beneath the table the second girl's leg wrapped itself around it.

'No,' she snapped. 'Fuck off.'

I let go and raised my hands. 'Sorry – didn't mean anything. Fine with me. Just – don't I recognise youse from somewhere? Do youse not work up the road there in—'

'No – now fuck the fuck off. Okay?'

I backed away, all the way to the bar. I stubbed the cigarette out in an ashtray. Beside me, a sixtyish guy with red cheeks, a stained black suit jacket and blue jeans, a roll-up burned almost to the quick between his fingers, sniggered and said, 'You'll never get anywhere with them.'

'Lookin' that way,' I said. 'Know them?'

'You could say that. In fact, half the men in this bar

probably know them. Word's out.' He gave a theatrical wink, then suddenly shook his hand and threw the tiny stub of his cigarette into the ashtray. 'Fuck,' he said. He raised one of his fingers to his mouth and delicately licked at the burn.

'Word . . .?'

'Aye. Just watch – you'll catch sneaky glances across.'

'Men will do that,' I said. 'They're good-looking girls.'

I turned back to the bar and took another drink. He was as drunk as I was, his words thick and slurry. The smell of smoke and weed was beginning to make me feel sick. That and the wine and the whiskey and the beer, and the three fat and indulgent courses on room service. My new friend leaned in beside me and said, 'Aye, they are lookers, the both of them. And every once in a while one of us will make an approach, just like you, and they'll bark like fucking Jack Russells. Half the men in here are here because they know the girls sometimes drop in for a drink after work. And not just these two, the rest of them too.'

'Rest of them?'

'Aye, they work just up the street. All day and all night. On their backs.'

'You mean they're . . .?'

'Aye, and no.' He had a fresh pint of Guinness before him, which he took a long sup of. When he left it down he had a moustache on his moustache. He wiped the back of his hand across his mouth, glanced back at the girls, then leaned in even closer and said drunk-quietly, 'See the one on the left? With the glasses?

'Safternoon I watched her stick a ten-inch dildo up her hole. And it didn't cost me nothin'.'

He nodded, pleased with himself, and added another wink for free.

'Good to know,' I said.

He showed me on his phone what they were up to, although the service wasn't really set up for mobiles. But it was eye-watering stuff. Then we were distracted by the girls finishing their drinks and getting up. I finished mine, thinking I would follow, see where they were going, try and get another word, ask about Billy the Bear, even though by now I only had a vague idea why I would want to know anything about him. I could barely stand. The bouncer let them out, but then closed the door after them and stood in front of it. He said, 'I don't think so.' My friend at the bar came over and put his arm around me and said, 'He's new . . .' So the bouncer looked at me with a mix of pity and sympathy and said, 'You need to give the girls five minutes to disappear.'

'But I wasn't . . .'

'That's what they all say. They just want left alone, so give them a chance to grab a cab.'

My friend guided me back to the bar, and against my better judgement I accepted a pint of Guinness and then bought him one back when the time came. Someone came and joined our conversation and handed me a joint, so I took a hit on that and then, when it came round again, another, and another, and by the time I went back to negotiate with the bouncer I realised the place was mostly empty, he was long gone, and the door was just on the latch. I staggered outside into a winter wonderland and immediately went on my arse. I started laughing, and then decided to roll all the way down the hill. It was exhilarating. At the bottom I threw up. Then I tried to remember what the hotel was called and where it was and who I was and what country we lived in and why I was out in the snow at all and why anyone would want to stick a ten-inch dildo up their arse.

16

I was freezing, and my head was pounding, and there was wind howling, and the hotel room curtains were flapping madly, but I couldn't get my eyes open because they'd been stitched shut by demons from hell. There was a horrific rushing sound in my ears as if all the blood in my body was frantically searching for an escape route and getting more and more frustrated. I could just about summon the power to feel about in the dark for the bedside light but I couldn't find it, or the wall, and somehow I'd lost the sheets and the mattress was as hard as concrete and the pillows were missing and my throat was like razor blades and I could hardly breathe through my nose stuffed with snot and vomit and if Christine had rolled up and told me she could work a miracle and make me feel better in exchange for conversion to the cause I would gladly have embraced it and lived my life as a missionary in

Indo-China or Strabane, and as soon as I thought that I was regretting it because suddenly there was a light and a hand on my shoulder shaking me and I said, 'What the fuck . . .?!' and recoiled as someone said, 'Sir, you can't sleep here,' and I bellowed, 'Get out of my fucking room!' and then two big hands grabbed me and hauled me to my feet and my eyes were magically open and I was wincing, wincing against the tiger-strong beam of a flashlight and seeing nothing but its big-bang brightness until whoever it was moved his head to the side and said, 'You're not supposed to be in here,' and I saw that he was wearing the uniform of an officer of the law, that in fact I was not in my hotel room but in some kind of tent, and the flapping was the opening to that tent, and I came to realise that the rushing sound was not in my ears but the River Foyle charging past, and that I had chosen to sleep in or been inexplicably drawn to the Peace Bridge where Moira Doherty had met her fate. The cop said, 'Sir, this is a crime scene, I should arrest you for—' But I cut him off by jabbing a finger at him and snapping out, 'I'm a private investigator trying to solve a crime! You wouldn't arrest Sherlock Holmes!' He shook his head and said, 'If he was contaminating a crime scene I probably would. Did you also remove the crime-scene tape at the foot of the bridge?' 'I didn't do fucking nothing!' My head was *literally* going to roll off. I clutched at it and tried to sit down again, but he caught me by the arm. 'Now, sir, let's not be doing that. I can point you in the direction of the homeless shelter if—' 'I'm not fucking homeless!

I'm a private detective!' 'Sir, you need to watch your language or . . .' There was laughter from outside the tent. I staggered forward and through the flap and said, 'And what the fuck are you laughing at?' to another cop with a stupid grin on his stupid face and he raised his hands and said, 'Nothing, Columbo . . .' 'Oh – fuck off!' I started walking back along the bridge. I stopped, turned: 'And Columbo wasn't a fucking private detective!' They were now both laughing at me, laughing policemen. I shouted, 'Why don't you go and catch some terrorists!' back at them, but they continued to find me hilarious. By the time I got to the end of the bridge I was marvelling at how Columbo had so entered the cultural lexicon that even bum-fluff-faced cops had misheard of him and also decided that I was never drinking again. By the time I got to the hotel I decided that it wasn't the drink, which I was well used to, but the drugs, which I wasn't. Cut that shit out and I'd be fine. I staggered past the reception desk to the elevators and pushed the button. As the doors opened, Sara Patterson was standing there. She looked surprised, stepped out and said, 'Have you eaten already?' I said no, I was just on my way to knock her up and she said, 'What?' and I said, 'Chance would be a fine thing, but actually you need to go back up and get your laptop, I have something to show you.' She studied me and said, 'You look terrible. Have you slept?' 'Absolutely,' I said, and it wasn't a lie.

I said to the waitress when she asked if I wanted coffee or juice what the chances were of getting a Bloody

Mary and she looked confused. I gave her my most serious face, and begging puppy eyes, and said, 'It's quite simple – it's a medically approved cure for Spanish flu, which I'm in the grippe of . . . with me?'

'Yes, sir . . .' she said, though her eyes roved for tactical support; she didn't look more than sixteen, olive skin.

'You get two ice cubes, lemon juice, Worcestershire sauce, Tabasco sauce, tomato juice, a pinch of salt and freshly ground black pepper, and vodka. With me still?'

'With you.'

'Repeat it . . .'

'Ice cubes, lemon juice, Worcestershire sauce, Tabasco, tomato juice, salt and pepper, vodka . . .'

'Perfect. You get a tall glass and add the ice and vodka. Squeeze the lemon juice in, six dashes of Worcestershire, three of Tabasco, go a bit mad with the tomato juice and make it a double shot of vodka. You got that still?'

'I have it, sir.'

'You think you could make that for me now?'

'Yes, sir, absolutely, sir. With the exception of the vodka; we're not allowed to serve alcohol before eleven thirty.'

'Oh for Jesus' . . .'

'Do you still want me to—'

'No!'

She took a step back. She said, 'Please help yourself to the breakfast buffet.'

'Brilliant,' I said. 'Thanks.'

I put my head in my hands and wished for the world to end. When it didn't, I got up and went to the buffet and filled a plate with everything that would fit on to it. I forced it down, at speed, tasting nothing, fighting the urge to retch the whole time. I was just finishing when Sara arrived back with her laptop. She apologised for the delay, she had to return a call, and as she sat she put four headache pills beside my plate. She poured me a glass of water. I swallowed them one by one without comment. I took a deep breath, forced my head up and reached across for her laptop.

She *almost* moved to stop me.

I opened it up and looked at a screen saver of Nelson Mandela, and groaned. Then I asked for her password.

'If you think I'm giving you . . .'

She pulled the laptop back, typed, entered and returned.

I opened her Google Chrome and said, 'How do you feel about sex in a public place?'

'I've nothing against it, but not on a first date.'

'I mean, are you easily embarrassed?'

'Not especially.'

'Good, then take a look at this . . .'

I spun the screen around. She half smiled at me and focused in. Then she let out an almost involuntary 'Jesus Christ!' and would have snapped the laptop shut if I hadn't pulled it back out of her reach. I half closed it.

'Starkey, for fuck . . .'

Her eyes were darting about to see if anyone was watching.

'Well that certainly put colour in your cheeks,' I said.

'What the fuck . . . I mean, why the fuck would you show me that . . . what's *wrong* with you?'

'Many things, but this is work.'

'*What* is . . . what are you talking about . . .?'

'*This*,' I said, and opened it up again.

'Jesus! It's a fucking breakfast buffet, Starkey, you don't have to . . .'

'You'd rather we watched it in your room? Lead the way.'

'Jesus.'

I adjusted the angle. 'Don't worry, no one can see. Just . . . tell me what you're see—'

'You know what I'm seeing! She's . . . with her hand . . .' Her brow furrowed, she glanced about again, and then leaned forward, her eyes narrowing as she studied it in a little more detail. 'Okay, and there's dialogue boxes down the side . . . comments . . . people . . . *men* . . . encouraging her to . . .'

'Encouraging her, yes, but also paying her to . . . look . . . see at the bottom . . . no, not that bottom, lovely though it is . . . here . . . here's the amount she's trying to raise . . . here's the amount she has raised . . . and this is what she's promising to do if she hits her target . . .'

'Is that . . . even possible . . .?'

'Depends on the size of the fist,' I said.

'Fascinating as this is, why exactly are you showing it to me, apart from the fact that you're still drunk and don't know what you're doing and probably getting a kick out of it?'

'Bear with me. I'm not drunk, I just had a bad pint, and sixteen good ones. I'm trying to explain something to you that has . . . relevance to you and what you're writing about. Porn. Porn, okay? Understand that porn is big business, whether it's on the internet, DVDs, in sex shops or on hotel pay-per-view, not that I would ever dream of doing that, unless someone else was paying for it. It's worth billions. But it's like a black economy, because nobody really knows; it could be bigger than Hollywood, bigger than Microsoft.'

'Don't they exaggerate everything in porn?'

'Yes, of course, but believe me, I'm a single man, living alone, and I've done the research, and the biggest part of porn at the moment is this . . . interaction. Instead of remotely watching some hugely proportioned porn stars going at it, you get to talk to ordinary women, or men, for that matter, good-looking usually but not gods or goddesses, and you encourage them to do what you want them to do with their bodies, almost anything you can imagine. And however extreme that is, double it or triple it and I guarantee you there's someone out there willing to do it, perform it, insert it, and many, many men, or women for that matter, willing to pay to watch you do it, willing to pay to talk to you and direct you while you do it. And it's safe – the performers aren't in danger of physical abuse or catching anything and the customers hide behind fake names. It's perfect. It's wanktastic.'

'You think it's harmless?'

'Largely.'

'You think there are no victims?'

'Not obviously.'

She pushed her chair back and stood up, face like thunder. 'I'm going for an omelette.'

'What?'

'What *what*?'

'What's got you annoyed?'

'Nothing apart from you being delusional. Harmless!'

Sara walked up to the buffet. I noticed that she had rather carelessly left her phone sitting on the table. I reached across and lifted it, and was pleased to see that it wasn't password-protected. I checked that she was still busy collecting her breakfast and then made an adjustment to it. It was in her own best interests, or possibly mine. When she returned with her plate, the phone was back where she'd left it.

I said, 'How do you mean, delusional?'

She sighed. 'Starkey – it's way too early in the morning to get into a debate about the mores of the sex industry. You're not stupid. You know it debases women, it exploits them, it does them untold psychological damage.'

'I thought it was too early to get into—'

'Starkey, shut up.' She nodded at the screen. 'I know about porn. But *this* is new to me.'

'Well there's a lot of it around. You could argue that

these women are the ones exploiting poor vulnerable men . . . that has to be better, right?'

She leaned across the table. 'Are you fucking joking?'

'Maybe,' I said.

There was, at last, some little relief from the pain and nausea.

'You don't think they're forced into this – by men? By economic circumstance? By mental illness?'

'They might just be exhibitionists making a bit on the side.'

'Starkey – what is the point in this? Why are you showing me hard-core pornography with my breakfast baps? Where's the relevance, or are you just—'

'Did you catch the name of the website?'

'No, I . . .' She sighed. She looked at a passing waitress, my Bloody Mary. 'Okay. Right.' She studied the screen again and then raised an eyebrow. 'Stroke City Girls. That's very location-specific.'

'It's a specific business.'

Political correctness required that the Maiden City was referred to as Derry/Londonderry, Derry *stroke* Londonderry, but it had quickly been rechristened Stroke City by local wags. And it had caught on. It wasn't so much a play on words as a play on punctuation. The genius behind Stroke City Girls had taken it one step further.

I said, 'Stroke is also a euphemism for—'

'I know what it is . . .'

'Abusing the wicked stick.'

'There's no need to—'

'Badgering the witness.'

'Starkey, you don't—'

'Just so that we're clear.'

She sighed. 'So what about Stroke City Girls?'

'It's run from two apartments not a stone's throw from here, if it was a small stone and you had a big, heavily muscled arm.'

'Right. Again, it may be a story for someone, but why me?'

'Because Stroke City Girls is being run at least in part from Billy the Bear's apartment. And it may also have at least one satellite in Castlerock . . .'

'In Castle— You mean . . .?'

'In Moira Doherty's holiday rental, from which she was probably lured to a meeting on the Peace Bridge, shot in the head and tipped over into the river. And after which her killers went to her cottage and removed the hard drive of her computer, because it contains the details of the Stroke City Girls set-up, the vast amounts of money they're making and where it's actually ending up.'

It was a bit of a stretch, and just one of any possible number of scenarios. But worth mentioning.

Sara was staring at me, completely oblivious to the fact that on the laptop sitting between us, and open to be seen by anyone passing, a red-headed, freckle-faced colleen was taking on board one of her five-a-day fruits in a highly unconventional manner and loudly appreciating it.

'Starkey, are you just guessing, supposing and imagining? Because it doesn't sound to me like you have any facts at all.'

'None,' I agreed.

Sara sighed. Her eyes flitted to the screen.

'Fuck me,' she said, 'but that's a powerful big banana.'

17

On the whole I prefer to plough a lonely furrow, but I'm not averse to the odd strategic alliance. Patricia says I'm not a team player. That I use people and discard them. That I lie and cheat and deceive. I don't deny it. She would concede that this behaviour is usually in aid of the greater good, and a way of protecting those very people from bad stuff. I had worked with Sara before, so she at least knew the way of me. Ostensibly we were on the same side, but there would be bruised lips and swollen eyes before we were done.

The strategy was: Sara goes and talks to her journalistic comrades and calls in favours with her police contacts. I pursue the naked cam girls. When I wasn't doing that, I'd be finding out more about Jacko and Moira. Then we'd meet up again and share, or trade, or tease.

Before I could drive to Shipquay Street, I had to

cough up thirty quid for the overnight stay at the Foyleside car park. The shopping centre itself wasn't open yet, so there were just a few cars scattered about, including one on either side of mine. I whistled up to it, aware that I was still probably two or three times over the limit. When I put the key in, the radio came on, a Christmas tune, so there was some life in it, but it just wouldn't turn over. I got out and opened the bonnet, just in case there was something obvious, like the engine was missing. As I peered in at it, I was aware of the door opening on the car beside me. Two men got out. I smiled hopefully at them and said, 'Any chance of a push?'

The closest, in a beige suit, with a thin face dominated by a thick black moustache, said, 'Not a problem,' and gave me a push, right back against the car.

As I bounced off it he said, 'Dan Starkey?'

The other guy came up beside him. Black suit, grey tie. They had neat hair and were the shape of people who went to the gym on a regular basis.

I said, 'Who wants to know?'

They moved right up close.

Doors opened on the other side and two more suits got out. They came round, so that there were four of them facing me.

The one who'd pushed me held up some ID and said, 'Detective Inspector Davies, Strand Road. Raise your hands so we can search you.'

Having not much else to do with my time, I raised my hands.

The cop in the black suit frisked me. He looked mildly disgusted as his hands roved up and down inside my jacket. 'Have you been drinking, sir?' he asked.

'Yes, but only since nineteen seventy-eight.'

'Last night, you mean?'

'Yes,' I said, 'in a world where there are seventy-eight minutes in an hour.'

He started to respond, but DI Davies waved him away. He said, 'Get in,' and indicated his car.

I got in the back. He got in the other side. We shut our respective doors.

'Your pals are going to feel excluded,' I said.

He studied me. It was probably meant to intimidate.

'These days it's all about inclusivity,' I said, with some difficulty, before adding: 'Also, caring is sharing.'

I looked out at his colleagues. I gave them the thumbs-up. I was contrary by nature, and drunk by design. I returned my attention to the detective inspector and said, 'Very impressive. It's that Movember thing, isn't it? The moustache? I tried growing one but it looked like someone had glued a gerbil on to—'

His finger shot out lightning fast and jabbed me in the Adam's apple.

Not that hard, but it didn't have to be.

I lurched forward, grabbing and coughing and choking and gasping.

While I spluttered he said, 'You know what this is about. She was in your car, you were seen with her in your car.'

'So what? Jesus!'

'So you admit it?'

'Yes! What's the big deal?'

There was no reason not to admit it. It would be on a camera somewhere, my number was on her notepad, on her mobile phone. I rubbed at my throat. His colleagues were watching, unmoved by the assault.

'Where did you take her?'

'I dropped her at Victoria bus station in Belfast, far as I know she got the bus up here, that's the last time I saw her.'

'Just tell us the truth, Starkey.'

'It is the truth.'

'You're only going to make things worse for yourself.' He shook his head slowly. 'Why was she in your car in the first place?'

'She wanted me to work for her.'

'Doing what?'

'I . . . look into things.' I still found it quite hard to tell anyone that I was a private detective without grinning stupidly. 'She had a problem she wanted solved.'

'Which was . . .?'

'Which was between me and her.'

'Try making it between you and her and me.'

'You know I can't do that, it would contravene the hypocritic oath.'

'The what?'

'The something like that. Look, Detective Inspector – I'm sorry she's dead and all that, but it has nothing to do with me.'

I trailed off because his mouth had dropped open

and the blood had suddenly drained from his face. He felt around for the door handle without taking his eyes off me. 'You wait here,' he said, opening it and backing out without breaking the connection, at least until he'd gathered his colleagues together. Almost immediately they all turned to look at me. I raised my hands in a helpless gesture.

A pick-up truck pulled up behind my car. One of the detectives spoke briefly to the driver, who then jumped out and began attaching the cables that would allow him to winch it up.

I rolled the window down and said to DI Davies, 'Aw, come on, you're not taking my car. I need my car.'

He came to my window. He crouched down, bending his knees carefully and keeping his back straight. 'We'll take what we want,' he said. 'This is a murder inquiry.'

'Yes, I know that, but—'

'You're going to burn in hell.'

He straightened and turned away.

The car was lifted and then lowered on to the flat bed of the truck. As I hadn't been arrested or otherwise restrained, I got out of the vehicle. They were talking animatedly amongst themselves and didn't notice me at first. Maybe it was the whistling that gave me away. But then Davies himself saw me, gave a sudden start, and they all reached for their weapons.

I raised my hands and said, 'Easy there. It wasn't that out of tune, was it?'

I had been whistling the 'Londonderry Air', the posh title for 'Danny Boy'. I thought it might ease the tension.

It did not.

One of them said, 'We should just do him here.'

Davies looked like he was giving it serious consideration.

Then he said, 'Do yourself a favour, Starkey – what have you done with the body?'

'*What* body?'

'Christine's body!'

That took me by surprise.

And when things take me by surprise, like news of death or mayhem, I have a tendency to laugh, or at least smile; it's a reflex, a gag reaction. It doesn't mean anything, at least to me. Others don't take it so well. The grey-suited cop punched me in the guts. I sank to my knees. Somehow, despite the pain, I laughed.

He stood over me and hissed, 'You sick son of a bitch.'

But I couldn't help myself.

Davies came up beside him. 'What's so funny, Starkey? Tell us now, or by God I'll let them kick you to death right here, right now.'

'Christine,' I said. 'Christine. You're looking for Christine.'

'Yes! Now you tell us what you've done to her or where you've buried or left her or—'

'I haven't fucking touched her, you stupid pricks! I thought you were talking about Moira Doherty!'

'Moira . . .?'

'She's the one I gave a lift to the bus station.'

The other cop was about to give me a kick, but Davies stayed him. He stared down at me. He grabbed me by

131

the lapels and dragged me up. He stared into my face. 'We don't give a shit about that old hag,' he growled. 'We want to know what you've done with Christine.'

'And I'm telling you, I haven't done anything.'

'You kidnapped her from Ballyferris . . .'

'No, she skipped there under her own steam.'

'You drove her in this direction but got caught in a blizzard on Glenshane.'

'Yes, I did.'

'Where you told the owners she was your daughter.'

'No, they presumed it and I couldn't be bothered correcting them.'

'Then you drove off with her in the morning, and she hasn't been seen since.'

'No,' I said, with a sigh, 'I walked her from the car to the river, she wanted to go across but the Peace Bridge was shut down because of the murder, so she went one way, I went the other. I'm sure there's cameras in here and out there, and the boys in green and the world's press were everywhere. Go and check. She walked off, happy as Larry.'

Davies was still scowling at me, but his eyes were no longer as inflamed. He glanced back at his colleagues. 'Check the security cameras inside and out.'

Two of them immediately set off.

Davies finally let go of my lapels, while managing to give me a shove backwards at the same time. I banged into the back of one of their cars and then stood there, massaging my stomach, thinking that their anger seemed more personal than official. And now that they had failed to get anything from me, they suddenly looked a bit unsure of themselves. I straightened up and pushed off the car.

'So how come you're so interested anyway?' I asked. 'Twenty-four hours, that's nothing for a missing person.'

'But not for a kidnapping,' said Davies. 'Not for a murder.'

He wasn't even looking at me now, but watching his two colleagues cross the car park.

'Has someone reported a kidnapping? Or a murder?'

'That's none of your business.' He turned back towards me and looked surprised to find me so close. He softened his voice a little. 'Look, we just want to make sure she's okay.'

I noticed for the first time a pinprick of metal on his lapel, and before I really knew what I was doing I reached out and turned it over. He quickly slapped my hand away, but not quickly enough to stop me from seeing what was there, hidden from public view but there all the same – a small metal cross with a sun behind it.

'For fuck sake,' I said. He was a cop for sure, but a New Seeker too. 'Are you all . . .?'

His colleague looked shifty enough to confirm my suspicion.

'We're investigating Christine's disappearance,' said Davies. 'She's sixteen years old and she's vulnerable and—'

'And she's more than capable of looking after herself,' I said. I shook my head. 'You boys have some fucking nerve, doing Pike's dirty work for him . . . isn't that right? He put the word out and you think you can just—'

'It's not like that . . .'

'It's exactly like that!'

'Starkey, you were with her, we still haven't seen any evidence proving that you really . . .'

'Oh shut up,' I said.

Davies looked a bit stunned. 'Don't you—'

But I cut him off.

'No,' I said, 'why should I? It's not like you're here on official business, is it? You're doing a homer for Pike, so unless you're going to shoot me, I think youse can just fuck off.' He opened his mouth, but nothing came out. It was time to press home the advantage. 'So here's what we're going to do. I'm going to walk into that shopping centre and buy myself a Twix. You and your pals from the God Squad are going to get my fucking car off that fucking truck and put it right back where it was, or I'll have you fucking chancers all over the fucking internet in about three minutes flat, okay? All right?'

'Starkey, you can't speak—'

'I *fucking* can!'

I turned and strode away towards the shops.

No move to stop me.

'Starkey! We're not finished with you yet!'

'Yes you are,' I called back, 'and give it a fucking turtle wax while you're there, you fucking spanners!'

18

I was still spitting nails as I walked towards Shipquay Street. I wasn't the slightest bit concerned about Christine, but I couldn't say the same about the cops. They might only have been local plods, but their willingness to use their position on behalf of their church was extremely worrying. Religion had always played its part in recruitment and policy, but it used to be so easily defined, as obvious as black and white, or orange and green; the New Seekers were adding new and camouflaged colours to the spectrum.

And I didn't like how quickly Pike had pointed them in my direction either.

As I began to move up the hill, I took out my phone and texted the teenage Messiah.

How's it going?

The man from the Mace was fixing a display in his window. He looked at me and I looked at him and I took the mature decision not to attempt to procure the Twix in his establishment, because it was bound to end in a bloodbath. I crossed the road to the café, but there were no free tables. I stood outside for a bit, looking up at the apartments across the way. The curtains were drawn at all of the windows, with no obvious signs of life. But I knew they were in there, flashing, touching, fingering, thrusting and sucking for the benefit of all mankind. It was just after nine a.m. If they stuck to yesterday's pattern, it would be twelve before their shift ended. I started walking again. A pound shop on the brow of the hill was just opening. I went in and bought a can of luminous orange spray paint. At the counter I asked how much it was. The boy in a red apron blinked at me. I said, 'Do you get asked that all the time?' He said no. 'What if something is worth *less* than a pound, do you put the price *up* just so that you can still say it's a pound shop?' He said no. I rattled the spray can at him and said, 'I hope this works. I bought bin bags in a pound shop once and they were rubbish.' On the way out he said he hoped I had a nice day. I told him it was a bit late for that.

I took the steps up on to the old wall, and walked along it as far as the Verbal Arts Centre, just off Bishop Street. There was a Siege-era big black cannon opposite, pointing out across the Bogside. There were some who probably wished that it still worked. The ramparts gave me a head-on view of the disassociated gable end marooned on a traffic island, which was Free Derry Corner. Behind it the old slums that had led to half the

Troubles had long since been bulldozed and replaced with modern state housing. These newer gable walls boasted murals that looked fresh and new but still harked back: a teenager wearing a gas mask and holding a petrol bomb, with police in riot gear behind him; a second showed more rioters, one of them with a megaphone, directing the trouble, and a woman on her knees in the act of banging out Bogside semaphore with a metal bin lid on the tarmac road.

I stepped off the wall and down the incline towards Free Derry Corner. As I approached, a small minibus pulled up opposite it and half a dozen Japanese-looking tourists got out and began to snap away. I obliged when one asked me to take a group photograph. I didn't know exactly when Moira Doherty had taken her photo of the graffiti announcing the death of her son, Billy the Bear, but there was no sign of it now. In fact, there was no sign of any graffiti, which was a shame. So I took out my can and spray-painted in luminous orange:

Is the Pope Catholic?

After due contemplation, and aware of the stares of the tourists, and the fact that their driver was on his phone almost as soon as I started, I took up my can again and sprayed:

Do bears shit in the woods?

The driver quickly shepherded his charges back on to the minibus, gave me a filthy look, and sped off. I tossed the can into some bushes, then stood and admired my handiwork. A couple of minutes later a red Volvo cruised slowly past, stopping about twenty metres along.

Two guys got out, one in a shirt and tie with a too-tight collar, older, fifties, the other in a black zip-up Harrington jacket that looked older than he was; he was probably still in his twenties, with a Sidney side-sweep. They sauntered across and stood behind me, one on either side. They studied my handiwork.

The guy with the tie said, 'You do that?'

'Nope,' I said.

The other fella said, 'You've orange paint on your hands.'

'Dammit,' I said.

'Are you fucking mental or something?' the tie asked.

'It's an art installation,' I said, nodding at the wall. 'I think it works. The orange is supposed to be symbolic.'

'It's fucking sym-bollocks,' said the Harrington. 'Round here, fella, this could get you shot.'

'This is sacrilege,' said the tie, 'I mean, Jesus, it's like pissin' on the Turin Shroud.'

'Tried that,' I said, 'but they have better security.'

'Fella . . .' the tie began.

'So are youse the monkeys, or are youse the organ grinders?'

'You wah?' said the Harrington.

The tie said, 'I'm the curator of the Irish Republican Archive.' He nodded ahead. 'It's just up there. This wall is a National Heritage Site.'

'Yeah,' said Harrington, 'so you better fuck off before you're done for vandalising it.'

I ignored him and said to Tie: 'And what did you do

before you became curator of the Irish Republican
Archive? Did you serve a long apprenticeship in
academia to prepare you for this important task, or just
heave a few petrol bombs?'

'None of your fuckin' business.'

'Thought not,' I said. 'Anyway, this is the score, lads
– I'm investigating the murder of Moira Doherty and
her son Billy.'

Without actually looking at them, I was aware of
them exchanging glances.

'Are you a peeler?' Harrington asked.

'No,' I said, 'I'm a private investigator.'

'What's so funny?' the curator asked.

'Nothing,' I said. 'I'm just blessed with a sunny person-
ality. Fact is, lads, my name's Dan Starkey and I'm from
Belfast, I don't have any connections here at all. But
Billy the Bear's death was announced on this wall.'

'What the fuck about it?' said Harrington.

'Well, I want to speak to whoever sanctioned the
announcement. In other words, who's in charge round
here?'

'Are you serious?' the curator asked. 'Who's in
charge? No one's in fucking charge, that's the problem.'

'Okay,' I said, 'let me put it another way. Who's
everyone scared of?'

The curator looked at me for a long moment, then
gave a shake of his head and produced a phone.

'Right. Well you asked for it,' he said and raised it
to his ear.

*   *   *

Moira Doherty had been an agitator, and in my own way, I was as well. Journalists are taught to always try and confront those who actually wield the power rather than spokesmen paid to spin, but even towards the end of my career in newspapers that had become increasingly difficult and it was nearly impossible now; you found out what they wanted you to find out, and there was rarely the time or the resources to dig deeper. But if Londonderry was anything like Belfast, if the Bogside was anything like the worst of Turf Lodge, then there would be nothing to be gained from hanging out in the pub trying to chat up the locals, I would stick out like a sore thumb. These places were always insular, paranoid and violent; you needed the nod from whoever was in charge if you wanted to get anything, including out with your life.

The curator and Harrington walked me to their car. The curator opened the driver's door and Harrington went to get in the back.

I said, 'Sure let me in the back.'

Harrington said, 'I'm always in the back.'

'You're fine up front with me,' said the curator, indicating for me to take the passenger seat.

I said, 'Really, I'd prefer the back.'

'I'm not your chauffeur.'

'I know that, but I'd prefer the back. I get carsick in the front.'

'Right. Get in the back beside him then.'

'I'd prefer not. It makes it look like I'm your prisoner.'

'Then get in the front.'

'Nope. I've seen *The Godfather* too many times.'

'This isn't the fucking seventies.'

'Really? In the back, by myself, then I'm just like a friend, getting a lift.'

The curator sighed. 'Right, Tommy get in the front . . .'

'But—'

'Just do it, or we'll be here all fucking day.'

Tommy got in the front. I got in the back. I sat in the middle, which gave me a good view of where we were going. The curator started the engine and we pulled out.

'It's great having a chauffeur,' I said.

They took me to a strip of shops and offices just a couple of streets away. All of the premises had very small windows. Cheaper to replace come riot season. The curator parked and pointed towards a blue-painted double shop front that shared a single door: one side with *McBride and Sons, Funeral Directors* and the other *Lovely Flowers.* He said, 'In there.'

I said, 'Are you kiddin'?'

'How do you mean?'

'The most feared man on the Bogside is a funeral director? Or a florist, for that matter?'

'No, but he happens to be in there.'

'Okay,' I said, 'very good – so who am I looking for?'

'You'll know him when you see him,' said the curator, and raised an eyebrow.

'Cryptic,' I said.

I got out the driver's side and stood expectantly at his window. When it came down I said, 'Are you not coming to make introductions?'

He said, 'I don't know you from Adam.'

'Well are you not waiting around to give me a lift back?'

He smiled and said, 'You may not need one.'

His window moved back up.

By the time I got to the other side of the road my chauffeur had already zipped away. I opened the shop door and entered a small vestibule, with a door to the right for the flower shop, and one to the left into the funeral parlour. As I opened the funeral parlour door a small bell sounded. The walls inside were suitably grey and austere. They were adorned with framed certificates, which gave me confidence that they would know how to bury me so that I stayed buried. Someone was standing facing an unmanned office desk. He turned as I came in and said, 'Mr McBride is just fetching something from upstairs.' He indicated some stairs to the left of the desk.

He was a smallish man, perhaps pushing sixty, in a black sports jacket with a black tie and a shirt that was a little loose around the neck. He looked like someone who had lately lost a lot of weight but his wardrobe hadn't had the chance to catch up.

As I sized him up, he sized me.

After a bit he nodded and said, 'Funeral for a friend.'

I said, 'Elton John.'

His brow furrowed. Not everyone got my obscure

song references. Maybe only Trish. This guy didn't look especially threatening, but experience told me that the worst ones rarely did.

He said, 'It's a bad business.'

I said, 'I'm a private investigator,' and this time, for some reason, possibly fear, I didn't smile.

'You don't meet many private investigators.'

'Nope,' I said, 'I have the market cornered.'

He said, 'Is there a market?'

'Nope,' I said.

We both nodded.

I said, 'I'm not looking to cause any trouble, but when I take on a job I always like to see it through even if the client dies before she has a chance to brief me properly. I'm not interested in the back story or how Billy ended up dead, I just want to know where the body is.'

He nodded sagely.

'Well,' he said, after a bit, 'I think they keep them in the back.'

I did some sage nodding myself.

I said, 'Are you, in fact, the most feared man on the Bogside?'

He said, 'I wouldn't have thought so.' He gave a tired shrug. 'I'm in TV licensing, I doubt there's a single one in the entire estate.'

'Starkey?'

There was a man standing at the bottom of the stairs. He might have been there for a while. He was wearing a black suit, and black tie, and black shoes.

I took a wild guess and said, 'Mr McBride?'

'You were looking for Danny?'

'I don't know. Is he the most feared man on the Bogside?'

'Is, was, and ever shall be.' McBride thumbed behind him. 'You've got five minutes.'

I looked at the TV licence man. His eyes had widened somewhat, and his cheeks had coloured. He looked at the funeral director and said, 'Danny Lynch is here?'

'Aye,' said the funeral director, 'we have him on commission.'

He gave me a wink, and stepped aside.

Danny Lynch.

I was wrong about Londonderry.

I didn't think I knew anyone in the city.

But I knew one person.

I knew Danny Lynch.

19

I said, 'I thought you were dead.'

'Just politically.'

Danny Lynch was sitting on a windowsill in an upstairs office, coffee in one hand, cigarette in the other. He didn't look much older than when we'd last met, some twenty years before. He'd been famous then for his striking red hair; now the colour had faded and it was speckled with grey. He pushed off the sill, put the cigarette in his mouth and came across to me with hand outstretched. He was astute enough not to register the brief moment of hesitation before I extended mine. I hesitated because I always hesitate to shake the hands of spot-changing cheetahs. If you're a terrorist, and turn political, you still always carry that history, that capability, that threat. Danny Lynch had been part of the IRA, but had also helped broker the peace agreements that brought our edgy peace. He had prospered in our new

Assembly, achieved a ministerial position, while all the while denying the obvious and well-documented fact that he had once masterminded murders and bombings on an industrial scale; and we had been so desperate for a cessation that we'd been prepared to overlook it. In the end, what had brought him down had not been his own violent history, but his cousin's – a rapist he'd tried to shield through political influence, a rare but career-ending misstep that had forced his own party to order him to resign. I'd lost track of him since he'd stepped off the national stage, but here he was, hale and hearty and asking me what the hell I was doing in his heartland and what my interest was in Moira Doherty and Billy the Bear, and all the while still shaking my hand with a good firm grip and strong eye contact you would expect of a politician, or of someone who was aware that he had once been known as the Butcher of the Bogside.

He said, 'Long time.'

I said, 'Never mind that, there's someone downstairs enquiring after your TV licence.'

His eyes twinkled at that and he gave me a thin-lipped smile as he finally let go of my hand. He had always been quite the charmer, certainly when he was a functioning politician and quite possibly even when he'd been a terrorist, the IRA's Londonderry commander and the man credited with inventing the concept of kneecapping as punishment for relatively minor indiscretions. Thousands of young men over the past forty years had Danny Lynch to thank for their inability to play five-a-side football.

He said, 'Dan Starkey, ever the rapscallion.'

I was allergic to both rap and scallions, but I decided not to mention it.

I just said, 'It has been a long time. Where was it, High Court in Belfast?'

'How sweet of you to remember.' He finally let go of my hand, which felt crushed. 'Coffee?' He turned towards an espresso machine sitting on a sideboard and began to fiddle with it before quickly letting out a frustrated growl. 'It can't be that hard to work, can it?'

I came up beside him and looked down at it. 'Where's George Clooney when you need him?'

He smiled, and finally pressed a button that did something right, and it resulted in a look of what appeared to be genuine pleasure.

'Ah,' he said, 'isn't it great when something goes to plan?'

'Aye,' I said.

'As I recall,' he said, turning now with my espresso, 'you were rather kind to me way back when.'

'I doubt that,' I said. 'Professional.'

There was a litte more small talk. Then I explained about my work as a private investigator, about Moira coming to see me about her son.

He said, 'Poor Moira. Interfering old busybody, but I'd a soft spot for her.'

'So any ideas who'd want to shoot her in the head?'

'Not exactly, though I admire their style. Doing it on the Peace Bridge. That's a statement.'

'The statement being?'

'We haven't gone away.'

'The Peace Bridge angle I get, but not shooting an old woman. That's not going to help your PR.'

'They're not so concerned about PR these days.'

I said, 'It's definitely *they* and not *we*?'

'Really? You think I'm into all that again?'

'I've no idea. All I know is I asked to see the most feared man on the Bogside and they brought me here.'

Danny shook his head. 'Sure – a fella as old as I am brought you here because he remembers the good old bad old days. No, Dan, that's not me. Not any more. I'm retired from everything.'

'And working in a funeral home.'

'Not working, but I've a few business interests that help keep the wolf from the door, that's all.'

'But you must still know who does what to whom and why.'

'I'm not unaware. Bitter old men and young bucks schooled on Chechnya and Columbine. Not sure if Billy Doherty qualified on either count.'

'So tell me about him.'

He had lifted his own coffee and taken a seat at the desk. His feet were resting on it, soft shoes on a hard man. He was framed by the window and I could see the Bogside streets rising up the hill behind him like furrows in a paddy field. He said, 'Now why would I want to do that?'

I said, 'For old times.'

He smiled at that and said, 'It's maybe not something you want to be looking into.'

'Why so?'

'Because Billy the Bear was an arsehole who rubbed a lot of people up the wrong way. And there are a lot of people out there who won't take kindly to you asking questions about him or them.'

'People like . . .?'

'Starkey, you're wasting your time.'

'Have you ever heard of Stroke City Girls?'

'Stroke . . . No, what are they?'

'*It* is a website, you get to watch local girls frig themselves for money.'

'No I haven't, but I will certainly look into it.'

'Billy ran it in partnership with Jacko. Do you know Jacko?'

'Do you think I know everyone? Jacko who?'

'Haven't the faintest.'

'No, I don't know Jacko.'

'But you knew Billy.'

'Yes, I knew Billy.'

'So he's definitely dead.'

'I have no knowledge of that, but a lot of people seem to think so.'

'What sort of people?'

'The people who might know these things.'

'Did you allow the news of his death to be posted on the Wailing Wall out there?'

'Allow? Nothing to do with me.'

'They wouldn't have done it without your nod.'

'You think?'

'Billy recently did some time in Magilligan for having

a gun. He was certainly involved in the old days; was he still involved?'

'I really couldn't say. But then there's a lot I'm not aware of. Forgive me for asking, Starkey, but is this turning into some sort of an interrogation?'

'It's a friendly chat. You wouldn't have invited me up here if you weren't curious yourself.'

'Just wanted to see how you've aged.'

'And?'

'Eventually it catches up with you.'

'Like a past.'

'Like a past, indeed,' said Danny. He turned his swivel chair a little so that he could look out of the window. 'Ah, if only we could change it. Guess I'm never going to have the chance to turn down that knighthood now. Tell you the truth, Starkey, I hardly knew Billy the Bear. In the old days we wouldn't have given him the time of day; he was just a fuck-up – bright enough, I suppose, but always managed to shoot himself in the foot. Once, literally, as I recall. So he'd no place with us. The Proddies would have welcomed him with open arms, though!' He let out a little chuckle. 'And eventually they did, and literally . . .'

'They . . .?'

I was surprised because in all the history of terrorism, nobody ever changed sides.

He saw my confusion.

'You do know about Billy, don't you, why he was called Billy the Bear?'

'Only that he was a big guy, I thought . . .'

'Starkey – he was a fruit.'

'He . . .'

'Bear is fruity parlance for a big hairy man who likes big hairy men.'

'Right,' I said. 'I did not know that.'

'You should get out more. You really don't know this? Back in the day, when Billy was in prison in Belfast, he fell in love with some huge muscled guy in the UVF, I mean like real love, not just fucking; they used to pay one of the warders to take each other wee love notes. Then one of them couldn't pay one week so Billy threatened the warder, told him he'd let his boss know he'd been making deliveries, so the warder took the note but then accidentally on purpose delivered it to the wrong cell, and ten minutes later it was public knowledge and the both of them got the heads kicked off them. That was pretty much the last time Billy was any use to anyone on our side, and soon as they're out he's shacked up with his hairy friend on Shipquay Street.'

'Not that you were keeping tabs on him.'

'It was common knowledge – all anyone could talk about for ages.'

'Was the UVF bear called Jacko, by any—'

'Nope, someone else, can't even remember who; he had his head caved in by his own side, this is years ago now. But once Billy was out, Billy was out and there was no stopping him. He was a bit of a joke really. Back then he was dealing, I know that, Ecstasy, dope, coke, anything he could get his hands on, expect he was taking the half of it himself, and that's what did for him. You want to get mixed up with them lot, be my guest, but it's not my area of expertise.'

There were footsteps on the stairs. The funeral director appeared in the doorway. He said, 'You said you'd give him five, and its fifteen now, and the rest of them have arrived.'

Danny glanced at his watch, nodded, and gave me apologetic hands. 'Sorry, Starkey, bloody board of directors. The business of dying really is a business.'

Danny got up from the desk. He pulled the sleeves of his suit jacket down over his exposed white shirt cuffs. McBride looked at me expectantly.

'Okay,' I said, 'fair enough. But we hardly talked about Moira. You must have known her pretty well.'

'Better than most. Slept with her.' Danny raised an eyebrow and added a proud little smile. 'Years ago. She was quite the girl. Could eat you for breakfast. And several times, she did.' He gave me a wink even as he began to shepherd me towards the stairs. 'But I'd had nothing to do with her for years. She moved out of town, last I heard.'

'From what you know of her, do you think she'd have had anything to do with Billy's Stroke City business?'

'Moira? She was in the bra-Ra in the seventies . . .'

'The bra . . . sorry, I don't speak the Irish . . .'

'The burn your bra wing of the IRA, Starkey, feminist to the tits, so it sounds unlikely . . . but you never know, people change, and family is family. Anyway . . .'

He nodded towards the stairs. McBride stepped back to let me go down first.

'Well, cheers anyway,' I said. 'I appreciate the info.'

'It wasn't info, Starkey, it was gossip.'

I was about to take the first step, but I stopped. McBride sighed.

'One more thing,' I said. 'Just occurred to me – someone was spotted coming out of Moira's house soon after she was murdered. Some fella with like a birthmark on his face. May have nothing to do with anything, but any ideas?'

Danny had been a terrorist, trained not to give even the slightest hint away under interrogation, and a radical politician schooled never to look flustered, so all he gave me was a slight shake of the head and a 'Nope'.

But not McBride.

Despite all his years as a funeral director who had to mask his emotions, he couldn't help himself: the glance he gave Danny Lynch was pitched somewhere between surprise – and panic.

20

It was one minute past opening time when I crossed the threshold of the Pub and spotted the closest thing I had to a friend in Londonderry sitting at the bar, pint in front of him and paper open to the racing. There was a roll-up between his lips and his cheeks were flushed. I said, 'You're either an alcoholic or a sexual deviant, or both.'

He looked at me, gave me a stupid grin, took a drag on his cigarette.

'I'm the owner.'

'Oh,' I said.

'Plus I'm an alcoholic and a lover of beautiful women made up entirely of pixels. Sit yourself down and I'll get you a pint.'

'Actually,' I said, 'I was just going to have a Diet Coke. The old head is a bit—'

'Shite!'

He was up and behind the bar and pouring me one

before I could pretend to stop him. He came round with it and got back on his stool. He asked me what line I was in and I told him. He asked me if there was money in it and I said no. I asked him if there was money in the Pub and he said no, he was losing it hand over fist. He tapped his paper and said he made more on the horses. He asked me why I kept doing it and I said I had absolutely no idea apart from the fact that I had a weird compulsion to help people, people who usually turned out to be spanners. I asked him why he kept doing it and he said, 'Because I can. Won the Lotto eighteen months ago. Bought this place. Thought it would be fun to have my own pub.'

'And is it?'

'No, it's miserable, the staff are thieving scumbags and the customers are always sucking my toes for a hand-out because they know I'm loaded.'

'How depressing,' I said. 'And you couldn't see your way to lending me . . .?' He raised his pint. I raised mine. We clinked. I said, 'Do you mind me asking how much you won?'

'Thirteen million.'

'That's a lot.' I nodded at the paper. 'And these horses you bet on – do you own them?'

'God, no, who wants to deal with horse shit and midgets?'

'You should try my job. And do you bet extravagant amounts?'

'God, no, it's a mug's game. I bet fifty pee each way, mostly.'

'So what do you do with your millions apart from owning a pub and betting on horses?'

'Nothing much. Just sit here mostly. About once a week I've to fend off hellions looking for protection money. And actually I should just give it to them, because it costs me more to hire people to chase them off, but it's the principle.'

'It's a vicious circle,' I said.

And it being very much still on my mind, I asked him if any of the hoods who were trying to strong-arm him happened to have a birthmark on his face and he shook his head. I asked him if he knew Jacko up the hill and he said met him once, didn't like him. I asked him why and he shrugged and said, 'Struck me as a sleeked wee fucker.' I asked him if he knew Billy the Bear and he said yes, he used to come in all the time.

'He drank with the girls quite a bit. He was very protective of them. He tried to pay me a little extra so my bouncers would keep an eye on them.'

'Tried and failed.'

'Well, I'm rolling in it, and they should be safe wherever they are and whatever they stick up themselves for a living.'

'What're they like, the girls?'

'You mean are they like hardened street-corner hookers?'

'Not exactly . . .'

'Well they're not. They're just trying to earn a living. And they're young, they don't have the same inhibitions we have. I say, more power to their elbows and other bits.'

I asked him the last time he'd seen Billy the Bear. He said about six weeks before. He said he knew Billy used to be a bit of a hard man, had done time, but usually he was just a big friendly guy. 'I don't think you'd want to cross him, but in here, he was great, great with the girls, big laugh on him, big laugh.'

'And he kicked with the other foot.'

'Protestant?'

'Gay.'

'Yeah, saw him with his boyfriend the odd time.'

'Jacko, you mean?'

'Nope, definitely not. Jacko's a scrawny wee runt. Think that one was strictly a business partnership. The boyfriend's another big fella, camp as Danny La Rue. Remember him? Last I heard he was working in the Forum, round the corner. Something theatrical. Make-up or costumes maybe.'

I glanced at my watch. It was almost twelve. Shift change for the cam girls. I drained the half-pint that was left and told him I had to go, and that it had been a pleasure talking to him. We shook hands. He said his name was Pearse Dunbar. I told him mine. I said I was sure I would be back. As I was heading for the door he said, 'Dan? You know, if you do need a few quid, it's not a problem.'

I said, 'You don't know me from Adam.'

'Maybe not, but you seem like your heart's in the right place, and that's important.'

I laughed and said, 'Tell my wife that.'

He smiled and turned back to his pint. I opened the door, but before I could get through, Pearse said: 'Oh. Dan. The birthmark . . .?'

'The . . . what about it?'

'Are you sure it was a birthmark? Just there's a fella runs one of the protection squads, bad bastard so he is, though he's not got a birthmark – but burns all down the side of his face. Maybe it's him you're looking for?'

'Maybe,' I said. 'Does he have a name?'

'Don't know his real name, but I do know they call him Sunny Jim behind his back.' He said it with a smirk. I nodded my thanks and stepped out into the crisp morning air. One pint of Harp and a handful of useful leads, including two pointers to someone going by the unlikely nickname of Sunny Jim.

Not such a bad morning after all.

I leaned in a doorway across from Billy's apartment. When I wasn't keeping an eye on the door I kept an eye on my phone and the Stroke City Girls website. I scrolled through the girls who were working until I came to one I sort of recognised, though it was discon-certing to see her with her clothes off. Last night she'd been the one with the short dark hair and the designer glasses I'd bummed a cigarette off. According to the site, her name was Pamela Canal. I suspected it was a stage name. Her stage was a bed, and at that moment she didn't appear to be doing much beyond lying with her legs spread and waiting for customers to pony up.

At the bottom of the screen it said *fingers in ass at goal/suck dildo*. On the right-hand side the customers were writing flattering comments about how beautiful she was, how lovely her pussy was, and what they'd like to do to her with their big hard cocks. Apart, that is, from the ones who were calling her an ugly whore they wouldn't touch with a bargepole. Pamela's expression remained unchanged, except for when someone paid a tip, which was in the form of tokens purchased from the website. To do the sucking dildo thing Pamela required five hundred tokens. She was currently languishing at twenty-five, so I guessed I hadn't missed many of her smiles. I checked my watch. It was exactly noon. Pamela's eyes flitted somewhere off camera, and a moment later her screen went dark and a notice came up saying *This show has ended*. This left the customers who'd paid tokens expecting to see her sucking a dildo as her target was reached rather hard done by. But I was sure Pamela wouldn't be losing much sleep over it, and that they wouldn't be pursuing her through the small claims court for recompense.

Five minutes later, the door to the apartments opened and Pamela came out. She was accompanied by the same girl she'd been with in the Pub the night before; they hugged briefly, then parted company. I crossed the road and followed Pamela into the Diamond, a small shopping square dominated by a department store and featuring several small coffee shops. Pamela joined a queue in one of these. She was dressed in blue jeans and a black puffa jacket; the only thing that made her stand out from anyone else in the queue was the pair of sunglasses she'd slipped into on her way up the road. I waited outside until she emerged, already biting into a sausage roll poking out of a small paper bag. I fell into step beside her, though she was well on to Bishop Street before she realised it.

I said, 'Remember me?'

She shook her head and kept walking.

'Last night in the bar, I asked for a cigarette and your mate told me to fuck off.'

'Right,' she said, not slowing at all, while surreptitiously moving her handbag round and opening it. Her hand slipped inside.

'I was just wondering if I could have a wee word with you.'

'No, fuck off.'

She glanced at the road behind, preparing to make a dash across.

'No, really, seriously – Pamela . . . I'm not one of those guys . . .'

'No one is ever one of those guys!' She stopped suddenly and her hand emerged from the bag, clutching a fork, which she poked towards me. 'Yet here you are, following me up the street with your tongue hanging out! Now fuck off or I'll ram this in your fucking eyeball.'

I took a step back and raised my hands. 'I know wankin' makes you blind, but that would be ridiculous . . .'

'Don't you fucking tempt me . . .!'

She moved closer, brandishing it. She probably wasn't much above the fighting weight of a pixie, but I had learned never to underestimate the huge physical clout of an angry woman. So I took another step back and said, 'Whoa, take it easy . . . this really isn't about you . . . it's about Billy, Billy the Bear.'

'What about him?'

'I'm trying to find him, that's all.'

'And who the fuck are you?'

'I'm a private investigator.'

'This isn't funny!'

'I know that . . . sorry . . . look . . . *look* . . .'

I produced a business card from my wallet. She had a fork in one hand and half a sausage roll in the other, so I held it up for her to read.

She read, *'Dan Starkey, Private Investigator . . . a bespoke service for important people with difficult problems . . .'* She looked at me over the top of it and said, 'That's quite a mouthful.'

I said, 'People in glass houses . . .'

Her eyes narrowed.

'There's not even a photo of you. You could be anyone.'

'It's a secretive business. But call the number there – my phone will ring.'

'It still doesn't prove anything.'

'I know that. It's completely meaningless. But that's what I do, and I really am trying to find Billy the Bear.'

'Why?'

'Because his mum asked me to.'

And with that her face began to crumple. Tears sprang from her eyes and her shoulders began to shake.

'I really miss him,' she cried.

She staggered forward and there was nothing else for me to do but open my arms so that she could fall into them. I held her while she roared against me, all the time aware that her sausage roll was being crushed into my jacket, her fork was pricking into my chest and only a matter of minutes before I'd been casually perusing her furry triangle via a website for cock-handed perverts.

21

We backtracked to the Diamond and the coffee shop where she'd bought the sausage roll. She was shaky and nervous and full of lingering suspicions. I could be as flaky as the pastry that still adorned my jacket, but for now I was doing my best to be reassuring and supportive. She said she'd been working for Billy the Bear for over a year, that she was a single mother and had been largely homeless when he'd taken her under his wing, sorted out somewhere for her to live, got her work on the website, no pressure, good money, lots of love. I said that someone less sympathetic could describe that as grooming and pimping, but not me, clearly, and she understood that, nodding through her tears, but that wasn't how it was, there was no pressure at all and she really loved her work. I asked how much she was earning a week and it was more than I was getting in a good month. I asked her how she justified what she did in her own head, and she said, it's precisely that, my own head, it's nobody else's concern and she didn't have a problem with it.

She said, 'Billy *saved* me, do you understand that? Saved me. And his mum was as tough as nails but she was good to us, to the girls, but then when we heard what happened to her, Christ, it's like a morgue in there.'

'Tell me about Jacko. Real name?'

'Andrew Jackson.'

'Like the president.' She blinked at me. 'Sorry. He's no Billy the Bear, I take it?'

'Nope. He's a shite-hawk.'

'How come?'

She sighed and studied the table. She flicked at imaginary crumbs. She finally took off her sunglasses and set them in front of her. Her dark eyes flitted back up to me. 'I'm not stupid, I know Billy's no angel, he's done stuff, but as long as he treated us right then none of that really matters, does it? But Jacko's different. He just turned up one day and said he was in charge now and it's all changed. It used to be fun. A laugh. All of us girls doing this mad thing and getting well paid for it, and the parties, Billy loved a party . . . Look, it sounds stupid to say we were like a big happy family, but it was a bit like that. And then Jacko comes in and he's just a nasty little man and he's making us work harder and stopping us talking to each other. And you know, making us do . . . more . . .'

'More . . .?'

She glanced around the café, which was lunchtime busy, and then folded her arms and rested them halfway across the table, with her head following. Given that she didn't look much more than twenty, we probably looked like a father and daughter having an intimate conversation.

'Look,' she said, 'we're all in it for different reasons, and we've all got our limits, what we will or won't do or show or insert.'

'As in . . .'

'As in whatever you can imagine, but he wants us to do it all. As far as the shows are concerned, we all start in one place, and then end up in another, and it's always been up to the girl where the start and finish is. I mean, start of my shift I'm in a bikini, twenty minutes in as long as the tips are coming in I'm naked and spread, and then it's a gradual build to the dildo.'

'Uhuh,' I said.

'That's what I do. Nobody ordered me to do it. But one of the other girls – she starts in a bloody duffel coat with about four layers underneath and the climax of her show, five hundred tokens and three hours later, is she gives the tiniest flash of nipple. It's each to their own. But Jacko comes in and changes all that – he wants us to put everything up there from the start, then crank it up. He wants us to go girl on girl, fine if you're into that but it's not for me; neither is peeing or pooing to order, thank you very much. Nor is bringing in his mates to fuck us on camera. We're not whores.'

In the court of public opinion, they probably were.

Not that it mattered.

I said, 'So do youse not just say no?'

'But then what, out on our ears and back on the dole or flipping burgers in McD's? And he's not making us do anything, not physically forcing us, but it's like the girls that do more get the better shifts, the girls that don't mind some fanny-licking or sucking off one of his mates, well their show gets better prominence on the site, so they get more money, and so where we all used to get on great, make mostly the same dough, now the half of them are at each other's throats and the atmosphere's all shit and . . . well, it was different under Billy. Of course he was in it to make money, he wasn't a fucking charity, but he understood us and why we were doing it. We were all in it together. Not with Jacko. Not with fucking Jacko.'

She said Billy was good with ideas, but looking back on it, maybe he couldn't cope with the day-to-day slog of running a business. He liked to party with his girls, and he liked to party with his boyfriend Harry, and he liked to go clubbing and pick up guys. He liked his drugs. And then he got into crush and he was out of it more and more. The last few weeks before Jacko arrived the girls were virtually running the business themselves.

'So what did Billy say about Jacko?'

'Well, that Jacko was his new business partner and together they were going to take over the world, but from day one you could see Jacko was in charge, and more and more Billy wasn't around or was off his tits.

Jacko brought new girls in, too, European girls who don't even pretend to be Irish, they go further, work longer. Used to be we just operated out of those apartments, there's eight bedrooms between the three of them, but soon Jacko was opening other houses, other apartments, and there's a lot of girls who don't even bother coming in now, just do it from home.'

'But all the money still goes through Jacko.'

'Exactly.' She sat back again and sighed. 'I'm stopping it. In a few weeks. I've been saving. Going to quit Derry. More and more people are starting to recognise me, schoolboys shouting stuff. I don't want my kid hearing any of that. So I'm going to Belfast, maybe Dublin. Maybe set up my own website, my own cams. How hard can it be?'

I nodded and said, 'Don't ask me, I can't wire a plug.'

I asked her if she wanted another coffee and she checked her watch – she had to pick her boy up from the child minder; he was five years old – but then she nodded. When I brought it back from the counter she was dabbing at her eyes with a napkin.

'Just tell me,' she asked, 'do you think Billy's alive?'

'I don't know. Everyone's saying he's dead but you never really know until a body turns up. Like his mum's.' She shook her head and another tear appeared. 'Tell me about her. Moira.'

'She was just lovely. She loved her boy.'

'How long had she been involved in the business?'

Pamela thought for a moment. 'I don't really know. I mean, she was always in and out of the apartment, but then I think – yes, she was there more when Billy started to get bad with the crush, and I think that's when she started to help out . . .'

'As in . . .'

'Just looking after us girls. And things like rotas and shifts, Billy was always hopeless with that . . . half the time you didn't know if you were coming or going.' I gave her a look and she rolled her eyes and said, '*Please,*' but she also managed a smile.

'But presumably you saw less of her when Jacko came in.'

'Uh – no, in fact. More probably. She didn't seem to mind him as much as we did. She was still doing the books, but she also became more like the public face of the business. I mean, she'd go out and rent apartments, she was just like this little old lady nobody would blink twice at, nobody would demand to know what she wanted it for. She'd move in for a few weeks, make sure everything was running smoothly, and then move on to somewhere else. Honest to God, I don't know where she got the energy. But as long as she was there we could put up with Jacko. I don't know what's going to happen now.'

'And what about Billy disappearing? How did she react to that?'

'She was in bits. I don't know how she was able to work.'

'She was still coming in?'

Pamela nodded. 'I suppose it was because him disappearing wasn't like . . . sudden? More like gradual, because he hadn't been around much or was staying with his fella so we just thought he's somewhere else, and then as the days went past it just started to dawn on us that something might actually be wrong.'

'And what about the last few days, before she . . . passed on . . . anything out of the ordinary?'

'Not that I'm aware of, but then she wasn't in much because she was setting up a new office out in . . .'

'Castlerock,' I said.

'Aye.'

'And how did you hear the news about her, were you in work?'

'I was just starting, and one of the girls came running in crying her lamps out saying it was on the news. We'd heard about the shooting but thought nothing much of it, but then when they said it was Moira everyone was in bits. We were all gathered round the telly, couldn't believe it.'

'What about Jacko? How'd he take it.?'

'He seemed just as shocked as we were. Some of the girls wanted to go home, but he wouldn't let us, straight back to work. He's a heartless bastard.'

'And he actually lives there, doesn't he?'

'Sure he does. So he can keep an eye on us. Honest to God, these past few weeks he's there twenty-four-seven, we never get a fucking break.'

She said finally that she had to get back to her kid, and that she hoped she'd been of some use but for Jesus' sake not to tell Jacko I'd spoken to her. I said I wasn't sure Jacko even existed because he never seemed to leave the apartments. She said, 'Oh he exists all right.' But then she shook her head and said, 'How is it it's the good ones like Moira and Billy get taken away and the shit-bags that get left behind?'

I had absolutely no idea.

But I'd been asking the same question for a long, long time.

22

I was to meet Sara in the Tower Museum at Union Hall
Place. I was early for once, and spent ten minutes
wandering around the exhibits looking in vain for a
tribute to the Moondogs, but there was only crap about
the Siege and a Spanish Armada shipwreck, the *Trinidad
Valencera*. It had been discovered by the City of Derry
Sub-Aqua Club in Kinnagoe Bay, which was just around
the coast, after nearly four hundred years underwater.
Now its many treasures were exhibited over four floors
of the museum, which was three too many.

Then Sara was behind me saying, 'They should have
you stuffed and mounted in here, Starkey, a perfect
example of the punk rock generation gone to seed.' She
smiled winningly. She was very attractive. I said, 'I'm
very pleased that you're thinking about mounting me,
not to mention my seed.' She shook her head and said,
'Are you always thinking about sex?' I said yes. Her eyes

fixed on some trinket or other, but I was pleased to see a slight hint of colour appear on her cheeks. I get to people eventually. I grind them down. They either fall in love with me or they try to kill me. Quite often both.

I said, 'Did you have a good day?'

'Not bad. You?'

'Not bad.'

We nodded at something rusty.

'Are we sharing?'

'After you.'

'No, after you.'

'No, really.'

'Starkey, you have form with lies and half-truths and avoidance.'

'I promise not to tell lies or half-truths or avoid anything.'

'Sometimes,' she said, 'I don't know why I bother.'

'Why're you always looking for an argument?'

'Only with you, Starkey, only with you.' She was looking at a depiction of the beginnings of the Siege, with King James and his army approaching the walls, and the group of thirteen young tradesmen's apprentices who took it upon themselves to seize the keys to the gates and lock them to prevent him taking the city. She nodded at these Apprentice Boys and said, 'Wouldn't happen today. They'd be too busy looking at their phones. James could just canter in.'

'They'd say *cba*.'

'And when they realised the city had been seized, text *lol*.'

'Listen to us,' I said, 'all groovy with our kidspeak.'

'Groovy,' said Sara. She kept her eyes on the Siege, but said: 'I deal with Belfast cops all the time, they're fairly relaxed these days. Derry cops – they're nervous.'

'Nervous generally, you mean?'

'No – that something big is happening and they don't quite know what it is.'

'What did they have to say about Billy the Bear?'

'I didn't ask them about Billy the Bear. I asked them about Moira Doherty, which is the story I'm writing.'

'Which is intrinsically connected to Billy the Bear's disappearance.'

'Chickens, eggs, you know that for a fact?'

'Nope. But you could have asked. What did they have to say about Moira?'

'Not very much. That they're following several possible leads.'

'That's what your connections told you? You could have read that on their website.'

'And I'm telling you they're tight, very tight, which means they're really worried.'

'Worried, tight – okay, I get it. So what else have you been doing with your day? Nice lunch somewhere?'

She rolled her eyes and led me up the stairs to the second floor. There were more Spanish treasures that probably wouldn't have been considered treasures in their day, or indeed anywhere outside of the museum. They just looked like scrap.

Sara said, 'I talked to the editor of the *Journal*. He's ex-*Telegraph* and he's still a local stringer for us.'

'I hope he has better connections than you do.'

'He's worried too.'

'About?'

'Escalation. He says the problem is there's all sorts of new wee groups . . .'

'*New wee groups!*'

'His words, not mine . . . new wee Republican groups and they've all got about half a dozen members and the only thing they can agree on is that they don't like each other. He says that till now they've been scrambling around doing Mickey Mouse stuff, and they're aware of it, and they know they need to pull off something spectacular, something that'll make disaffected youth flock to join their group rather than one of the others.'

'It's like Merseybeat and the Beatles.'

'I don't even know what that means.'

'Everyone's vying to be top dog in the new scene. Like punk and the Pistols. Ska and the Specials.'

'Starkey, I don't think analogies are your strong point. All I'm saying is someone is planning something, and something more spectacular than shooting an old woman in the head. That's the start of something, not the end.'

'But why Moira Doherty?'

'No idea. He knows who's who here and he says she hadn't figured for years.'

I stood nodding at some pewter dishes and marvelling at why anyone would want to marvel at them, while aware that Sara was now studying me.

She said, 'Unless of course you know different.'

'Not really, no.'

Nevertheless, she raised her eyebrows expectantly.

'What?'

'Your day, Dan. What did you find out, private eye?'

I hadn't quite decided whether to keep my powder dry or not. I liked Sara and her spirit and tenacity, but I didn't trust people who didn't trust me. I was, conveniently, saved from making a decision by my phone ringing and a name coming up that was both unexpected and, in its own wee way, entirely expected.

I said to Sara: 'I'm sorry, I'm going to have to take this.'

She said, 'Very convenient.'

I said, 'That's exactly what I was thinking.' I gave her my smile. I answered the phone and said, 'One minute.' Then I held it to my side and said: 'I've two words for you, Sara Patterson.'

'Fuck you?'

'Close. Sunny and Jim. Sunny Jim.'

'What're you talking a—'

'Sunny Jim, that's your lot. I'll take this outside, and I'll be back in five. Is that long enough?'

As I turned for the stairs she said after me, 'Sunny Jim – they're fucking firelighters!'

I gave her the thumbs-up, and continued on.

Halfway down, I raised the phone and said, 'Sorry about that, now what can I do for you, my old buddy, my old Bailey and Loan?'

'Starkey, this is serious,' said Rev. Pike.

'It always is, mate,' I said. 'It always is.'

*　　*　　*

A freezing wind was sweeping around the square in front of me, and the clouds above were heavy with snow, the first flecks of which were already descending. A little to my right was the city's orange-hued Guildhall, where Derry Council met. It had also been the venue for the pre-Jimmy Savile Saville inquiry into Bloody Sunday, two hundred million spent to discover the bleeding obvious. We were a crazy, mixed-up, contradictory province of a fading colonial power but still largely intent on resisting the lure of the leprechaun. Rev. Pike wasn't worried about minor territorial, political or religious squabbles; he was consumed by the fate of all mankind and his meal ticket. I could hear him saying, 'Starkey, are you there?'

'I'm here,' I said, 'there, and everywhere.'

'What're you doing up there?'

'Waiting.'

'Waiting? Waiting for what?'

'An apology for setting your police dogs on me.'

He sighed. 'Starkey, I haven't time for this.'

'Clearly, you have.'

'Starkey – okay. Fine. If I have concerns for Christine's safety, then you must understand that I have to follow every possible line of enquiry. I know you're very close to her and while I don't necessarily approve of that, I have to respect her wishes. But when she's spotted in your company, and then suddenly disappears without trace, it's natural to think that you may have something to do with it. However, since you have now been largely exonerated, and as I'd like to think that we both have

Christine's best interests at heart, I thought we might perhaps co-operate in an effort to discover where she is or what has happened to her.'

I cleared my throat.

He said, 'Well?'

I said, 'That was one of the worst apologies I ever heard.'

'Starkey . . .'

'In fact you should apologise for that apology.'

'Starkey! Christine is missing!'

'Do you ever think, Pike, that maybe she just doesn't want to talk to you?'

'She—'

'That you smother her, you keep her prisoner in your castle, you don't let her out, you don't let her have friends, you put this colossal pressure on her to be something she probably isn't?'

'Did she say . . .?'

'Nope, I'm just speculating.'

'Starkey . . .'

'Are you aware of what I do for a living?'

He sighed. 'Yes, Starkey, you're some kind of journalist.'

'No, I'm some kind of private investigator.'

He couldn't see me smiling.

'Which you know. Because I've already fucked your life up once with my amazing investigative powers.'

'That's ancient history, Starkey, we've both moved on.'

'Really?'

'This isn't about us, it's about Christine. I have genuine concerns.'

'If you have genuine concerns, why don't you drop what you're doing, whiz up here and we'll look for her together? Be a classic movie – two guys who hate each other at first but they experience all kinds of dangerous scrapes together and that hatred gradually changes to mutual respect and then full-on buddy love. We'd be like *Lethal Weapon*. Or *Turner and Hooch*.'

'Starkey, I want to hire you to find her.'

'Well why didn't you say that in the first place?'

Across the way, I caught the eye of someone who caught the eye of me. He looked away. He had his hands thrust into the pockets of a too-thin hoodie and looked half frozen and miserable, standing in a shop doorway with a fag hanging out of his mouth. He glanced back into the store behind him.

Pike said, 'How much would we be talking about?'

'Special offer, one thousand a day, plus expenses.'

'A *day*?'

'Special offer just closed. That'll be two thousand a day, plus expenses.'

'Starkey, this—'

'Pike – you take ten per cent of everything everyone earns who signs up with you, you're rolling in it. You wouldn't blink at paying two grand for a decent barrister or someone to feng shui your cloisters, so stop being so tight. And as she's probably wandering around looking at the architecture, it's not going to take me very long.'

'Okay,' said Pike, 'two grand a day.'

'And what if it takes forty days and forty nights?'

'Whatever it takes.'

The fella across the way threw down his fag, gave a resigned sigh, and turned into the store. There would be a girlfriend inside with a screaming toddler in a pushchair.

'Are you really worried? I asked.

'About what?'

'That something has happened to her.'

'Yes, of course I am. We have our disagreements, we have our arguments, but she's never not in contact. Starkey – you know her, she's very wise, but also quite naïve, not exactly worldly. She's sixteen. She's alone. And no one has heard from her since you saw her at the Peace Bridge. Now where should I send the money so you can get started?'

'You shouldn't.'

'Sorry, I don't under—'

'Pike, I just wanted to know if you'd pay it. But do you seriously think I'd ever, *ever* work for you? Answer to you? No chance. Keep your money. I'll have a look for her off my own bat, not because some fucking Moonie is throwing cash at me. Now who're your people up here, who should I be talking to?'

'Starkey, there's no need to—'

'Just the facts, ma'am,' I said.

When we were done, I turned back into the museum. My five minutes had turned into ten. I checked every floor, but there was no sign of Sara. I phoned her without response, I sent her a text, asking where she was hiding, but nothing. It was now late afternoon, I hadn't eaten and was still exhausted from my night's drinking. A room-service meal and a doze on a comfortable hotel bed suddenly seemed very appealing. It wouldn't be wasted time, it would be thinking time with my eyes shut. And there was plenty to think about, not least why the hell I'd turned down two grand a day to look for Christine.

23

I have been beaten, shot and left for dead on many occasions. It instils in you not only an aversion to being beaten, shot and left for dead, but also the importance of being aware of what is going on around you. On the whole, bad guys don't telegraph their intentions or book an appointment. They come at you every which way. Soon as I stepped on to the Peace Bridge and he stepped on after me, I knew he was following me.

Of course, it helped that I recognised him.

Sleep had proved elusive. I had half a bottle of wine in my room, and a glass of whiskey in the bar. I called Sara up to see how she was getting on with her homework, but no response. There was a light snow falling, and it had been for a while. It was lying, and the air was freezing, but the wind had dropped so it wasn't an unpleasant walk. It was getting dark and there were only half a dozen others on the entire length of the bridge;

four coming towards me, two immediately behind – plus the impatient shopper I'd spotted outside the museum tucked in behind them. He was still underdressed for the weather. He appeared to have the build of a starving sparrow. I'm not much of a fighter, but I could probably have taken him. Instead, I picked up my pace. You don't have to be that strong to pull a trigger or slip a knife between someone's ribs. And as I was approaching the spot where Moira Doherty had been plugged and tipped, sudden death was kind of on my mind.

I thought at first that there was no visible sign of what had happened to her or the police activity that had followed, that it had all been swept efficiently away by the combined forces of the tourist police and Mother Nature. But as I passed what I supposed was the exact spot, I saw that someone had propped a small bunch of flowers against one of the metal posts. I glanced behind, saw how far back my follower was, and then quickly crouched down. They were red roses, half a dozen of them, but they were barely more than buds, bound with an elastic band and with a sticker on the cellophane surrounding them that showed they'd been bought for £2.99 in a Maxol garage. No note. I walked on. When I looked back, I saw the two pedestrians immediately behind me pass the flowers without pause; when I checked again, my follower was crouched as I had been, checking them out.

As I reached the end of the bridge, Ebrington Barracks was immediately in front. I turned to my right on to Browning Drive and continued around a bend that skirted the barracks before bringing me on to the shops on a Limavady Road slushy with going-home traffic. With the snow getting heavier and the car lights dazzling, it wasn't difficult to slip into a side street, duck behind a parked car and watch as my follower trudged on past. I continued along the side street and turned right, intent now on approaching my target by this less direct method while using the red beacon light on its spire to guide me in.

I emerged back on to the main road directly opposite the red-bricked St Comgall's, checked for but found no sign of my follower, and then darted across the traffic. I passed the church, which was closed and dark; but there was a hall behind it which was brightly lit. Half a dozen women were standing in the car park chatting and waiting for the minister, just visible through a glass panel, to release the kids lined up behind him. Within a few moments the minister opened the door and called out, 'Careful now!' The kids paid him no heed, immediately skidding down a short disabled ramp into the snow and charging about excitedly while their mothers finished off their gossip before setting about trying to rein them in. Although the kids were all wearing different-coloured winter coats, they were also all sporting blue and white neckerchiefs clearly emblazoned with the New Seeker logo. Football teams, Hitler and God liked to get them young.

The minister, fiftyish, plump, came down the ramp and helped with the gathering, laughing and joshing with the young mothers as he did. He finally noticed me as he waved the last of them off. His smile faded and he stood looking uncertainly at me, this stranger in the snow. He said, 'Can I help you?'

'Sure,' I said, 'I'm looking for a teenage Messiah, was wondering if you had any ideas?'

'You mean . . . are you the police? I – I told them everything.'

'Nope, not the police.'

'Pike, then? Did he send you? I told him everything as well. Not that there's anything to—'

'I'm a friend of Christine's.'

'Friend? How do you mean, friend?'

He glanced behind him, somewhat nervously, as if he was calculating if he could get up the ramp and inside to lock the doors before I would be on him, which made me think that he had lately been scared by something or had something to hide, because I'm about as intimidating as a pickled mackerel.

I said, 'Friend as in friend. We hang out, face-bake, needlepoint.'

'And what . . . exactly can I help you with? Like I say, I've told everyone . . .'

He took a step back. One hand felt about him for the rail.

'Just a chat.'

'That's what you said last time, and you smashed the hall up.'

'Not me.'

'People like you.'

I reached inside my jacket for my wallet and he took another two steps back. I produced one of my cards. 'She really is a friend. But I'm also a private detective. I'm working on a different case but I gave her a lift up here and now she's dropped out of sight, so I'm just a little worried.' I stepped forward. He stepped back. 'Relax,' I said. 'Here . . .' I held the card up for him and moved closer. He hesitated, but allowed me to come right up to him. He took the card. As he read it, he mouthed the words. When he was done, he said, 'Can I keep this?'

I shook my head. 'It was a special offer, I only got twenty-five, so they're rare as hen's teeth.'

He said, 'Are you serious?'

'Rarely,' I said.

The hall was large and modern with a pale wooden floor set out with lines of tape for various sports. There was a basketball net at the far end and chairs scattered about. There was a plastic box crammed full of small plastic balls. Children's toys lying around. There was a pool table with the balls in a triangle ready for a game. I already knew that he was the Rev. McCutcheon, that he'd been *in situ* for nine years but only turned Seeker in the past six months. As he scurried about tidying up, I asked him how he'd been converted and he said Christine had appeared before him and he'd known instantly that she was the Messiah. I said, 'Appeared like in a vision?' and he laughed and said, 'No, on Skype. Just called up and we started talking and next thing you know . . . I can't really explain it.' He gave a slight shake of his head. 'It's a feeling . . . no, more than that, an absolute conviction. A warmth. A warmth of the soul.' He recommenced his tidying. He said, 'And you say you're friends with her? You don't get that?'

'Nope, to me she's just your average obnoxious teenager.'

He sucked air in through his teeth. 'Please, don't say that. Does that mean you're not even one of us . . .?'

'Just an ordinary lapsed Presbyterian.'

'Well, you'll see the light. Everyone will.'

'Including whoever smashed your hall up?'

'Especially. Oh, it doesn't look now like there was too much damage, but we've cleaned it up so you'd hardly know. And people are very generous. Windows were replaced free of charge; part of the floor was burned – you see there, the wooden tiles are fresher-looking? They're new. And the pool table . . . look.' He moved across to it. I joined him. 'You wouldn't know it was ripped up – all repaired by our loyal congregation.'

I lifted the black ball and began to transfer it between my hands as we talked.

'When was this?'

'About a month ago. But it had been building. When a church converts – well, it's not always a hundred per cent, and those who are . . . disaffected are naturally angry. We reach out to them, but . . . well, they're very set in their ways; they spread stories, corrupt the truth, and suddenly what we're doing here isn't good and pure but repainted as brainwashing and evil and next thing you know you've a mob rampaging through and you're lucky to get away with your life.'

'That bad?'

'Oh yes, I had to be smuggled out. Otherwise I dread to think . . . but here I am, still fighting the good fight.'

'You think that's wise?'

'Of course it is. The people have to be ready for what's coming.'

'And what *is* coming?'

'Why, the Rapture, of course.'

'I don't suppose that's the Blondie single?'

'The . . .? No, I mean it's the—'

But I held up my hand. 'Please,' I said, 'I understand you believe it, and that's fine. But I just want to know where she is.'

'And I've absolutely no idea. I told the police, they were here last night.'

'You haven't seen her or heard from her?'

'No, absolutely not. I wish I had. To have her here in person? That would be splendid. We dream of that. But no, I didn't even know she was in Derry.'

Rev. McCutcheon began to pick some flecks of dust from the green baize.

I said, 'She was coming to see you. She said there was a problem with the church in the city and she was going to come and help sort it out.'

'Well there is a problem, but she hasn't been to see us about it.'

'So what about the people who caused the trouble? The disaffected? Could she have gone to see them?'

'I don't know. It's possible.'

'They have someone in charge, a ringleader?'

'Well, I don't wish to cast dispersions.'

'Aspersions,' I said.

'Aspersions?'

'You cast aspersions, not dispersions. A small point, but it might save your life one day.'

'It . . .'

'Aspersions have already been cast, Rev. I just need a name.'

'Well. It was young thugs who did the damage. They came in with balaclavas on, but even with that, I knew the half of them from the neighbourhood. But you can't pick on them, they're just doing what they're told. You really want to talk to Peter Quinn. Peter was a lay preacher with us, and like many lay preachers he came to it via a stint in prison. He rather likes the sound of his own voice. He's a big noise here on the Waterside, and not a man you'd want to cross.'

'And what's his problem with Christine? He doesn't think she's the Messiah?'

'The opposite, I'm afraid.'

'How do you mean? He *does* believe she's the . . .?'

'He believes she's the Antichrist.'

'Ah,' I said.

'And that does concern me a little bit. If Christine came up here without protection and someone like Peter Quinn heard about that, well, I dread to think what he might do. I sent the police off in his direction too, but they didn't get very far. If you can do any better – then God bless you, Dan Starkey.'

It wasn't a phrase I'd heard much before.

I said, 'Rev., likelihood is she's fine, just doing her own thing, clearing her head, and she really hasn't been missing for that long. So I wouldn't worry about it overly.'

He began to flick the hall lights off, which was quite a broad hint that my time was up. I moved to the front door and he came with me. I stepped outside into the snow and he followed, closing and locking the door behind him.

'Walking my way?' I asked.

''Fraid not.'

He nodded across the car park towards a largish-looking three-storey property in complete darkness. 'One advantage of being in the God business – you usually get to live on site. One disadvantage?'

'You get to live on site?'

'Exactly.'

'Did they smash your home up as well?'

'Nope. Better locks.'

I gave him a nod and turned away. But I hadn't gone more than a few yards before he called after me.

'Mr Starkey?'

'Yup?'

'Do you have a lot of success as a private investigator?'

'Fair to middling,' I said.

'Well, if Christine is in any trouble, I hope you find her safe.'

'With the Lord's help I will,' I said, 'and a little luck.'

24

It wasn't quite the retreat from Moscow, but I did feel
a tiny little bit sorry for him, pacing at the foot of the
Peace Bridge while the snow fell even more relentlessly
around him and clearly scared of what might happen
if he confessed to losing me. He had deduced that I
would return whence I came, but not that I might say
sod it, I'm not walking in that, and choose a different
mode of transport. As my taxi cruised slowly past him
and he clapped his hands together, his woollen hat
sodden and his breath coming in great misty clouds, I
rolled down the window and, making sure he had a
good look at me, gave him a big thumbs-up and yelled,
'It's Chrissssttmasssssss!' as close to the way Noddy
yelled it as I could, although still impossibly short.

The taxi driver nearly lost control of the vehicle.

He shouted, 'What the fuck?!!!'

I was rewarded with a look of utter surprise and then

complete consternation from my follower, who immediately started to run after the car but then went flying on his arse in the snow.

I sat back, laughing, and suggested to the driver that he get with the spirit of Christmas and he said it was more than a month away yet, and besides, he was a Muslim. I asked if he was a Protestant Muslim or a Catholic Muslim and he said he didn't understand what I meant, that such a thing was impossible, and I said, there, in a nutshell, was the problem with the Middle East and he said, *What?* and I said, 'No sense of humour.'

He decided to concentrate on the road.

I checked my phone. I called Sara.

She answered quickly, her voice low.

'Starkey,' she said.

There was music on in the background, a DJ talking.

'Aw,' I said, 'you're thinking of me.'

'Your name came up on the screen. What do you want?'

'The love of a good woman, but I'd settle for a steak with you and then a roulade in the hay after.'

'I'm busy.'

'I know that. How is it out there?'

'Out where? I'm working in my room.'

'No you're not. I just had them let me in.'

'You . . .'

'Told them you had a history of epileptic fits. You might have drowned in the bath. But apparently not. Nice undies, by the way.'

'Starkey . . .'

'So you're out at work. You're parked and watching someone.'

'How could you poss—'

'I can hear your radio on in the car, the presenter has just trailed his own station, so I know it's one of the local commercial ones. I also know that none of them have been able to afford to switch to digital, so they're still FM, but the radio in your hotel room is digital, so you couldn't be picking it up unless you were in your car. I can hear that you have your heater on high. But your wipers are only on intermittent, so you're parked up somewhere watching someone or something and you have to keep the windscreen clear enough to see what's happening.'

'All right, Sherlock, very good. So tell me where I am then.'

'Really? You don't think I know?'

'I know you don't know.'

'I'd have to concentrate.'

'You're such a bullshitter.'

The taxi driver looked back at me. 'City Hotel?'

'No,' I said, 'change of plan. Millennium Forum.'

He nodded and we drove past the hotel. I said to Sara, 'You took my tip on Sunny Jim and ran with it. You found out where he lived and you've followed him to where he is now. How am I doing?' She sighed. 'Okay. I'm seeing a Spar shop somewhere near you.'

She said, 'There are hundreds of Spar shops, there's one on every corner.'

But I could hear a little nervous skip in her voice.

I said, 'It's almost like I'm flying, I'm floating past Free Derry Corner, I'm turning, I'm turning into Westland Street . . .'

'Starkey . . .'

'. . . and there, there you are, in the car park of the Welcome Inn, all alone in your wee smelly dog car, Sara Patterson hot on the trail of Sunny Jim . . .'

'Starkey, you bastard, where are you, where the fuck are you?'

I could just picture her, twisting and turning in her seat, trying to catch a glimpse of me.

I laughed, told her I was downtown but had spies everywhere, including squirrels on skis, and not to get her knickers in a twist. We should meet later. I suggested Badgers. Eleven p.m. I hung up while she was in mid refusal. Borrowing her phone at breakfast and changing her phone finder app so that it allowed me to track her had been easy, and simple, and was already bearing fruit. It unsettled me a little that she was poking around the Bogside at night. She had grown up in the bucolic north-west. Londonderry in general and the Bogside in particular was a law unto itself. I had made some inroads there by getting Danny Lynch's tacit approval to ask questions; the same courtesy had not been extended to Sara. But she was a big girl, and she did the crime beat so she had to know how to handle dangerous people. And I had my own agenda, which for the moment involved getting dropped outside the Forum and giving my driver a modest tip for putting up with me.

The driver said, 'Merry Christmas,' as I climbed out.
I said, 'As-salamu alaykum,' which surprised him.
He said, 'Slainte!' and I told him not to push it.

The audience was just getting out of the last night
of the punk musical, wave after new wave of them
chatting happily and singing snippets from the show.
It was an impressive turnout for a filthy night. I pushed
in amongst them and as a man with receding hair spiked
up for the occasion struggled back into his leather jacket
I managed to swipe a programme out of his pocket. I
moved right and down some steps by the side of the
theatre, which gave me a view of the stage door, which
was at a lower level again. While I waited, I perused
the programme. The main cast and crew all had photos
and short biographies. I was looking for Harry, the
costume designer. Turned out his full name was Harry
Lime. Really. Big round face, bald as a coot. He was
from Belfast originally but had trained at the Bristol
Old Vic and specialised in designing costumes for large-
scale musicals. He had worked on all the greats, and
Mamma Mia! too.

After about ten minutes a large group emerged from
the stage door and moved as one up the steps past me.
Last night of the show and the cast and crew were intent
on celebrating. But no Harry Lime. When they turned
the corner, I continued down to the next level and walked
up to the rear doors, which were lying open. As there
was no security, I just walked on in. As I stood pondering
where to go next, swing doors to my left opened and a
teenage waiter came through carrying a bottle of wine

and a glass on a tray. I asked him the way to the costume department and he said he was just going there. I said I'd save him the trip if he pointed me in the right direction. He accepted gratefully. I took the tray and followed his instructions.

The costume department's doors were also open. I saw a large, brightly lit room packed tight with racks of clothes. A man was putting plastic covers on various punk outfits and labelling them. Harry Lime was fleshier than his photo.

I said, 'Not going to the party?'

He said, 'I wish!' without looking up.

'This must be for you.'

He looked round and then smiled broadly. 'There is a God! Usually they're in such a rush to get to the bar they forget all about me.' He fitted a studded leather jacket on to a hanger, hooked it on to a rail and came towards me. As I set the tray down on a counter, he lifted the bottle, briefly examined the label, and then twisted the top off and began to pour. 'So who're you when you're at home?' he asked and took a healthy swig, which came right back out again as I said, 'I'm looking for Billy the Bear.'

'What the fuck?'

'Relax,' I said, 'his mum asked—'

Before I could finish, he jabbed the flat end of the bottle straight into my nose. It was such a shock and so fucking sore that I let out a yelp, and staggered back. Blood was already cascading down my chin. As I cupped my hands over it Harry vanished through the door. I tried to go after him but felt so woozy that I just sank to my knees and then crumpled over until I was on my back looking at stars dancing above me. And then there was a change in the light and he was back, looming over me, screaming: 'Do you see this, do you fucking see this?' He was brandishing something I couldn't quite make out, at least until he pressed it against my temple and experience told me that it was a gun. 'How did you get in here?' he yelled. 'How the fuck did you get past security?'

'There was no—'

He hit me with the barrel.

'When are youse going to leave me alone? I haven't done nothing!'

The blood was now pouring down the back of my throat. I rolled over and started coughing. Then something landed on the back of my head and I let out a yell before I realised that it was soft and it hadn't hurt. I raised my hand to it; it was a cloth or a towel. I pressed it against my nose and tried to stem the flow. I rolled back over and he was right there again with the barrel pressed into my cheek.

'I know what you're thinking,' he said, 'you're thinking this is just a stage gun . . .'

'I wasn't—'

'And yes it is, it's from the musical, and sure, it only fires blanks, but this close? This close the charge will blow a hole in your head the size of my fist. Do you want me to do that?'

'Why would I want that?' I said. 'Although it would fit in perfectly with the pattern of my life.'

A little clarity was beginning to return. He said '*What?*'

I turned my face towards him, so that my cheek was actually pressing into the gun barrel. I said, 'Harry, I've been doing this for a long time. Generally if people ask you if you want something unpleasant done to you, it's just a threat. You've reacted to something, over-reacted, because you're scared, but I'm not here to cause you any trouble, I'm just looking for Billy. His mum hired me to find him and I need your help. But at the end of the day, it's your call. So either pull the trigger or get that fucking thing out of my face.'

His mouth opened a fraction and he bit into his bottom lip as he pressed the gun even harder into my cheek. His finger began to squeeze the trigger.

I have a habit of tempting fate.

25

'The thing about producers,' Harry Lime was saying, 'is that while the show is on, you're all part of one fabulous big family, and God knows I've been involved in enough productions so I can say it's the same everywhere, all over the world, but as soon as that final curtain comes down and they have all the money they're ever going to wring out of you, then all deals are off. This lot, load of Paddies from Galway, I told them I was scared, told them there were these people after me, trying to get at me, and they said, not a problem, they'd double security, make sure no one got near me for the entire run of the show. And they were true to their word. But as soon as that curtain came down, they pulled their guys *instantly* and that's why you were able to just walk in. It was a surprise. You can't blame me for being jumpy.'

I gingerly touched my nose. It had stopped bleeding but I could feel it swelling and my eyes puffing up.

To his credit, once Harry Lime came to his senses, he was genuinely concerned and suitably apologetic. He whisked me off to the theatre's basement bar. He was a big guy with a big smile that struggled to be anything other than fleeting on his troubled, baggy-eyed face. He said he'd been virtually living in the building since this had all blown up.

'This?'

'Billy disappearing, them'uns coming after me. I should have taken myself back off to London, could have disappeared there rightly, but I'd committed to this crock of shit . . .' he thumbed around him, 'and couldn't let them down, so I've been working here, sleeping in the department, and I *did* feel safe. Now I'm going to have to do a runner, not even bother going home for my gear.'

'You mean to Shipquay Street?'

'No! That hole? No chance. Billy didn't mind slumming there, but mostly we were at my place. I'm a surfer at heart, so I've a caravan up at Sunnylands? You know, on Benone Strand? The waves are epic. And all that rubber's quite flattering too.'

He gave me a wink. He was, I supposed, quite camp. When he'd had the fake gun pressed to my head and was threatening to blow a hole in me, he hadn't sounded camp *at all*.

I said, 'It must be Baltic up there, this time of year.'

'Tell me about it. Park's all closed down for the winter, but because I'm not here that much, I sneak in when I'm home and play cat and mouse with the warden.

It's *hilarious*. Speaking of which . . .' He reached up and gently peeled my hand away from where it was feeling the contours of my reshaped nose. 'It doesn't look so bad, and you know, in your trade it might actually help, gives you a tougher kind of a look.'

'Lucky me, then,' I said. 'So tell me about Billy, and how you met him, and what you're so scared of.'

We were drinking whiskeys. Doubles. The only other customers were half a dozen overweight, balding middle-aged punks moaning about the travesty of a musical they'd just witnessed as they sipped their cocktails and perused the late-night tapas menu.

Harry took a sip, nodded in appreciation and said, 'Ah – Billy. Billy. Billy the Bear. Never was a man so aptly named. Soft and cuddly, loved to hibernate, but you make him angry, he could tear your arms off. It's just a pity he . . . let himself go.'

'How do you mean?'

'That drug, that crush? See – I go away, months at a time, touring with shows. Every time I came back it was always lovely, at first, absence makes the heart and all that, but then gradually I'd see he'd gotten a bit more into it, or out of it. He used to be a bit of a whirl-wind, life and soul, finger in every pie, but more and more he just withdrew, let others do the work, said he was delegating, enjoying life more, but when you dele-gate to scumbags, you get ripped off . . .'

'Scumbags like Jacko.'

'You know Jacko?'

'Only by reputation.'

'Scumbags like Jacko . . . I mean, man, you know about the cam girls?' I nodded. 'That was a licence to print money, but Billy managed to fuck it up and next thing you know Jacko steps in and snatches it all away.'

'So they weren't business partners?'

'Absolutely not. Billy handed it over, paying a debt.'

'A debt for drugs?'

'Far as I know. A deal that went wrong. By and large, I've nothing against drugs, but there's a time and a place. He always told me he did a wee bit of dealing, but gave the impression it was never much more than getting some gear in for your mates, not real big deals. I suppose I had the old love goggles on. Thing with drugs, whether you're taking or dealing, if you've that kind of personality, maybe enough is never enough.'

'So you think the drugs are the reason he's disappeared, or *been* disappeared?'

Harry turned the now empty glass in his hand. I signalled the barman for two more. 'I don't know. There was something going on with him the last few times I was back. You know, sometimes you think you know someone, just because you lie on a couch with them to watch *Corrie*. Just because you like dancing or lifting weights or . . . but I suppose I never really knew him. Maybe because I'm away so much we were like a holiday romance and I never really got to see the flaws until it was too late? Anyway – last year was a bit of an eye-opener. I was in London, *Phantom*, and I get a call from him says he's been arrested, the police had raided the apartments thinking it was a brothel. He got off that, nothing illegal, but in the course of searching the place they found a gun, which had a history, and so he was sent off to Magilligan for three months. And the funny thing is, I could almost wave to him from the caravan, the prison's only along the beach a bit.'

The barman came across with the drinks. Harry reached for his wallet, but the barman said, 'On the house, Harry.'

Harry nodded his thanks.

We clinked glasses.

'But the charge was dropped?'

'Yup. The gun was found in the roof space, wrapped in a twenty-year-old newspaper, so the argument was it belonged to some previous tenant. They didn't think there was much chance of getting a conviction, so they had to let him walk.' Harry shook his head sadly. 'But there was something different about him when he got out, and that's really when he started getting heavier and heavier into the old crush. I'm just sorry I wasn't there to help him, but I was away on tour so much and . . .' He swirled the whiskey. 'To tell you the truth, towards the end he was getting so bad with it maybe I found excuses not to come home so much? I feel like shit now he's gone.'

'Addicts are hard work,' I said.

'Do you have someone close who's . . .?'

'Aye. The ex-wife. She's something shocking with the drink. Anyway – he wasn't really alone, was he? The girls seemed to help him, and then his mum stepped in.'

'Yup, good old Moira.' He took another drink and said, 'What a cow. She didn't have anything to do with him for years, broke his heart so it did. Then when she heard there was a bit of money around, she swept right back in. Stroke City Girls was Billy's idea, then Jacko was wheedling his way in, and next thing you know she's at it too. Like fucking maggots.'

'Maybe she was just trying to help him . . .'

'No, fuck that, she was a prize cow. He told me, soon as he came out as gay – soon as he was forced out, I suppose – she wouldn't touch him with a bargepole. I couldn't believe it – I got home from a gig, called up to the apartments to see him, prepared for Jacko, but then I find her there as well, virtually running the place, business suit'n'all.'

'Really? Sure she was about seventy or something?'

'I know she was getting on, but you know she had Billy really young? Like fifteen or something? So she really wasn't that much older. And she was that kind of a woman – one minute she could look some dowdy oul' bag, and next you'd see her all glammed up like an Avon lady. She was a fucking . . . what's it . . . chameleon?' And then he began to hum 'Karma Chameleon', smiling at me and looking a bit misty-eyed. 'We danced to that. A lot. That was our generation. Even up at Straightshooters, they'd play that for us once in a while, then laugh at us oul' codgers cutting a rug to it.'

'Straightshooters . . .'

'Aye . . . just up the hill a bit. It's a club. For us. It's where we met, in fact. Wasn't called Straightshooters then, but these places are always changing their names. Met him in the dark room and it was love at first bite.' He saw my face and said, 'What? Does it make you uncomfortable?'

'No, I . . .'

'Oh yes, first night, he fucked me twice.'

'I . . .'

'He widened the circle of my friends, so to speak, did big Billy the Bear. He wasn't long out of prison for robbing a shop. He was, literally, an arse bandit. He still went there, two or three times a week.'

'To dance and . . .'

'To pick someone up and fuck 'em.'

'But weren't you two . . .'

'Dan, whatever works, and it works for us. This world, the rules are a wee bit different.'

'Okay. I probably knew that.' I took a sip of whiskey. 'When was the last time you spoke to him?'

'I was on the train, to Manchester, job interview. Didn't get it. I called him up to whine about it, but he was off his head. I told him to go up to Straights, get his head golden-showered.'

'He . . .'

'Figure of speech. Far as I know, he went, and I never heard from him again. I was back home here in a couple of days, thought maybe he'd met someone else, but then this gang of hellions came to the caravan and I knew something really bad had happened to him. I mean, if you're twelve years old and a gang comes calling for you, they want you to come out and play. If you're my age – you get the fuck out of there. And that's exactly what I did, I squeezed out the back window and hid in the sand dunes till they'd gone.'

'*They*, as in . . .'

'Christ, I don't know, they were all in balaclavas.'

'What did they want? Were they looking for Billy?'

'Who knows? Like I said, I didn't hang around.'

'And what did they do when they couldn't get hold of you?'

'I don't really know – they broke the door, for sure, I could see them inside.'

'They take anything?'

'I don't know, I haven't been back. I may sneak back before I go, see what I can rescue.'

'Did Billy keep anything with you? Anything to do with the cam-girls business or his drug deals? Something they might have been looking for? Anything on a computer or . . .?'

'If they wanted to know how much it cost to outfit a pantomime dame in 1995, then they might have hit a gold mine, but otherwise, absolutely not.'

'No hidden stashes of crush . . .'

'No, no, and no. Never.'

'But they weren't to know that.'

'Nope, and I wasn't hanging around long enough to point it out. I was in those sand dunes for fucking hours.'

Harry shook his head.

'Poor Billy,' he said. 'Do you really think he's . . .?' There was suddenly a tear in his eye.

'I don't know. Maybe I'll find him yet.'

Harry dragged an arm across his face. 'Well if you do, give him one for me. I miss the stupid bugger.' He drained his glass and stood up. 'Now, if you'll excuse me, I have to finish packing the gear. And then I'll have to think about somewhere to sleep, for sure as hell they're not going to let me kip here again tonight. I'll maybe nip home, pick up some essentials, then get the hell out of Dodge. You don't want to buy a caravan, by any chance?'

I smiled. 'It might come to that yet.'

Harry nodded down at me. 'And really sorry about the nose. I'm just a bit jumpy.'

'No bother,' I said.

I took out my card and gave it to him. He was one of the lucky ones. I asked him to give me a call if he noticed anything missing from the caravan, just in case it cast any light on why exactly they'd come for Billy or why they were still pursuing him.

Harry examined my card, flicked it between his fingers and said, 'A real live Irish private eye. Sam Spud.'

'That's me,' I said. I took a note of his number as well, because I know how lazy people can be. As he turned to go, I said, 'Harry? The name – Harry Lime? It's a nickname or a stage name, right? From *The Third Man*? Orson Welles?'

Harry smiled. 'Most people think that,' he said, 'given that I work in showbiz. My *real* name's Harry McIlroy. It was my dad started to call me Harry Lime when I was a kid, and it stuck.'

'Because he was a fan of the movie?'

'No,' he replied. 'Because from an early age he knew I was a fruit.'

Harry gave me a wink and sashayed away.

26

I sat in Badgers, nursing a pint, waiting for Sara – I'd a lot of names to chase and a mountain of second- and third-hand information on two disparate cases to think through. But the music was too loud and the company too raucous. The cast and crew of *It Makes You Want to Spit* had taken over the bar, and they'd a nasty habit of bursting into classics from the Andrew Lloyd Webber songbook, which annoyed my brain sufficiently to get up and out as soon as it became clear that Sara wasn't coming. I was sure she'd have realised by now how I'd tracked her to the Bogside and amended that function on her phone – but when I checked it was still showing her there in the pub car park. If she was waiting for closing time so that she could tackle or track Sunny Jim, she might be in for a surprise – as I'd recently discovered, Londonderry bars don't always adhere strictly to the licensing laws. I tried calling her, but it went to voicemail: I told her she could be there all night and to wise up and get back to the hotel for a hot whiskey and romance, and then I might see her after that.

I returned to the hotel, ordered up a bottle of wine and sat by the window looking out at a Peace Bridge that was barely visible through the snow. I FaceTimed Trish. She said, 'What the hell happened to your nose?' I told her a gay costume designer had smashed me in the face with a bottle of Blue Nun, and we agreed to put it down as another black mark against the Catholic Church. She was in bed, face scraped, hair back, tired but smiley. She said the kids with the kid were back in the nest. I asked how they were taking to parent-hood and she said like ducks to water, if one of those ducks was a lazy waste of space. Bobby had more important concerns, which mostly revolved around *Call of Duty*. And Lolita?

'Yup, she's a natural, she's beautiful and she's tough. A real Belfast mum, do you know what I mean?'

'Cow and Gate in one hand, Lambert and Butler in the other?'

'Exactly. She takes no prisoners. Especially with Bobby, which is no bad thing. He's huffing at the moment, but as soon as he's put down the al-Qaeda threat, I'm pretty sure he'll pitch in. Speaking of threats and internecine warfare, how's the Maiden City treating you?'

'Fine, apart from the fact that I'm starting to look like the Elephant Man.'

'C'mon,' she said, 'and tell Trish everything.'

So I did. I always had told her everything, or parts of everything, or mere hints of everything, mixed in with lies and half-truths nestling in a bed of fabrication; it was usually to protect her, or to protect me. But here and now, with nothing to hide, I told her everything. She was mature and knew me better than anyone. She listened. She nodded. She made sympathetic faces at the right time, and rolled her eyes when I deserved it. I took her right back to the start, to Moira Doherty arriving to recruit me into the hunt for her missing son, an ex-terrorist and sometime gangster, drug dealer and gay boy who had launched a cam-girl wank site on the internet which, being a licence to print money, seemed to have attracted even more insalubrious types, including Jacko, who was too scared to leave his apartment, and Sunny Jim, a Republican whippersnapper who was probably responsible for her murder. I told her about my teenage Messiah friend cadging a lift and then disappearing, and about our old friend Pike setting his convert cops on me, and getting followed through the snow to a reverend who had suspicions about an ex-con turned preacher who thought Christine was the Antichrist.

At the end of it all she nodded sagely for a bit and then said, 'So this Sara Patterson, are you doing it with her?'

'No, Christ.'

'This Christ, are you doing it with her?'

'No, God, she's barely sixteen.'

'Yet there's definitely something going on.'

'We're friends, that's all.'

'A grown man and a barely sixteen-year-old travelling the country together. Tie a yellow ribbon round the old yew tree, my love.'

'Don't be ridiculous.'

'I wonder what Freud would make of it.'

'He'd make a meal of it. Or are we not talking about Clement?'

'Christine, young, beautiful, tempting, powerful, available. You probably have her locked in a basement somewhere.'

'Well,' I said, 'you've been a big help.'

She said, 'As always, Dan my love, there's a lot of shit happening. But you could just walk away, you don't owe anyone anything. But . . . that's not going to happen.'

'Of course not.'

'You like working things out. But you know, honey, these things, they're like Christmas lights – sometimes they can just never be untangled. Sometimes you have to go out and buy new lights.'

'And sometimes you just persevere. Unless, of course, we're talking about marriage.'

She sighed. 'So, you're not having sex with Sara Patterson.'

'No.'

'I like what she writes in the paper. She reminds me of . . .'

'Don't . . .'

'. . . a young you . . . And she's single . . .'

'I have no idea.'

'I'm not asking, I'm saying, she says so in her column.'

'Don't believe everything you read in the papers.'

'She does hard news well, and has a good turn of phrase in her column. You've so much in common.'

'Sigh,' I said.

'But does she have these?' said Trish.

'These?'

'*These*,' said Trish, and lowered her camera angle to show me her naked breasts.

'I have no idea,' I said.

She caressed them.

'Or this . . .'

She lowered it again, lower and lower.

She said, 'It's been a long time.'

'Yes it has,' I said, 'but I always love coming home.'

Later she said, 'You shouldn't let other people do your dirty work for you.'

I said, 'FaceTime isn't perfect, but it—'

'I mean your girlfriend, Sara, sending her after Sunny Jim like that. You should have done it yourself.'

'She's a big girl . . .'

'With a big ass . . . but still, it used to be you wouldn't have fobbed it off.'

'I'm older and wiser.'

'No, you would have wanted to know first hand, because you always say the devil's in the detail. See what you told me about the look that passed between the funeral director and the other guy, what's his . . .?'

'Danny Lynch.'

'Danny Lynch . . . you picked up on that, and who knows what else you're missing by having her out there while you're in here having virtual sex.'

'Are you complaining?'

'Not at all. I'm very happy. It's the perfect relationship. I can have my way with you and then literally switch you off. Just like this.'

She cut the line.

I couldn't help but smile.

My Trish.

I looked at my watch. Somehow it was now three in the morning.

I phoned Sara. There was no response.

I checked the app again.

She was still in the car park of the Welcome Inn.

I did not think this was a good sign.

I sighed and said, 'No rest for the wicked,' out loud.

I pulled my collar up, thrust my hands deep into my pockets and stepped out of the hotel. It was coming down heavier than ever. There was no traffic at all. The silence was pierced only by the crisp snap of my feet in the virgin snow, and the equally crisp snap of the footsteps following behind.

Our relationship wasn't exactly the same as before. This time, as I chanced a quick glance back, I noted that my follower was wearing gloves. And that he had acquired a friend.

27

It was just ridiculous pretending they weren't there. The streets were deserted: no pedestrians playing in the snow, no cars on the road, just us, three dark specks on a whiteboard. I was outnumbered, and one of them had at least twenty-five years on me; I hadn't had a proper look at the newcomer yet. I slowly upped the pace from a determined trudge to something like a speed walk, and then a jog that progressed into proper long strides. When I glanced back, they were right there with me, no further back, no closer, just there. I darted across roads, ducked into side streets, backtracked and circled, but they remained equidistant. While it felt like they'd been behind me for hours, and we had covered several miles, the truth was that it was barely ten minutes and not much more than a mile and I was gasping for breath like an asthmatic in an asbestos factory.

And then I just stopped, in the middle of a pristine road, caked cars on either side, shops shuttered, doubled over with my hands on my knees, greedily sucking for oxygen while they came to a halt about ten metres away, themselves breathing hard but not as bad as I was.

I said, 'I don't know about you . . . but I'm fucking fucked.'

They said nothing.

The other guy was taller, beefier, beanie hat pulled down to his eyelids, jacket zipped up to his nose. They had their hands in their pockets. No obvious display of weapons, but that hardly lessened the threat.

I said, 'Okay, it's my turn to chase you two now. I'll give you a head start, I'll count to ten.'

Still they just looked at me.

I had recovered my breath a little, but not enough to take off again.

'Well,' I said, slipping my hands into my own pockets, 'this is a bit embarrassing. Tell you what – let's forget guns and knives and adapt to our surroundings, settle it with an old-fashioned duel.'

I lowered myself to one knee and began to gather together a snowball.

My original follower said, finally, 'Are you fucking mental or something?'

'That's a matter of opinion,' I said.

I stood, snowball in hand, and then moved closer.

I knew that if I took the bigger, stronger-looking one out of the game first, I'd have a much, much better chance of survival. But I would only have one chance to take them by surprise.

'Come on,' I said, 'gather your ammunition, then we can discuss the rules.'

'Rules?' said the other one. 'In a snowball fight?'

'Like fucking what?' said the first one.

'Like protect yourself at all times.'

I pulled my arm back and hurled the snowball with all the strength I had. The bigger guy was already starting to laugh at the ridiculousness of it when the snowball smashed into his face, taking out his top row of teeth and knocking him clean out in the process. He fell straight back and landed with a *whump* in the snow and lay there unmoving while blood spurted out of his broken mouth. His companion stood staring at him, open-mouthed. By the time he looked at me, I had a second snowball ready.

He said, 'How the fuck . . .?'

I showed him the second snowball. 'It's just snow,' I said, 'wrapped around a snooker ball.'

He looked at the ground, and the black ceramic ball lying in a patch of red snow with one jagged tooth attached to it.

When he looked back at me, I had the second snowball pulled back and ready to fire.

I said, 'So, will we continue?'

He raised his hands. 'No fucking way. But what the fuck did you want to do that for?'

'May have escaped your notice, pal,' I said, 'but youse were chasing me.'

'Only because you ran off.'

'Okay. Youse were following me. Now I want to know why, and who you're working for.'

I pulled my hand back a little further.

He said, 'Don't, mate . . .' He took a step away. 'I didn't fucking sign up for this.' He looked down at his pal again. 'Jesus,' he said.

'I'm warning you,' I said, with another small thrust of my hand.

'Okay . . . all right! There's nothing . . . no harm meant . . . Danny just said he'd give me fifty quid if I'd follow you around, see what you were up to . . .'

'Danny Lynch?'

'Aye.'

'He wanted you to put the frighteners on me, warn me off, beat me up?'

'No! He just said, tell me where he goes, who he meets . . .'

'And what'd you tell him?'

'Nothin' . . .'

I fake threw it again.

'Swear to God!' he cried. 'There's nothing to tell. You looked around the museum, you walked back to your hotel, you came out, you crossed the bridge, I lost you, you drove past, I hung about outside, you came out and then you started running so we ran after you. That's it mate, honest.' He looked down at his friend. 'There was no need to . . .'

I said, 'You better put him in the recovery position.'

'Wah?'

'Turn him on his side, make sure his airways are clear.'

He looked confused.

I rolled my eyes and crouched down.

His face was a mess.

His mate said, 'Is he all right?'

I said, 'Well he won't be eating toffee apples for a while, but he seems to be breathing okay.' I set the snowball down carefully before turning him. He let out a groan and his eyes fluttered. I looked up at his friend and said, 'You might want to get him to a hospital.'

I picked the snowball up again and stood.

His friend took out a mobile phone, but then stopped as I clicked my fingers.

'Let me,' I said. 'Wouldn't want you calling in the flying squad by accident.'

'I wasn't—'

'Give.'

I had the snowball poised and ready again.

He handed the phone over.

I held it in my left hand and jabbed the keys with one finger of my right while still holding the snowball. The operator asked which service and I said ambulance. The ambulance service asked what had happened and I said someone had suffered a sports-related injury. I gave her the location but not my name and hung up. My friend put his hand out for his phone and I said, 'I don't think so.' I slipped it into my pocket.

I said, 'What's your name, anyway?'

'Michael.'

'Michael what?'

He looked a bit shifty.

'Michael Lynch.'

'Right. And him?' I asked, nodding down.

'Patrick.'

'Patrick *what*?'

'Patrick Lynch.'

'Right,' I said, 'a pattern emerges. And was he getting paid fifty quid to follow me as well?'

'No, he's my mate. I was starving so he brought me a Subway.'

'Expensive Subway,' I said.

I turned and started to walk away.

Michael immediately came after me.

I stopped and said, 'What are you doing?'

He stopped and said, 'Following you.'

'Michael, that job's over. Now look after your cousin or your nephew or whatever the fuck he is.'

'Danny told me to—'

'Fuck Danny.'

I raised the snowball.

Michael looked at it, and looked at me. 'Danny's not going to like this,' he said, then let out a sigh and turned back.

'Hey, Michael?'

He turned.

'Catch!'

I threw the snowball as hard as I could; he raised his hands to protect himself, but too late, it slapped into his face. He let out a cry of pain, but then stood there, somewhat puzzled why it hadn't hurt more.

But it was snow, just snow.

I was strictly a one-ball wonder.

28

From my position on the city walls I looked down on Free Derry Corner, and off to its left the Welcome Inn with a vehicle sitting seemingly abandoned in its car park. Even from such a distance I could see enough of it to know that it was Sara's, and that if she was still inside it watching out for Sunny Jim she would have to be using X-ray specs to see through the snow-covered windscreen. There were no exhaust fumes, no hint of a light from within or without. I phoned her again, but straight to voicemail.

I supposed she might have considered the conditions too dangerous to drive in and decided to walk back to the hotel. But she would surely have taken her phone with her, and it was still showing up on my app as being right there in front of me. She might have gone inside to see if she could talk to him and stayed for a lock-in; I already knew it wasn't exactly uncommon in these parts. Or maybe Sunny Jim was extracting her teeth with pliers in a back room. You met all sorts in bars.

After looking around in vain for a biscuit tin lid with which to toboggan down the hill, I settled for an ungainly slither. By the time I reached the bottom, my arse was damp. I continued on across the blanketed grass to Free Derry Corner. I noted that my graffiti had been expertly removed from the wall. I continued on along Lecky Road and turned right on to Westland Street, my eyes peering ahead towards the bar, which was in darkness, and Sara's car. There was no movement anywhere, no sound. It felt like I was the loudest man on the planet as my feet crunched into the snow. I approached her car on the driver's side. I knocked gently on the plastered window. When there was no response, I scraped the snow away and peered inside, a large part of me fearing that Sara would be staring straight back at me, frozen solid. But the car was empty. I tried the doors, but they were all locked. I looked across at the bar. I studied my surroundings. Still no one moving, still just the silent snowfall. I walked across to the bar and listened at the doors. Nothing. I tried opening them, but they were also locked. I put my ear to the door, but no twiddly-dee, no raucous laughter; just a bar, shut for the night. I checked the windows, but they were shuttered. I stood, pondering. I didn't doubt that the phone app worked – but I called Sara again just to be sure. It immediately began ringing from her car, the sound carrying perfectly. I stepped back across and peered through the driver's-side window again. But I realised that the ringtone wasn't coming from inside. I moved around the car.

There.

A slight glow from under the snow about five metres away.

I hurried across, crouched down and pushed my fingers into the fine powder. I pulled Sara's phone out and wiped it on my jacket. The screen was badly cracked, but it was still displaying my name as it rang.

I cut the line and stood looking at the bar, and then past it at the lights flickering through the snow from the trellised houses of the Bogside on the hill beyond. I wondered if she was up there somewhere, having a cosy fireside chat with Sunny Jim, or if she was gone, murdered and disappeared like so many innocents before her.

And if that was indeed the case, if it was, once again, entirely my fault.

Danny Lynch answered on the third ring.

'Michael,' he growled, 'this better be important.'

'It surely is,' I said.

'Michael?'

'Nope, he's indisposed.'

'Well who the fu—'

'It's Dan Starkey.'

'Dan . . .?'

'As a tracker, your Michael is hardly Hawkeye.'

'Hawk—'

'Though since *MASH*, the two often get confused.'

'What the . . .?'

'*Last of the Mohicans*! I was just saying, the late lamented Michael is really crap at—'

'Late and lamented? You mean he's . . .?'

'When I say late and lamented, I mean freezing cold and embarrassed that he was spotted so easily, disarmed so quickly. You sent him out after me with hardly a jumper on.'

'Starkey, what the fuck are you doing with my nephew's phone? And why are you calling me at three o'clock in the fucking morning?'

'I've just told you. He's useless, verging on gormless. But that's the problem with nepotism. Or do I mean incest? Anyhow, I need your help.'

'My . . . Starkey, have you lost your fucking mind?'

'No, but I have lost my girlfriend.'

'Your . . .?'

'She was in your neighbourhood and now she's disappeared. And I suspect you're probably the only person in this shithole of an estate who might be able to help me.'

'And why the fuck would I want to help you?'

'Because I think it's Sunny Jim who has her.'

There was a pause then. The creak of a bedspring. A sigh.

And then he said, 'For fuck sake, youse can surely pick your battles. Right. Come up to the house.'

He cut the line.

Ten seconds later, I phoned him back and asked for the address.

His house was about as far up the hill as they went. On a good day there might have been a splendid view, but now it was lost in the low-hanging clouds. It looked like just another two-up two-down in a nondescript terrace. There was a battered Audi in the driveway and a kid's trike on its side in the front garden. For the most feared man in the Bogside, it wasn't very impressive. But perhaps that was the point. He had always sold himself as a man of the people, and maybe he was just that.

The door opened before I could ring the bell. He thumbed up the stairs and then put a finger to his lips. He was wearing a towelling dressing gown and had a cup of coffee in his hand. So far, so Soprano. He led me through to a smallish kitchen made larger by the addition of a sun room. There were fridge magnets, cereal boxes, and plates on a drip-rack by the sink.

'You sound wired enough, Starkey, but coffee?'

I nodded. He fixed it. He brought it to a kitchen table sticky with jam. He immediately turned for a sponge to clean it.

'Grandkids?' I asked.

'Nope. Surprise late package.'

'That must be fun,' I said.

'I'm shattered. But yes. Now tell me about your girlfriend.'

'Fiancée,' I said.

'You let your fiancée have *anything* to do with Sunny Jim?'

'This isn't my town and the only player I know is you. How was I meant to know who Sunny Jim was?'

'All you had to do was ask.' He pulled a chair out and sat opposite. 'You know for sure he has her?'

'All I know is she set out to track him down, and now her car's abandoned at the pub at the bottom of the hill and her phone smashed beside it.' I took a sip of my coffee. His grey chest hair was showing through the opening in his dressing gown.

He was studying me, his cup raised to his lips but not quite drinking. He said, 'What are you up to, Starkey?'

'I'm just concerned for the missus.'

'I thought you were looking for Billy the Bear?'

'I am.'

'So why the interest in Sunny Jim?'

'I told you earlier. He was spotted at old Ma Doherty's.'

'It may not have been him.'

'We both know it was.'

'You don't even know who he is.'

'Then tell me. But first help me find Sara.'

He pondered that. Then he took his phone from his dressing gown and stood up.

'Let me make a couple of calls.'

He began to move out of the kitchen.

'You don't have to leave,' I said.

'Yes I do.'

He left. There was a maroon-coloured school blazer

hanging over the back of his chair. It had a New Seeker emblem on the lapel. I sighed. I sipped. I took out my phone and texted Christine: *Are you (a) hiding? (b) trapped under a large wardrobe? (c) with your Father in Heaven?*

There was no response by the time Danny came back in. He sat down, took a sip of his coffee, made a face and then pushed the cup to one side.

'My people are checking,' he said.

'Okay. Appreciate it.'

'They might be a while. Why don't you go back to wherever you're staying and I'll give you a bell once I hear anything? I'd give you a lift but I don't think anyone's going to be driving in this.'

'No. I'm fine. I'll wait.'

'Right. Okay. I thought you were married.'

'I was.'

'But you're doing it again?'

'That's the plan.' I nodded at the blazer. 'One of your kids is a New Seeker.'

'Aye. Our Claire. Overnight she went from Lady Gaga to what's her name . . . Christine? All a lot of bloody nonsense, but what do you do? Have you tried grounding a teenager these days?'

'Tell me about it,' I said. 'But wouldn't a good knee-capping slow her down?'

'Ah, the good old days.'

'You should have patented it, you could have been rolling in it by now.'

'I should have. And it really worked. We had the lowest crime rates in Europe.'

'Apart from the murders and the bombings.'

'Those were political.'

'Terrorism.'

'Political. And if you want to find your fiancée, perhaps we should agree to differ on this and try and work together?'

'Ah, Northern Ireland in microcosm.'

'Exactly.'

'And how's that working for you these days?'

'Pretty shit, to be honest.'

'Yeah, me too.'

'We had good Troubles.'

'We were in our prime.'

'Well don't worry, Starkey, they may be coming back for an encore.'

'Which brings us handily back to Sunny Jim.'

Danny drummed his fingers on the table. 'You really sure you want to get into this?' he asked.

'I'm already into it.'

'No you're not, though your girl may be.'

'We're one and the same. So who is he? What does his mother call him?'

'James Owens, Jimmy, born and bred just around the corner from here, and a right wee gobshite from an early age.'

'So you know him well enough?'

'Kind of. When he was a kid. Then I lost track. Starkey, you've got to understand – the days when I was running things around here are long gone. When we gave up the guns, all our kids had seen enough of the violence to know they preferred peace. But the next generation of kids – they were brought up on stories about their old men blowing this up, blowing that up. And they started to think, well, what's really changed? We're still ruled over by the Brits, we still have no jobs, and the Bogside is still the Bogside. And they got angrier and angrier about it, but they didn't know what to do about it, and there was no one to show them – all the old hands like me had given up, were dying out, moving away, all the old guys who could make a bomb or snipe a soldier were too arthritic or apathetic to get involved. So they've had to start figuring it out for themselves.'

'And Sunny Jim was one of those kids.'

'*Is* one of those kids. He's still in his twenties.'

'So he joins an organisation . . .'

'Joins a few, leaves them just as quick. See, Starkey, a firebomb in a sports shop or hijacking an Ulster bus is nothing to the likes of Sunny Jim – they're into spectacular. They're post 9/11, bigger and louder the better. But how do you do something big if you've never been out of the Bogside and know nothing about anything?'

'You get out.'

'Exactly. And traditionally – boxing? Soccer? Or . . .?'

'Or the army,' I said.

'Exactly.'

'And where better to train you how to be a terrorist. So Jimmy Owen joined up. And I'm betting he didn't go for the Irish Army. They make the Swiss look like the three hundred Spartans.'

'Yup. Jimmy joins the old enemy, and gets the best training in the world. He was away for two years. Given to understand he did very well too. Sergeant Jim Owen. Right up to the point when his army personnel carrier hit a roadside bomb, and the whole thing went up in flames. Three soldiers died – Jimmy was badly burned. He spends a long time in hospital, is eventually invalided out, comes straight back here, and first day one of his mates sees the state of his face and just says without thinking, "All right, Sunny Jim, how's it going?" and the name stuck.'

'He mind being called it? To his face.'

'Seems to revel in it. Does half the work for him, his face the way it is – scares the shit out of people before he even opens his mouth.'

'I thought with the army – I mean, it's been going on for generations, local kids, maybe been in a bit of trouble, they join up and when they come back they're all grown up and sorted and focused on living a good life, contributing to society. But not Sunny Jim?'

'Maybe it's the bomb fucked up his head, or maybe it's knowing he's going to look like that for the rest of his life, but the only thing he came back focused on was starting up the war again, and he's been building it ever since. I've done my best to calm him down, to talk it out, but he's really not interested. He's earnest, he's committed, and he's planning something. I'm pretty sure of that.'

'Something like . . .?'

'No idea. But something big, something people will remember.'

'So if he was spotted at Moira Doherty's, what do you think that's about?'

Danny gave a little shrug. 'I was thinking about that after you left – if she was somehow tied up with the porn business, the Stroke City whatever, and if porn is the licence to print money like they say it is, well maybe that's his interest. Money's not easy to come by in the terror business these days – the Americans, the Arabs, they're gone for good, and you sure as hell can't raise anything more than buttons here, people just aren't interested – maybe porn's financing whatever the hell he's planning.'

I looked at him across the table, shaking his head, the skin on his face slack, his bed-head hair flat on one side, frizzed on the other. He looked about as old as I felt.

I said, 'You're telling me he's planning something, something big, for a reason. You think I can do something about it.'

He smiled. 'It's good to have a healthy ego, Starkey – but the fact is I'm telling everyone. My former colleagues at Stormont; my former brothers in arms; the police. I've even made coffee for MI5; they sat just where you're sitting and they listened and they nodded and they went away and did bugger all. I speak to journalists all the time, they're happy to pick my brains about the bad old days, but when I start warning them it's all going to come back, they just look at me like

I'm some crazy old man who misses the spotlight.'

'And do you? Miss the spotlight.'

'Aye. Well. I can't deny it had its moments. But I have different priorities now, a crying, shitting little mistake who just happens to be the greatest thing that has ever happened to me. So I might miss the spotlight, but it doesn't mean I want to step back into it. Far from it. But it does mean I've an even greater interest in peace. So I keep telling people something big is coming down the line. Which is exactly why I'm telling you too.'

His phone, lying face down on the table, began to vibrate. He raised his eyebrows at me and turned it over. He squinted at the screen, then raised it to his ear. He said, 'Well?'

He listened, he nodded; I could hear the voice at the other end, but couldn't make out the words. Eventually he thanked them, then took several moments to locate the button to cut the call. He placed the phone face down on the table again. He looked me in the eye. His mouth curled down at the corners as he said, 'This isn't good.'

29

Danny knew short cuts that made the trudge down the hill less arduous, but it was still hard going, because although the snow had now stopped, it was quickly hardening underfoot. A couple of times one of us had to reach out to stop the other from falling. When we were still a couple of streets away, I was able to see that there were now lights on in the Welcome Inn. There was another vehicle just inside the entrance to the car park. As we drew closer still, I saw a fresh set of footprints leading across to Sara's car, around it, and then across to the pub doors, which were now open.

As I started to follow Danny in, it suddenly struck me that he could be leading me into an ambush, that actually he'd been on the phone with Sunny Jim and they were working together on that something big, that spectacular, and they wanted both the reporter and the private investigator who had started poking around out of the way. He wouldn't have wanted to do anything at his house, but once at the bar . . .

'Starkey?'

He was looking back at me as I hesitated, with one hand still on the swing door. There was a smallish guy in a denim jacket with a fur collar behind the bar clearing away glasses. There didn't appear to be anyone else. I could still take a step back and start running.

'This is Carl,' said Danny, 'he manages the place.'

Carl looked up and nodded. He said, 'Close the door, mate, it's cold enough.'

I took a deep breath, and released it.

Danny was looking wistfully about him. 'Haven't been in here in years,' he said.

I approached the bar. There were a couple of pool tables off to the left, a small stage, a bank of slot machines. The carpet was thick underfoot. It smelled of cigarettes and spilled drinks. It was the kind of place I might have enjoyed a drink in under less worrying circumstances, if only it hadn't been on the Bogside. Even with pubs, it was location, location, location.

Danny joined me at the bar and said, 'Sorry to drag you out of your pit.'

'Not a problem, Danny,' said Carl. He gave me the eye. 'A private investigator? In Derry? Are you fuckin' kiddin'?'

'Yes,' I said.

Danny said, 'Tell us about the woman.'

'Sara,' I said.

Carl sucked in his lower lip for a moment, then

looked from Danny to me and back. 'Youse have to understand – I wasn't working last night. It wouldn't have happened on my watch – you know that, Danny, don't you?'

'What happened, Carl?'

'I spoke to . . . well, one of the girls. She said Sunny Jim and his crew were in, not causing any trouble or anything, but you know what they're like. Anyway, you don't see many strange faces in here, everyone knows everyone, so apparently this woman comes in, orders a drink, sits at the bar for a while, then goes over to Sunny Jim . . . don't know what was said, but she leaves pretty quickly. Then Jimmy and his crew . . . well, you're probably better looking yourself. C'mon round . . .'

We ducked behind the bar and followed him into a small office crammed with files, crates filled with empty bottles, a desk with a computer showing the feed from three CCTV cameras. Two of the pictures showed the inside of the bar, one along the front of it where the customers would sit or stand, the second behind the bar just over the till, to check that the staff weren't stealing money. The third camera gave a wide-angle view of the car park. Carl sat at the desk and tapped on the footage from the car park, which then enlarged to fill the entire screen. He began to rewind it. 'I already had a look, it doesn't make for very pleasant viewing. Let me just . . .' For what felt like a long time it just looked like we were watching a still image, because nothing was happening – at least until

I saw myself moving backwards from the bar to the car, and then out of the car park. Carl tutted and said, 'Sorry, there's a quicker way . . .' He fiddled with the touch screen for a bit and then the time jumps were more significant. Danny and I both moved a little closer when we suddenly saw the screen fill with moving figures. Carl stopped the rewind, and then began to play it at normal speed.

The picture quality was pretty good. Sara's car was just visible in the corner. There were half a dozen other vehicles parked. The snow was coming down steadily. Sara suddenly appeared, crossing from the bar to her car and getting in. She didn't make any attempt to clear the snow off the front or side windows, and she didn't start the engine, so we couldn't see what she was doing inside. After about another minute of nothing, a figure appeared, wearing a black jacket and woollen hat, and got in the passenger side. According to the clock in the corner of the screen he was only in there for three minutes. We got our first glimpse of his face when he climbed out: a red shadow from his brow and down one side of his nose and across his cheek. Then he moved back across the car park and disappeared inside the bar. The engine started, lights came on, but the snow was too thick on the windscreen for the wipers to shift; Sara got out and began trying to clear it with her bare hands. At first she appeared to be doing it at quite a leisurely pace, even stopping for several moments of hand-rubbing; but then she was glancing nervously back as people began to emerge from the bar and she started to work at it with more urgency. There was just two of them at first, then a larger group; several women amongst them; I thought maybe it was closing time. But then they began to move towards her. There was no sound, of course, but I could see that Sara was talking as she swept at the snow, and that the people were drawing closer. And closer. And then suddenly she was grabbed from behind and thrown backwards; she stumbled into the arms of two women; one of them yanked at her hair and the other punched at her stomach. Sara sank to her knees. One of the men came up and twirled into some kind of martial arts kick, which connected his foot to her head, and she fell over. And then the crowd was all around her, and I lost sight of her, but there was kicking, kicking and more kicking and it just didn't seem to stop.

Beside me Danny said, 'Christ.' Carl said, 'And there's a lot more of that,' and put his finger to the screen to fast-forward it, an action that also caused the attack to speed up. It was surreal and horrific. Carl stopped it again as a man wearing an anorak pushed through the crowd and knelt beside Sara, who I could now see was lying face down with the snow stained red around her. Another woman followed the man through the gap and crouched on her other side. The crowd began to drift away, some crossing the car park, others back into the bar. The man in the anorak and the woman turned Sara over, but then immediately leaned over her so we couldn't see the state of her face. Then they caught her under the shoulders and began to drag her across the snow. They stopped before a red car, and lifted her into the back. The woman got in beside her and the man opened the driver's-side door. Before he climbed in, I reached past Carl and touched the screen to freeze the picture so that I could get a proper look at him.

Danny immediately said, 'It's Frank Murray.'

'Is that bad?'

'Father Frank . . .'

'Is that bad?' I had history with priests.

'No, of course not. I didn't recognise him without the collar . . .'

Danny took his phone out and began to search for a number. On the screen, the car was driven out of shot, leaving behind it only a trail of blood, which was already beginning to disappear under the falling snow.

'Frank? It's Danny Lynch.'

He walked off with the phone.

Carl shook his head at the screen.

I said, 'If you have a Christmas club, I'm not fucking joining it.'

'Ninety-nine point nine nine nine per cent of the time they're all absolutely fine. But then something sets them off and they're like . . .'

'Animals,' I said. 'Fucking animals.'

I turned to walk out of the office, but then I turned back.

'I want a copy of that tape.'

Carl started to shake his head.

I took a step towards him.

He held his hands up and said, 'No, mate – you don't

understand, there are no tapes these days. And nothing ever disappears, so even if I wanted to delete it, I couldn't.'

Danny came back in.

'She's in Altnagelvin. They're going to operate on her.'

He reached up and tapped his head.

I said, 'Fuck.'

30

Carl said he'd drive me to the hospital. Danny waved us off from the Welcome Inn car park. He was up for coming with me, but I said no. It wasn't his problem. He'd never even met Sara Patterson. He said, 'One of my girls had an operation there last year, was nearly the end of me, I'm so used to being in control. Phone her family, let them know what's happening, they'll want to be there.'

'Yes, Dad,' I said.

'Frank Murray's there, he's a good guy.'

I got into the car. Carl started the engine. I rolled the window down and said, 'Somebody has to do something about Sunny Jim.'

Danny nodded as we pulled away.

My head was throbbing. It was hangover, lack of sleep, but mostly shock. And anger. Sara had been attacked by a mob and was now about to go under the surgeon's knife. I had sent her after Sunny Jim. Neither of us had known how dangerous he was. I hadn't told her to track him down, or get out of the car and walk into the lion's den, but I had nudged her in that direction. I swore at myself. Carl gave me a look.

Altnagelvin Area Hospital is on the Glenshane Road, on the other side of the river. We fell in behind a snowplough, which was virtually the only vehicle on the road. It led us most of the way there, only veering off when we came to the bridge. As we crossed the water, I managed to calm myself down. I thanked Carl for the ride and for driving in such conditions; he said it was no problem, he lived nearby.

'You don't live on the Bogside?'

'You joking? It's a job, man.'

'But isn't the Waterside largely . . .?'

'Proddy? Sure it is. And so am I. If they knew, they'd probably dance on my head as well. So keep it under your hat.'

He dropped me at A&E. I checked at the desk and they sent me upstairs. It was still the early hours so the wards were in twilight mode. A sallow-faced doctor asked if I was next of kin and I gave him the line about being her fiancé in case he withheld. He told me Sara was unconscious, but contrary to what I'd been told, a decision hadn't been made yet about an operation. A nurse directed me to a waiting room at the end of the corridor. Father Frank was sitting there. I sat beside him. He had his collar on now. I told him who I was and he asked if I wanted to pray with him and I said

I'd rather not. I thanked him for getting her out of there and he said he wished he'd gotten there sooner. He only lived a few streets away; a woman had come banging on his door, then driven him down. He shook his head and said, 'They are good people.' I said, 'You could have fooled me.' I asked how Sara had been on the way to the hospital, if she had said anything, but he shook his head.

The nurse came back in and said she understood I was Sara's next of kin. She said Sara had broken ribs and internal bleeding and a fractured skull and that they were going to keep her in an artificial coma and give her blood-thinners to prevent clotting. They hoped they'd be able to avoid an operation. She said she had to get some details.

'Let's start with her date of birth?'

'I'm not entirely sure.'

'Well, how old is she?'

'I'm not entirely sure. Thirty-five?'

'O-kay. Her home address?'

'Ahm, pass.'

'You don't know where she lives?'

'In Belfast. But not exactly.'

'Phone number? Email?' I was shaking my head. 'Do you know if she's allergic to anything?'

I shook my head. 'Look, I'm sorry if it seems like I don't know a lot about her. It's a recent engagement. And I'm not sure if it's relevant that you know exactly what date she was born on or what her fucking email address is . . .'

'Maybe best left to later,' the priest said to the nurse.

The nurse gave me an exasperated look, and then withdrew.

'Sorry,' I said after her.

I put my head back against the wall and blew air out of my cheeks.

'It's not her fault,' said the priest.

'No,' I said. After a minute I said, 'So whose fault is it? The people of Londonderry? The people of the Bogside? The people who frequent the Welcome fucking Arms? Or Sunny Jim?'

He said, 'I understand you're angry. I've been doing this for ever, I've sat in waiting rooms like this dozens of times. Sat with fathers and wives and sons and daughters who think running out there to take revenge will somehow improve the lot of whoever it is whose life is hanging by a thread. But it doesn't, it can't. You just have to wait and see what happens.'

I shook my head.

'How does he get people to do things like that? That mob thing.'

'Sunny Jim? I suppose he plays on their fears.'

'I thought that was your job.'

'I can see how it might look like that.'

I looked out of the door and along the corridor. It was starting to get a little busier. I said, 'Did you give her the last rites?'

'I gave her the next-to-last-rites.'

He gave a little smile then, and I managed one too. We got talking. I told him a little bit about who I was, and who Sara was, and what we were up to. It wasn't a secret. I told him Sara had been trying to find out about Sunny Jim because he was somehow connected to the death of Moira Doherty. We'd also heard there was something building on the Bogside, something bad. Father Frank nodded and said there was something in the air, but nobody was talking. I asked if nobody had spilled the beans in confession and he said, 'I wish.'

He said, 'I know Moira Doherty of old. *Knew*. Sad state of affairs.'

'She'd moved away from the city.'

'She had, but I'd still bump into her around and about quite regularly. I even had a wee joke with her – I called her the mother-in-law.'

'How so?'

'Well, you know the way kids move away from home, get married, whatever, but instead of seeing less of their parents they sometimes end up seeing more of them; they're always on hand, almost hovering, waiting to swoop in and help, even though they're not really wanted? That was Moira: away, but also somehow always there.'

'If you knew her, then you must have known Billy, too?'

'Of course. Billy the Bear.'

'Did you know he was gay?'

He smiled. 'Everyone is wise after the fact. You can piece it together if you look back, but why would you want to? It wasn't the fact that he was gay that bothered me, it was the fact that he was always in trouble, and into the drugs. A wayward soul was Billy.'

'Do you know if he had much to do with Sunny Jim?'

'Not that I was aware of. Different generation. Sunny has that fire-and-brimstone thing that young men always have; absolute conviction that what they're doing is right, and you can't argue with them. Billy had it once, but you lose it, don't you? I think actually that when he did come out, it opened his eyes a bit, whole new world out there. I even met his boyfriend once, he seemed like a good thing for Billy.'

I got up, and I paced a bit.

I asked after Sara again.

The same nurse told me there was nothing more I could do and I should go home and get some rest. But I just sat there, and the priest sat there.

I looked at my phone. It came back to me that she had family in Castlerock, and then the street where her parents lived, and I knew that I should call them and tell them what had happened and how she was – but I just couldn't bring myself to do it. I hadn't hurt her, but I might as well have – I'd flippantly sent her on the trail of Sunny Jim and now she was lying at death's door. In the end I asked Father Frank to do it. He said, 'No problem,' and took a walk down the corridor with his phone. I did something – I called the *Telegraph* and left a message. I didn't say who I was. I was a little bit ashamed of myself.

Father Frank came back. 'I got a number for them, but no reply – not the sort of message you want to leave on an answer machine. I'll keep calling until I get through.' I thanked him and asked if he wanted something from the machines at the entrance, and he said a coffee. He went to reach for money but I said, my treat. When I got there, there was a guy in a grey hoodie repeatedly pressing a button and swearing. I said, 'The machine says you need to put in another twenty pee.'

He turned and said, 'I don't have another fucking . . .'

I saw that it was Michael, my follower, my crap Hawkeye. His mouth dropped open a little and his eyes darted left and right of me, seeking an escape route. I inspire fear in few people, so it actually felt quite good, although, to be honest, he looked like he might also be scared of his own shadow, and the shadows of badgers and squirrels. I put my hand in my jacket pocket and his eyes widened, then looked relieved when all I produced was a handful of change. I reached past him and put the required 20p in and a Crunchie duly appeared. He nodded thanks and cautiously reached down for it without taking his eyes off me.

I said, 'I hope that's not for your mate.'

He shook his head.

I put my hand in my other pocket and he looked worried again.

Maybe it wasn't me, maybe it was the world he lived in.

I brought out his phone and handed it over.

'Oh. Thanks,' he said.

I thumbed behind me to a row of plastic chairs and said, 'Sure, take a seat, tell me the story of your life.'

He took a seat. I said, 'How's Patrick?'

'They're wiring his jaw. It was some shot.'

'It *was* some shot,' I said.

'What . . . what're you doing here?'

'Visiting a sick relative.'

'Bit late for that,' he said. 'I mean, you know, the time of night . . .'

'She's *very* sick.'

'Oh. Right. Well.' He looked at his Crunchie, debating. He looked at me and said, 'Do you mind?'

'Go ahead,' I said, 'it's your funeral.'

He hesitated for a moment, then ripped the top of the wrapper off and crunched into it.

'So anyway,' I said, 'tell me about Sunny Jim.'

His eyes flitted up. The Crunchie seemed to stick in his throat. He said, 'I don't, I mean, I . . .'

'Don't give me a lot of crap, Michael, I know you do.'

'I . . .'

'Word of advice – set a password on your mobile phone. And if there's any chance at all that someone else might get hold of it, and you don't want them going through your recent calls and texts, try deleting them as you go. So I know you've been on to Sunny J half a dozen times today; what I don't know is whether Uncle Danny knows you're in cahoots.'

Michael shook his head. 'I don't even know where that is.'

'Where what is?'

'Cahoots.'

'It's not a place, Michael, it's . . . it doesn't matter

what it is, what I mean is, will Uncle Danny be happy that you're working with Sunny Jim?'

'I'm not working with him. I just . . . I just help out. It's not like a job.'

'And your uncle's fine with that?' His eyes dropped and he shook his head. 'What do you think he'd say?'

'He wouldn't say anything. He'd kill me.'

'Okay,' I said. 'So we're back where we started. Tell me about Sunny Jim.'

'If I tell you about Sunny Jim, then Sunny Jim will kill me too.'

'Only if he finds out.'

Michael sat back and sighed. 'Fuck it,' he said.

I nodded. I said, 'Michael – what is it that you think I do? My job.'

'You're like an undercover cop.'

'Who told you that?'

'Uncle Danny.'

'What exactly did he say?'

'He said you were a private detective and to follow you about to see who you talked to and where you went.'

'And a private detective is a sort of cop.' He nodded. 'Okay. So who, who else do you normally deal with, what other cops?'

'Inspector Watts. Or DS Doyle.'

'And what exactly do you do for them?'

'They give me money and I tell them what's going on in the Bog.'

'Do they know you work for Sunny Jim or your uncle?'

'Nope.'

'But you tell them about them?'

'No chance. They're way too scary. I give them other stuff.'

'Okay. You're working for your uncle, you're working for Sunny Jim, and you're working for the cops. Is there anyone else you're working for?'

'The *Derry Journal*.'

'You pass them information.'

'No, I deliver it.'

'Deliver it? How's that diff— Michael, do you mean that you have a paper round?'

'Yup. I do seventy houses a night. What's so funny?'

'Nothing. Really. Nothing. You're a busy little beaver, aren't you?'

He smiled bashfully; crooked teeth stained with nicotine.

I said, 'Okay, Michael, let's go over what you know about Sunny Jim.'

He said, 'Do we have to?'

'Yes, we do.'

'Okay,' said Michael.

31

Poor Michael was now working for me as well. I wasn't sure how he was going to find time for his paper round. I asked him if he knew Billy the Bear and he got a bit sheepish. He said he knew he was missing, but that wasn't us, he got away. I asked him what he meant.

He said, 'We picked him up from this fruits' disco. We were told to give him a fright. Took him to the beach and pretended like we were going to shoot him and he took off. It was really funny. Ended up running into the sea. But, like, I know he hasn't been seen since.'

'So he could have drowned?'

'Nah, we kept an eye on him, he got out okay. Mission accomplished.'

'And who ordered that? Sunny?' Michael shook his head. 'Uncle Danny?'

'Aye.'

'How come?'

'I don't know. We just do what we're told.'

'And you enjoy it.'

'Beats following the likes of you around.'

I returned to the waiting room, and waited and thought about Billy the Bear and how he might yet be alive. The priest sat opposite me, sipping his coffee and flicking through a New Testament. I asked him if he was reading it for light relief, as the Old Testament was such hard going. He said no, for light relief he usually read John Grisham but he'd left the latest at home, so it was either the New Testament or the latest *Hello!*. We both agreed that the movie of *The Firm* was a good and faithful adaptation of Grisham's first big hit, but that it would have been rendered ridiculous if it had been set in Londonderry, with Londonderry accents. The American accent was crucial. We laughed a little. It was a relief. For me, at least. He probably dealt with hideous beatings all the time. He asked me again if I wanted to say a prayer with him and I said not particularly. But, seeing as how we were talking religion, I asked him if he knew Rev. McCutcheon at St Comgall's across the river – different church, same God. He grinned somewhat sheepishly and said, 'Yes, I know Gary.'

'Why the smile?'

'If you knew him like I know him, you'd smile too.'

'How so?'

'Is he a friend of yours?'

'Nope. Just met him.'

'Well – he's very nice. Very sincere. Very passionate.'

'I sense a *but* . . .'

'Not really. It's not a flaw. But I've known him all my life and I know what he's like. How old are you, Mr Starkey?'

'Dan, please, and old enough.'

'I only mean . . . well, we're probably of similar vintage . . .' which scared me, 'but way back in the seventies, and I know it's hard to believe now, I was a punk rocker.'

'Ditto,' I said.

'Ah good, you'll understand what I'm getting at then. Were you serious about it – punk rock?'

'Damn right.'

'Do you, for example, know what the B-side of "White Riot" was?'

'"1977".'

He grinned broadly. 'Good man. The point is, I was a punk, and if you really understood punk, then you were a punk for life . . . agreed?'

'Absolutely.'

'And it didn't matter what you became later, you know baker, butcher, candlestick maker . . .'

'Or priest . . .'

'Or priest . . . it stayed with you, you always lived by the punk ethos, at least in your head . . . anarchy, disrespect for authority, three chords and the truth . . .'

I nodded. I was liking him more and more.

'But then there were always punks for whom it was just a fashion. It was just dressing up and spitting a lot.'

'Gotcha. And Rev. McCutcheon was . . .'

'Gary was . . . a flibbertigibbet. One day he was a punk, hair spiked, winklepicker boots, skin-tight jeans, best of everything. Next day he was a Mod. Then he was into Ska. Before you knew it he was a New Romantic. Do you know what I mean?'

'I know what you mean. But how does that . . .?'

'We both took long and winding roads into the Church, but he's still the same as he ever was. Whatever is new and trendy you can be sure he'll embrace it. Maybe I'm just biased because the Catholic Church never changes, that's what makes it great, and fallible, but Gary – he went happy-clappy years ago, he invited in charismatics, spiritualists, ex-prisoners, dealers, dopers, even Cliff Richard. He speaks in tongues, he—'

'And now he's a New Seeker.'

'And now he's a New Seeker. And you know, whatever he goes for, he believes in it one hundred per cent, at least until the next thing comes along. The New Seeker thing will be the same: it's a fad, a fashion, couple of years it'll be nothing more than an embarrassing memory.'

'You're not a believer, then. Christine being the new Messiah.'

'No, of course not, it's ridiculous. Many of us are still struggling with the concept of the *old* Messiah. Last thing we need is some new kid on the block.'

'But do you think she's a threat?'

'To me? To the Church? To civilisation as we know it?'

'Any or all.'

'Well not to me personally. I'll just keep on doing what I do. And I won't deny we've had a few of our congregation slip away to *them*. But Derry folk are sturdy, and once they commit, they commit, and luckily we get most of them from birth. So the church here won't be that badly affected – but elsewhere? And civilisation as we know it? I think the New Seekers will be – and let's go back to the music here – I think they'll be like the Beatles. This phase is like Beatlemania. It's growing, it's growing, the music is catchy, melodic, kids love it . . . but it'll plateau, the kids will get older, start to question . . . it'll be like . . . the *White Album* . . .? Difficult, inaccessible, their popularity will fade, they'll split up, and eventually someone will get assassinated.'

'God,' I said, 'you have it all worked out.'

'God,' he said, 'usually does.'

It was just getting light when I finally left the hospital. I stood outside waiting for a taxi to take me back to the hotel. They said it would be a while. I could easily have walked, but I was knackered. And grey. And old. And depressed. Presently Michael and Patrick joined me. Michael looked a bit sheepish, Patrick just glared. I asked them if they were going back to the city side and Michael said yes. I said we could share. Patrick started to shake his head, but he was in too much pain. Michael, who had lacked 20p for the vending machine, seemed more inclined to accept.

I said, 'It's on me, my treat.'

Patrick said to me, 'Ishudbeatthefugginfaceoffyee.'

I said to Michael, 'Would you care to translate?'

He made Patrick say it again.

'I think it's: I should beat the fuckin' face off you.'

I nodded. 'He's so bitter and twisted.'

The taxi pulled up. An elderly couple climbed out, helping each other. I studied them to see if they looked at all like Sara, but couldn't decide. I said good morning to them anyway. They looked red-eyed. I held the door open for my new companions, but Patrick refused to get in. Michael looked pained, but elected to stay and wait for the next one. I gave them a wave as we pulled away from the kerb and Patrick gave me the fingers.

I told the driver to take me back to the City Hotel.

I sat back and stared out and ignored what he had to say about global warming. I wasn't seeing the snow, but Sara's bloated face and bandaged head, the drip and the monitors. We'd eventually been allowed in, the priest and I, and he said a prayer over her. Instead of a prayer, I made her a promise. She had wondered what the hell I was doing still in Londonderry when I wasn't being paid and there was nothing personal at stake, and I hadn't really been able to answer, or even understand myself beyond the fact that I was curious, and bored, and on the run from my own family, but now there was very definitely a reason. Not only was I absolutely determined to find Billy the Bear and work out who'd killed Moira Doherty, but now I swore that for what he had done to Sara, I was going to get Sunny Jim as well.

I was going to fuck him up.

32

I asked Trish if she still loved me, and she said she loved the maintenance, and child support that would doubtless be forthcoming. I said, no, really, and she said, yes, really and we could have gone on like that for hours but she stopped and asked me what was really wrong, because my voice sounded strange, so I told her what had been happening and she said, 'Do you love her?' and I said, 'Who?' and she said, 'Sara,' and I told her not to be ridiculous. She said then why was I telling people that we were engaged, and I said it was convenient, and just my way of winding people up, by appearing to be open with them when I was in fact protecting myself. Trish said there was no smoke without fire, and that she was very happy for me. Then she asked what Sara had that she herself didn't have and I said, 'Youth.' I called her back and said I was only joking, and swore that it wasn't that kind of a relationship, that she was

far too young, that she didn't get any of my references, that she wasn't even born when the Sex Pistols
split up and that we each had underpants that were
older than Sara was. Trish asked if Sara made me
laugh and I said yes. Then I phoned her back and
said but not the way you do, nothing matches that.
I told her that for maybe the first time ever I felt a
bit out of my depth. That I was used to being chased
and harried but this was different, there was something ominous in the air that I couldn't shake or
fathom; that my own beatings in the past had been
undoubtedly painful but also somehow vaguely
comical because I had largely orchestrated them myself
through stupidity and cheek, but that what had
happened to Sara displayed a raw viciousness I'd never
really encountered before. Trish said, 'You forget so
easily,' and reminded me about Cow Pat Coogan and
what happened to Little Stevie, way back when, and
I said, 'Sorry, you're right. What I mean is, they were
individuals, this was a mob, I've never seen anything
like it.'

'But a mob with a leader, a swarm with a queen
bee.'

'Sunny Jim,' I said.

'You're a fighter, Dan, but not a *fighter*.'

'I can hold my own.'

'When Sara's not holding it for you. But we both
know you couldn't fight your way out of a paper bag,
it's nothing to be ashamed of . . .'

'I absolutely—'

'Shhhh. There's nothing wrong with asking for help.'

'I'm not asking for—'

'What happens when the fuses go in our house?'

'Our house?'

'Or former house, or your current apartment . . .'

'Fuses . . .?'

'What happens when you lose the Sky signal, or the dishwasher stops working or a door comes off its hinges?'

'I see where you're—'

'You send for a man . . .'

'I send for *the* man . . .'

'The man who fixes things. I think that's what you need.'

'I don't need—'

'Yes you do. If it's as bad as you say it is, you need someone to watch your back while you do what you do. Someone who can fight off a mob single-handed, who can shoot a man in the eye from a hundred yards, who can rip the spine out of a cow without the cow even being aware of it.'

I said, 'We do know a man like that.'

'Yes we do.'

'But I couldn't just ask him to drop everything and—'

'No you couldn't,' said Trish, 'because men are crap at asking for help and directions, but I can. And I will.'

'Trish, I really don't—'

'I'm doing it. And you know why?'

'Why?'

'Because despite everything, despite the heartbreak,

the let-downs, the disappointments, the unfaithful-
ness, the lies and the betrayal, deep down I really, really
would find it difficult without the maintenance. So keep
your head down until I talk to him, and I'll let you
know what's what as soon as I can. Okay?'

'You're not the boss of me,' I said.

'Yes I am,' said Trish.

I managed an hour's kip, and then went down for
breakfast. When I left the hotel, I checked in every
direction to see if Michael or anyone else with an
unhealthy interest in my progress was there, but didn't
spot anyone. I skated along to a store for people who
loved Apple products but didn't like Apple prices, and
handed Sara's phone in to get the screen repaired. They
told me to come back in the afternoon. I walked back
to the shopping centre car park and was surprised when
my pride and joy started first time. I drove back across
the river and parked opposite a terraced house at Violet
Street. In fact, someone had used a black marker to
insert a small *n* between the last two letters so that it
now read Violent Street.

The ex-con and lay preacher Peter Quinn, who had
fomented rebellion in St Comgall's, lived at number
twenty-three, which was about halfway along a Victorian
terrace with quite a steep incline. It was a little after ten
in the morning and people were just beginning to get
about their business. The snow was sitting particularly
thick on Violent Street, which made it difficult to trav-
erse, with or without wheels. I sat for a while, just getting

my bearings and watching doors open and close, people chipping away at the snow-caked ice on their wind-screens and then searching for traction as they drove away. There was a shop on the corner doing a brisk business in steaming coffee. A light was on in an upstairs bedroom in Peter Quinn's three-storey house. Another light just visible through a dormer window in the roof space. After a while I trudged across and knocked on the door. No answer. The houses faced directly on to the street so I was able to peer through his lounge window from the footpath. Neat and tidy inside, leather sofa, large-screen TV, tropical fish. I succumbed to temptation and walked up to the shop and bought a coffee. I asked the girl behind the counter if Peter Quinn had been in this morning and she made a face like I'd asked her something deeply personal. I returned to the car and sipped the coffee and watched the house.

My phone rang and it was Pike's number. Having nothing better to do, I answered it with 'Speak of the devil.'

He said, 'What's that supposed to mean?'

'Wild guess,' I said.

'Starkey, it's too early in the morning for . . .' An intake of breath. 'Have you made any progress?'

'Yes I have,' I said.

'Would you care to elaborate?'

'No I would not.'

'Starkey . . .'

'Patience, my good man,' I said, in a hail-fellow-well-met kind of a way. Then I said to him, 'Have you any idea what hail-fellow-well-met actually means?'

He said, 'Starkey . . .'

'Never mind, suffice to know that as soon as I'm off the phone you'll be googling it. Sorry – it must be the coffee. Who knew it could do that to a fellow?'

'Starkey!'

'Yup?'

'What's happening?'

'Not much,' I said. 'But that's the nature of stakeouts.'

'A . . . stake . . .?'

'Yup. So can't stay on long.'

'This is in relation to . . .?'

'Yes, absolutely.'

'Starkey – we're about to go public with this. I know you think I overreacted when she first disappeared, but I hope you'll agree now that I was right, that there's been no word from her, no sightings . . .'

'I wouldn't do that,' I said.

'Why not? We've so many followers now that if we go public the chances of one of them spotting—'

'Pike, I can't believe I'm saying this, but I do know a little something about PR, and if I were you I wouldn't say a word, not yet. You'll damage the brand.'

'How do you . . .?'

'Christine is your figurehead, your Messiah, and as I understand that, she's meant to be like – perfection. If you put it out there that she's missing, then you run the risk of someone you can't control finding her and reporting what she's up to – if she's just thrown a teenage strop, if she's off her head on blue WKD, or getting a tattoo of Justin Bieber on her arse or just having loads of sex, you really don't want that out there; people will see that she's maybe not who they thought she was.'

'I understand that, Starkey, but what if she's in danger, what if every minute we waste not putting it out there . . .?'

'I'm just saying hold your water for twenty-four hours. By then we'll know for sure if it's an extended bender or something to worry about.'

'But . . .'

'Just do it,' I said.

I cut the line. I had been keeping an eye on the street, and the man who'd appeared around the corner carefully negotiating the footpath and carrying two heavy-looking Tesco bags. He stopped at Peter Quinn's house, put the bags down in the snow and then produced a set of keys from his anorak pocket and raised it to the door.

I set the remains of the coffee down and jumped out of the car. I immediately went on my arse on the foot-path, letting out an involuntary *whuumph* in the process. The man I presumed to be Peter Quinn looked across and laughed. He said, 'It's a bloody nightmare.' His smile faltered a little as I got up, wiped at my behind, and then began to slide across the street towards him. He had the door open and the bags up in either hand again, but then seemed to realise how defenceless he was like that and quickly set them down. As I stopped

before him, he brought his shoulders back in a way
that suggested that he was well used to confrontation.
And possibly violence. He was fiftyish, with short-
cropped hair; he was a big man, well built.

I said, 'Sorry to trouble you. Though usually when
people say that they're not really sorry at all. And I'm
not.'

He said, 'What?'

'Sorry. Peter Quinn?'

His brow furrowed. 'Who wants to know?'

His eyes flitted towards his open door.

I got out my card and showed it to him. He took
hold of it, though I held on to my side of it. He read
out my name and occupation.

He said, 'So what?'

There didn't seem any point in beating about the
bush. I took the card back and said, 'I'm looking for a
teenage Antichrist, any thoughts?'

'You wah?'

'Christine. The wee girl who those nutters think is
the Messiah. She's gone missing this neck of the woods,
wondering if you've seen her.'

'Missing? Up here? In Derry?'

'Aye. She was heading for St Comgall's but seems to
have got waylaid.'

'Right. I see. Goodness. I had no idea. And *have* no
idea. What's this got to do with me?'

'Well it doesn't, necessarily, I'm just checking with
anyone who might have an interest in her, just in case.'

'Just in case what?'

'They've seen her, talked to her, offered her sanctuary.'

'Sanctuary?'

'Can't be easy, people keep calling you the Messiah twenty-four hours a day.'

'Well for one thing, she's no Messiah.'

'I know *that*,' I said, while taking a quick glance down at his shopping. 'But she's sixteen, and missing; people are getting concerned. She might be in trouble.'

'If she was the Messiah and in trouble, she could work some magic, she'd be fine.'

'I think you may be confusing her with Harry Potter.'

'No, I don't think so. It's the same thing – witchcraft. The devil's work.'

I nodded.

'So, you haven't seen her?'

'Absolutely not.'

'She didn't call to discuss your issues with St Comgall's, with Rev. McCutcheon.'

'I should imagine this is the last place she would call, if she knew the issues, if she knew my views. They're all a bit mad, if you ask me.'

'Well, okay – what about your wife? Could she have seen her?'

'I'm not married.'

'Girlfriend, boyfriend, German shepherd?'

'Ger . . . Look, I've no girlfriend, certainly no boyfriend, and frankly I haven't time for this. I don't know anything about this Christine besides the fact that it's all a lot of poisonous rubbish. Now do you mind?' He indicated his open door.

I said, 'Not at all. I'm just asking around.'

I gave him the thumbs-up and turned back across the road.

By the time I was behind the wheel again, he was inside with the door closed. A moment later he appeared at his lounge window, looking out. I started the car and pulled out. As I drove, I wondered why, if Peter Quinn had no wife or girlfriend, he was buying *Grazia* and *Hello!* and Tesco own-brand coconut body butter moisturiser.

And then my phone pinged and I angled it towards me and saw that it was a text from Patricia that said simply:

He's on the train.

33

I waited at the top of Shipquay Street until Pamela
Canal came along. I almost didn't recognise her, with
her face scraped of make-up and her hair pulled back;
in fact, I was looking past her and it was she who said
hello to me.

She followed that with 'Are you waiting for me?'

'Nope,' I said, 'but I'll walk your way.'

I fell in beside her.

'Have you found Billy yet?'

'Nope,' I said, 'but working on it.'

She was wearing knee-length burgundy leather boots
that protected her against the slush splashes that were
peppering my trousers. It had started to rain in the last
half-hour; the snow was too thick and the air still too
cold for the ice to fully melt, but the process had begun.
She was wearing blue jeans and a black sweatshirt
under a thin-looking anorak.

She must have seen me appraising her. She said, 'Don't worry, I clean up well.'

I gave her an embarrassed smile.

'I know,' I said.

'Is it funny,' she asked, 'talking to a complete stranger, but knowing you've seen their bliff as well?'

'Strange rather than funny,' I said. 'Do you get approached by a lot of men who've . . . seen it?'

'Hardly ever. Because around Derry I don't go out with the war paint on or the hair done, or if I do, I look completely different. It's like an act, you know, like panto.'

'He's behind you,' I said, 'or wishes he was. Does it put you off men?'

'Not at all. They're just men. And they're customers. It's just playing the game, teasing tokens out of them. We compete. We might hate Jacko, but there's none of us were forced into it, and for the most part we enjoy it.'

We had arrived outside the apartment block.

I stepped up to the door with her and she gave me a confused and then concerned look as I said, 'I thought I might pop in and say hello to Jacko.'

'We have strict orders not to let anyone in.'

'Say I forced you. Say I put a gun to your back.'

'Do you have a gun?'

'Do I have a pistol in my pocket or am I just pleased to see you?'

'*What?*'

'Yes. I have a gun. Although it's very small and I don't use it very often.'

269

'*What?*'

'Just go on in,' I said, 'it'll be fine.'

She hesitated for a moment, then reached up and pressed the buzzer. She gave her name as Jenny, and we were in. There was an elevator directly in front of us. We stepped into it. She pressed for the second floor. As we rose up I said, 'Don't worry.'

'I'm not worried, and could you punch him as well?'

The doors opened and we stepped out. There was a woman standing facing us, heels, stockings, knickers, no skirt, basque, but her eyes on a clipboard. She was already saying, 'You're five minutes late . . .' It was only when Pamela didn't respond that she looked up and clocked me and before I could say anything she yelled: 'Jacko!'

I heard a scramble of feet on a wooden floor above. I raised my hands and said to the woman, 'I'm only here for a chat.'

There was a long hall behind her with doors on either side from which girls in various stages of undress peered out. I had expected Jacko to come flying down the stairs at me, possibly armed with a gun or a sex toy, but instead I heard, very clearly, the sound of a door being slammed shut upstairs and bolts being secured.

Pamela moved in front of me and said, 'Fiona – I'm sorry, he said he had a gun. But he only wants to talk to Jacko. I think he's okay.'

Fiona was Amazonian, with a pointy bra on her that could have lanced a Bengal tiger. She said, 'Is that right?' I nodded. She said, '*Do* you have a gun?'

'I have a pistol in my pocket, or maybe . . .'

'You can't shoot all of us.'

'Well, technically I can. But I really do just want to talk to Jacko. Are you his girlfriend?'

'No, fuck no.'

'Business partner?'

'I wish. I get a little extra for doing the rota.'

The girls were still watching me from their doorways. A couple had appeared at the bottom of the stairs. Outside of Stormont I'd never seen so many tits in one place at one time. I thumbed upstairs and said, 'What's he doing?'

'He has a panic room.'

'I've heard about those. Jodie Foster. How long's he had that?'

'A few weeks.'

'What exactly is he scared of?'

'Everything.'

I looked at Pamela. 'And this is the guy that bosses youse around?'

She gave a little shrug.

'Okay,' I said, 'okay. The bullied bully bullies. Is it like a proper panic room that would withstand a nuclear strike or Mormons, or just a room with a big door?'

'Big door,' said Fiona.

I nodded and moved to the stairs. The girls who'd ventured out to see what was up scurried away in front of me. As I began to mount the wooden steps I heard Fiona say, 'All right, ladies, targets to meet, let's focus . . . lube up and let's get busy!'

By the time I got to the top of the stairs, the girls had disappeared into their rooms. There was another longish corridor with doors on either side, with one right at the end that was both bigger and sturdier. I knocked on it.

Jacko told me to fuck off, his voice high-pitched and fearful.

I said, 'You're too quick to judge, you don't even know who I am or what I want. I might be here to tell you you've inherited a million pounds from your great-aunt.'

He said, 'Do you think I'm a stupid cunt or something?'

I said, 'There's no answer to that.'

I slipped my card under the door. I said, 'FYI, this is who I am and what I do. And FYI, if it was any kind of a panic room there shouldn't be a gap under the door because if I really wanted to get you I could just feed poison gas in.'

He said, 'Who the fuck uses poison gas?'

'Syrians,' I said.

He told me to fuck off again, but then said, 'Private investigator? Working for who?'

'Tell you the truth, Jacko, I'm not working for anyone. Or I'm working for justice. Have you ever heard the expression, your enemy's enemy is your friend?'

'No. What the fuck are you talking about?'

'What I'm saying is I'm not after you. I'm after Sunny Jim. Is that who you're hiding from?'

'I'm not hiding from anyone!'

'You're in a fucking half-baked Homebase panic room, Jacko. Wise up.'

'I'm protecting myself, that's all. I'm not scared of him. But I'm not stupid either.'

'Okay. I understand that. But open the door. Let's talk. Maybe we can come up with something that'll work for both of us. Get Sunny Jim off your back. Isn't that what you want? You're sitting on a gold mine here, Jacko, you really don't want Sunny taking it away from you, do you?'

There was an extended silence then – at least from him. There were groans of pleasure coming along the hall. Maybe they were fake. It was always hard to tell.

Eventually Jacko said, 'How do I know he didn't send you to kill me?'

'Because you'd be dead already.'

'How so? No one gets through these fucking bolts.'

'Jacko, forgetting for the moment the already much-discussed poison gas – you're standing in front of the door right now, aren't you?'

'What about it?'

'It's a big door, and I'm sure the bolts are impressive. But it's wooden, Jacko. Wooden. If I was after you, I'd just have shot you through the fucking thing.'

When the bolts were drawn back about thirty seconds later, and the door finally opened, the first thing he saw was me with two fingers pointing at him and a thumb up.

'Bang,' I said.

He said, 'You're not fucking funny.'

34

It was a small room with one shuttered window. There was a TV, a computer, a sofa, a mini-fridge with its door open, which contained Carlsberg, and a cupboard that was also open and stocked mostly with Pot Noodles and crisps. It wasn't so much a panic room as a den. Jacko pointed me towards the sofa, then looked down the corridor to make sure I was alone. He bolted the door again, then opened up a director's chair and set it in front of me and sat. He said, 'You don't look like a private detective.'

He, on the other hand, looked like the glorified pimp that he was. He was in a baggy T-shirt and sweats, with a three-day gingerish stubble and greasy hair. His trainers were untied, dirty grey laces flapping as he nervously crossed and uncrossed his legs. He lit a Marlboro Red, and showed me the box. I shook my head and instead indicated my business card, which he was still holding. I clicked my fingers. He handed it over.

I said, 'Sorry, what's a private detective supposed to look like?'

'I don't know. You should have a hat.'

'Well, I'll take that on board. But let's start by asking you what sort of shit you've got yourself into with Sunny Jim.'

'Seven shades of it. But why should I tell you?'

'Because I'm going to bring him down.'

'Aye, right, you and whose army?'

I said, 'Keep the faith. Now – Sunny.' I thumbed around the room. 'How'd he get involved in this set-up? And what's he got to do with Billy the Bear disappearing and his mum getting shot?'

'How do I know you're not wearing a wire?'

'I'm not wearing a wire.'

'Yes, but how do I know?'

'Jacko, do you really think anyone wears wires these days? Fuck sake, they've satellites that can record you having a piss from space, wires are so last century.'

'Maybe, but I still . . .'

I shook my head, and pulled up my shirt.

'Satisfied? Or do you want to check my pants as well?'

Jacko took a long draw on his Marlboro. 'Look, man,' he said, 'sorry, I'm just . . . I didn't ask for any of this. I was just looking to earn a bit of dough, I was just helping Billy out, but then it all went fucking pear-shaped.'

'Okay, tell it from the start – how'd you get involved with Billy?'

'I met him at Straightshooters, it's a—'

'I know what it is. You're gay as well?'

'Fuck no. But I *am* an entrepreneur. I was at uni doing—'

'You were at university? Studying?'

'Man, you're so judgemental. Did you never hear about books and covers?'

I raised my hands, placatory. 'Continue.'

'Yes, uni, masters, if you must know, computers . . . but I also like to earn a buck on the side. I was putting on gigs, and clubs, I started putting on events in Straightshooters, and that's where I met Billy . . . so I knew he was gay right from the start, and he was a big guy, and I found out he was pretty well connected, and when you hire a doorman that's what you need, not just that they can handle themselves, but they know who to talk to to smooth things over.'

'He was your bouncer?'

'Yeah, at the start, though to tell you the truth he was mostly in it to pick guys up. But we got on okay. So he was working for me a few months and he was always talking about this plan to make it rich and that plan to make it rich. He was a bit of a bullshitter, but you know, gradually he wore me down. He thought there was big money to be had in porn, and I was like, what, porn in Ireland? You're fucking kidding. But next thing he gives up the bouncing, his clothes get better, he's wearing all kinds of bling; still coming to the club but now he's throwing the money around, so it made sense to talk to him properly, see what he was doing . . .'

'See if you could get a piece of it?'

'Yes, of course, I told you, I'm an entrepreneur. And I know computers, and what he was doing was pretty primitive, wasn't much more than plugging cameras into a few laptops and hoping for the best. So I got involved, I set up this whole cam-girl thing as it is now.'

'In return for . . .?'

'An equal share. And he had no problem with that, he could see the difference I was making.'

'So what happened?'

'Crush happened. It started off slow enough, but then he just went for it and so he was off his head virtually all the time. A real fucking liability. Oh, those girls out there all loved him because he was like their gay best friend, a big gentle puppy with them, but it was no way to run a business. There was no work in him at all, and he had a big mouth, so he was out every night boasting about all the cash he was making, and people started to pay attention . . .'

'People like Sunny Jim.'

'Exactly. Look, I'm not a bad guy. I tried to help him, I even got his mother in to try and keep him on the straight and narrow, but talk about inviting the devil into your house – I thought she'd just nursemaid him, but next thing she's saying she's looking after his interests and she's making decisions and hiring girls and expanding us out and not even asking my permission . . .'

'So youse didn't get on.'

'No, we— Now, houl' on, if you're trying to say I'd something to do with . . .'

'Me? Not me, no.'

'Well I didn't, okay? We rubbed each other up the wrong way, that's all. Doesn't mean I . . . anyone's to blame it's her own son, it's Billy, what he got himself into . . .'

'Which was?'

'Well, getting sent to fucking prison for a start.'

'What was that about? There was a gun?'

'There was some oul' fuckin' antique in the attic. But the thing is, I was up in the attic a couple of days before, scoping it out in case we could have used it as another room for the girls, and I'm pretty sure there was no gun there. Then the cops come charging in, warrant and everything, they had a tip-off the gun was there.'

'So what're you saying, someone planted it, was trying to warn Billy, or warn both of you, what they could do?'

'I don't know. The likes of Sunny Jim, they don't need to go round planting evidence, they just come and blow your knees off. It was almost like they wanted him to go to prison, and Billy – it was almost like he *needed* to go to prison.' Jacko looked around him, then reached down to the floor and lifted a saucer he'd been using as an ashtray. He stubbed out his cigarette and immediately took out another. He rolled it between his fingers for a few moments and then lit it. He gave a little shake of his head, a laugh. 'You know – it even crossed my mind that he got himself sent to prison so that he could clean himself up? Get straight?'

'You mean he treated it like it was the Priory or something?'

'Exactly. It's the sort of fucked-up idea he'd come up with. And you know, when he came out, he was fit and far as I could tell clean and sober. He got back into the business, which his ma didn't like at all, and he was great. But it didn't last. He was back on that crap soon enough, worse than ever.'

'So what do you think happened to him? Is he still out there?'

'I honestly don't know. He was off his tits so much of the time he could just as well have fallen down a well as been shot up by Sunny Jim or any other of those hellions.'

He took another drag of his cigarette, then stubbed it out half smoked.

'You're hiding . . . you're protecting yourself here in this room from Sunny Jim, right?'

'Amongst others.'

'Others?'

'Who want a piece, or all, of what I have.'

'But mainly Sunny Jim. And he's threatened you?'

'He's threatened what he will do if I don't hand over what I have, the software, the hardware, the history of everyone who has ever paid to jack off on my site.'

'He just wants the business, or does he want to blackmail your customers?'

'Both, I expect.'

'But you can't stay here for ever. And if I can get in this easily, you can be bloody sure he can get in too if he chooses to.'

'Yes, of course he can, but he knows if he tries anything, I can just destroy it all, and then he'll have to start from scratch, which he won't be able to, because I've talked to him face to scary face, and he might be big and tough but he doesn't know shite in a shoebox about computers. He was waving a piece of paper around claiming Billy had signed over his half of the business to him. Since then I've been paying him what Billy would have made, but it's not enough for him, he wants everything.'

'So what's your plan? You can't hide out here for ever.'

'I'm not hiding. I'm just being sensible. Look, I've made plenty of dough, and I could make plenty more, but I'm getting out of it. I just need a couple more weeks, make sure my nest egg is big enough, then I'll up sticks, get into something less dangerous.'

'If cam girls are so lucrative, why not just set it up somewhere else, where Sunny Jim can't get at you?'

'Because to tell you the truth, I'm sick and tired of it. I am a heterosexual man. I love women, and even if they don't believe it, I do care about the girls out there, but it's getting to the point where I never want to see another pussy again. These last six months, I've been up to my neck in pussy. I've lived and breathed it, and I can't remember the last time I had a hard-on. Pussy should be a rare and beautiful thing, not staring you in the face every minute of every day God sends you.'

'It's a tough job,' I said, 'but someone has to do it.'

He smiled then. He said, 'Well I'm open to offers.'

The doors were all closed along the hall as I left.

Ooohs and *ahhhs*.

I took the elevator back down and stepped out into the rain. I slipped slightly on the pavement. As I righted myself, I happened to glance across the road and saw birdy-chested Michael standing there, leaning against a blue Jag, arms folded.

I said, 'All right, Michael, you back on the job again?'

Instead of answering, he took a step to the side and opened the back door of the car. The man who was looking out had a very obvious and very severe burn down the side of his face. He waved me over. There were two guys sitting in the front. I thought about making a run for it, and looked down Shipquay Street. There were two guys moving up the hill towards me. One very clearly had a gun drawn, which he was holding straight down against his side. He was the fella in the Harrington jacket from the Wailing Wall.

And I didn't know if he was coming to kill me or save me.

I stepped off the pavement into the slush and across to the car.

35

Sunny Jim was looking straight ahead, so that all I could see was the burned side of his face. I was sure it was deliberate. He would be aware of the effect it had on people. In the following minutes he only looked directly at me two or three times, and even then his head hardly moved. His scar looked ghastly and painful and fresh, though I actually knew it to only be ghastly. Sometimes you can judge a book by its cover, especially if it's been bought in a fire sale.

I said, 'It's nice to meet at last. We've been circling each other like agoraphobics at a Presbyterian disco.'

I make misjudgement calls. It's often not quite deliberate, more of a fake bravado, a mix of panic and disbelief that I've allowed myself to get into another stupid situation. Usually, inside, my cylinders are firing in a million different directions, looking for ways out, for flaws in the armour, and I cover it up with babble.

With Sunny Jim, even though I knew that I should play this sober and straight I still could not help myself. He gave me the heebie-jeebies all right.

He said, 'Give me one reason why I shouldn't blow your fucking head off.'

His accent was Londonderry, with a soldiery hint of Estuary English. It was deep, and gravelly, and intimidating.

I said, 'Well, I've just become a grandad, and you wouldn't want to deprive the poor wee fella of that. And of course a lot of people must have seen me get into your car, there's CCTV all over the place these days, so if you take me to some remote forest and do it there there'll always be that guilt by association and you wouldn't want that because it would screw up whatever it is you're really planning, what this is really all about. Because it's sure as hell not about cam girls. I mean, poor Jacko is hiding in there like Vincent Price in *The Last Man on Earth* and I don't doubt you could have blown his head off any time you felt like it but you're probably worried it'll disrupt your master plan, which makes me wonder why it is that Moira Doherty was shot because that's a real attention-grabber as well, so that kind of makes me think that you weren't responsible for that, that there's a bit of a power struggle going on and if I had to put money on it it's between Danny Lynch and you probably, the old guard versus the young pup. How am I doing? Usually there are denials or sighs or slaps but you're just staring ahead like I've got dementia or something.'

I could feel my heart pounding in my chest, and although it was still freezing cold my shirt was stuck to my back and my hair sat damp and dank on my head.

He said, 'You used to be a journalist, and now you're a private investigator.'

'Yes,' I said.

'And who are you working for?'

'I'm self-employed.'

'I mean . . .'

'And I'm not working for anyone. So I guess I'm just doing it for the good of all mankind.'

'Are you some kind of religious zealot?'

'Nope.'

'Because you've been hanging around with the New Seekers.'

'Well spotted. But no, I don't work for them either.'

'Then what exactly is it that you're after?'

'For the most part I'm just looking for Billy the Bear.'

'And no one is paying you to do this?'

''Fraid not.'

'So it's a cause, a passion project, a conviction.' He turned to me. 'Perhaps we have more in common than you think.'

'I would seriously doubt that.'

'Are you working with that cunt was beaten up in the car park?'

'Yes I am. She sends her best.'

'Is that not enough to scare you off?'

'No, it incentivises.'

He said, 'See, we are very similar.'

The ginger-haired driver was keeping an eye on me in the mirror. The beefy guy in a denim jacket beside him didn't look back once. We were just driving around the city centre, which was a relief. I thought that if we started to head towards the Bogside that might be the end of me, it would just swallow me up. If we did start in that direction I was planning to make a dive for the steering wheel. We'd go head first into a lamp post, the airbags would disable the driver and his mate, while I would use my fighting skills to take out Sunny Jim before he'd a chance to pull his gun. What could possibly go wrong?

But still we kept within the walls.

He said, 'I saw a lot of dead civilians in Afghanistan. Some of them I killed.'

'Uhuh.'

'I never liked to see people die who had nothing to do with the war.'

'Good to know.'

'But sometimes it can't be helped, they just get in the way. Difference between there and here is that for the most part they had no choice, they had nowhere else to go. Here, you have a choice to make. So you should make it.'

'What about you?'

'What about me, Starkey?'

'Well,' I began, without really knowing where I was going, 'I may not be the best private investigator in the world, but I do have a habit of screwing with people's master plans. But, say, if you tell me where

Billy the Bear is or what happened to him, then maybe
I'll go away. If you don't, I'm not going anywhere and
you'll always have that worry that I'll pop up and spoil
things.'

'You're really not in a position to be bargaining with
me.'

'I know,' I said, 'I'm just chancing my arm.'

There was a slight flaring of the nostrils.

After a considerable pause he said, 'Billy the Bear
was a fuck-up, when he could have cleaned up. He
owed me big time and handed over his share of the
business to me. I am currently in negotiations with his
partner for the other half.'

'I'm not sure Jacko looks on them as negotiations.'

'Well, if he would ever open his door to me he might
find that I'm not unreasonable. As for Billy – maybe
he came to his senses and got the hell out of here. He
owed people all over the place and any one of them
would have had the head off him if they could. And
think about it, Starkey – if he'd just handed half the
business over to me, why would I need to kill him? I
had no reason to.'

'Wild guess – it wasn't all done with legally binding
contracts? And maybe his mum wouldn't roll over the
way he did so you had to get rid of her as well?'

'I thought you said you didn't think that was me?'

'I did – but I'm just throwing stuff out there as it
comes to me. Americans would call it spitballing.'

He nodded slowly. 'Well, to be fair, Moira Doherty
was playing stick-in-the-mud. Actually, I did have the

contracts, all signed and legally binding, but she just wouldn't believe it.'

'You raided her house and stole her computer.'

'Yes I did. Once I heard she'd been shot, I seized whatever equipment she had before someone else did, because it was mine.'

'So basically you've done nothing wrong. A big boy did it and ran away.'

He turned towards me properly for the first time, and I got the full two-face effect up close. It was disconcerting, and creepy, and intimidating and not helped by the fact that his eyes appeared slightly jaundiced. There was a curl of contempt to his upper lip as he spoke.

'Starkey,' he said, 'let me just make this clear. This, what we're doing here? I'm giving you an opportunity to walk away. I don't have to justify myself to you, I don't have to explain, but the fact that I am is just my way of giving you a chance to live. As I've said, I had no reason to kill Billy the Bear or his mum – you, on the other hand, I have every reason to kill you because you're complicating my life, and I don't like complicating. I don't have to take you to some remote location and shoot you in the back of the head either, it's not my style. You'll just be found dead in your bed in the City Hotel, room 811, and nobody will ever connect me to it. Do you understand me?'

'I understand you,' I said.

'Good. So this is your one and only chance. Take it. Now where can I drop you?'

'At the train station,' I said.

'That's a wise decision. And one piece of advice? Don't get a return ticket.'

'I don't intend to.'

Sunny reached forward and tapped his driver on the shoulder. 'We'll drop him at Waterside,' he said.

It hadn't been officially called Waterside in years, but the locals persisted. The blue Jaguar pulled to a halt outside Londonderry train station five minutes later, nothing further said. I had not forgotten my revenge, but there was no opportunity here to take it; I had to play a longer game. And I should have held my peace, but I couldn't help myself. As soon as we stopped, I reached for the door handle, but then paused dramatically and jabbed a finger at him. 'I may be going home now, but we're not finished. That *cunt* you had beaten to within an inch of her life in the Welcome Arms car park? Her name's Sara Patterson. And that's one thing you will not get away with. And if anyone's a cunt, you're a cunt.'

I gave him a nod and went to push out of the car.

Except, of course, that the child lock was still on.

I know because I pawed at it three times.

Then I sat back and said, 'Well, that's embarrassing.'

36

Joe the Butcher was coming along the platform, sports bag over his shoulder. I was used to seeing him in a blood-spotted white jacket, but here he was in a stylish long black winter coat. I was used to seeing him with gory knives and cleavers in his hands, but here he was with his scrubbed pink paw extended and then pumping mine. I was hoping the knives and cleavers were in his bag, together with a gun or two. I was used to seeing him chopping things up. I was hoping that the threat of such would keep my enemies at bay. Enemies like Sunny Jim, whose parting words to me as I sat waiting for his driver to open my door were 'Starkey, if I ever see you again, I will kill you.'

Joe was saying, 'So how's it hangin'?'

And I was saying, 'Fine and dandy,' as if we were old mates reunited for a stag weekend.

He was aware that I was slowing down as we approached the station exit.

He said, 'What? Already?'

He dropped the bag from his shoulder.

I looked about me for a sign of the Jag, or Michael loitering with intent, but it appeared clear. It didn't mean someone wasn't watching and checking, though. I hoped not to tip them off too soon that I was still in town, and that I had back-up, but it was out of my control.

I said, 'No, no, it's fine.'

We got into a taxi. My car was still at Shipquay Street. I took Joe to the hotel and asked for a duplicate key for Sara's room. They were, literally, very accommodating. I said sure take half an hour to settle in and he said he'd see me in the bar in five. When he came down, he smelled of whiskey and I guessed he'd found the minibar. He was wearing the same big coat; it was impossible to tell if he was carrying a weapon, and maybe that was the point. He said, 'I appreciated the lingerie and perfume, but it really wasn't necessary.' I told him whose room it was and what had happened to her and he agreed that his comments weren't so funny now. And then we laughed about that. I thanked him for coming and he said a change was as good as a rest. I told him about Sunny Jim and his fearsome reputation, and he said that he never worried about reputations, that they were usually all tripe and he knew a lot about tripe even if it was unfashionable. He said he was loving Londonderry already because he'd been up to his elbows in mince all week. 'All the gore and none of the fun,' he added, with the twinkle of a born joker or serial killer.

He said, 'So what're we talking here? Proactive or reactive?'

'Bit of both,' I said.

I told him about the players and the places, about Danny Lynch and the curator and Harrington and Michael and Patrick with the busted jaw, about Harry Lime and Billy the Bear and the cam-girl business and how it all started with Moira Doherty travelling down by bus, and how I was second choice after Sara Patterson, and how that was the story of my life, and he said, 'Agh, you don't have it so bad, I haven't had my hole since 2007.'

He said, 'Okay, so where do you want to start, with yer man Michael? He seems like a good bet for getting us in everywhere we need to go, put a double barrel to Danny Lynch and have the truth out of him, or just blast away at Sunny D . . .'

'Sunny Jim.'

'. . . Sunny Jim so that he's off your back.'

I said, 'No, we should start with the teenage Messiah.'

And he said, 'What the fuck are you talking about?'

So I told him about Christine and he remarked on how I liked to keep myself busy. He said the New Seekers had come round his shop looking for a donation and he'd chased them. He said, 'Less smiley than Mormons, more bonkers than Jehovah's Witnesses.' I told him about the lift I'd given her to Londonderry, and her disappearing, and Pike – 'That wanker,' said Joe, who remembered him best as a puritanical but coke-sniffing politician – trying to blame me for her disappearance and then trying to hire me to find her. I told him about Rev. McCutcheon with the flibbertigibbet personality and the civil war in his church. I told him about Peter Quinn, the born-again lay preacher, and how he lived alone but still bought women's magazines and coconut body butter, which suggested to me that he might just be holding her hostage.

'So maybe that would be the best use of our time,' I said.

We had enjoyed a couple of hot whiskeys each by then. They took the edge off a cold, damp, misty kind of a day. We picked up the car and then drove to Violet Street. As we parked, I looked up at the amended street name and wondered if it was a sign of things to come. We sat in the car about twenty metres down from Peter Quinn's house, and noted the light was still on up in the roof space. I asked Joe if he had a plan.

He said, 'Let's review what we do and don't know. This guy, you say he's ex-paramilitary? Ex-prisoner? How long ago? Which organisation? What did he do for them?'

'I don't know. What diff—'

'If he was an enforcer, then he'll know how to handle himself; if he did the books or pressed their balaclavas, then maybe not. If he was recently inside, chances are he's fairly fit because there's nothing else to do in there.'

'He didn't look particularly fit. I think it's a while since he was in prison.'

'You think? Are you guessing?'

'I'm guessing.'

'When you talked to him earlier – you said he was just opening his front door? Was there more than one lock, any bolts, anything like that?'

'I didn't really notice . . .'

'Well think. Deadbolts?'

'No, I don't think so, he just turned a key. Why?'

'We're looking for anything that might delay us if he sees us coming or slams the door in our faces. If she's up there, there's no telling what he'll do if we go for her – if he's mad enough to kidnap a teenage girl then he's mad enough to kill her rather than let her give evidence against him. We don't want to be scrambling around with deadbolts while he cuts her throat. If he gets upstairs before we do, then we're in trouble. Chances are she's tied up, maybe drugged . . .'

'How can you know that?'

'She's a teenage girl, so she would be well capable of breaking out of anywhere unless she's restrained. He may be using the body butter for her wrists, ankles, so the restraints don't cut into her too badly. She's probably gagged as well – it's a terraced house; even if the roof space is soundproofed, a certain amount is going to carry. Nobody knew she was coming to Derry?'

'Not as far as I know. Why?'

'It means this wasn't pre-planned. He just seized his opportunity. But that means he's winging it, the house isn't set up for it so he's probably shit scared, hasn't slept, trigger-happy, he didn't have supplies in but is wary of leaving her alone for anything more than a quick trip to the corner shop.'

'How come you know all this stuff?'

He shrugged. 'Andy McNab mostly.'

'Andy Mc . . .?'

'*Bravo Two Zero*. Big fan. But I love all that SAS stuff, *Zulu*, man against overwhelming odds, man against the elements. I once survived in Tollymore Forest Park for a week living off berries and mushrooms.'

'Were you on the run or . . .?'

'Nope, just did it for a laugh, 'cos I was bored. Lost a stone and a half and got food poisoning, turns out some of the mushrooms were toadstools, but the point is I did it, I stuck it out. I'm sure and steadfast. There's a kind of philosophy with all of those SAS books – make your mind up, go in fast, go in hard, don't give 'em a chance to think. Have you checked out behind the house? Is there a garden? Maybe easier access?' I shook my head. 'Okay, I'll do that now. He doesn't know me from Adam so I can take a quick scout past. If there's any movement, anyone comes or goes, give me a bell. I won't be more than five minutes.'

Before I could say anything else, he had slipped out of the car and around the corner into Primrose Street.

I was thinking that maybe Patricia had jumped the gun by sending Joe the Butcher to help me. I hardly knew him at all apart from the fact that he'd been inside himself, seemed to have a good heart and had helped me out of a spot of bother in the past. But it wasn't inconceivable that he could get me into more trouble and worse situations. I was getting on in life and had managed to survive on shrugs and misplaced wit with only the occasional contusion to show for it; given the right conditions or circumstances, Joe the Butcher could take my misery to an entirely new level.

He was back in two and a half minutes, shaking his head.

'Big wall at the back, no door in it, glass along the top. Nothing suspicious about that, all the houses are the same, must have burglar problems. But it means we don't know what's on the other side and trying to find out might give the game away. So I think we'll aim for the front.'

'Okay,' I said. 'When? Now?'

'No. We wait. We observe. No point in starting a gun battle. There's a shop on the corner, do you want a sandwich or something? I'm starving.'

'No, I . . . Do you want me to go and get it?'

'Nope, if he sees you we're fucked. I won't be more than five minutes.'

And he was away again.

I was starting to think he might not only be gung-ho, but also suffering from some kind of attention deficit disorder. He walked past Peter Quinn's front door without apparently looking at it and disappeared into the corner shop. A few moments later my phone rang and he was giving me not so much a list of the snacks on offer as an inventory of everything on sale. I tried to interrupt him several times to reinforce the fact that

I wasn't hungry but he just kept rattling off possibilities, at least until I shouted: 'He's on the move!'

We'd only been on our stakeout for a matter of minutes, so we'd either been rumbled or we were extremely fortuitous. Maybe that was to be Joe's contribution: he was an unsuspecting catalyst, changing lives and history and tempting fate just by the very fact of his being there.

Peter Quinn was looking up and down the street. He had what looked like a Tesco Bag for Life scrunched up in his hand. He started towards the corner shop, but then abruptly turned and walked the other way, in my direction.

'Where is he?' Joe asked.

Peter Quinn began to cross the road on to my side.

I slithered down in my seat.

'Coming this way . . .'

I was about to find out if he'd clocked my car earlier.

'You acting normal?'

'If being curled up in a footwell is normal, then yes,' I said.

It was a narrow road with very little traffic, so as he approached I could actually hear his footsteps: alternately soft and squishy and hard and crunchy as he moved between patches of slush, hard snow and ice.

Then they were right by my window.

And passing on, with no obvious hesitation.

'Well?'

I slowly pulled myself up enough to look out, and saw his back disappearing around the corner.

'He's away on.'

'Okay!' cried Joe. 'Game on!'

As I got out of the car, Joe was hurrying down from the corner shop. We met outside Peter Quinn's house. Joe produced a gun from inside his coat. He held it straight down at his side. It was dark against the material; you would hardly have known it was there if you weren't looking for it. We faced the door.

He said, 'We haven't given any consideration at all to the fact that he might not be working alone.'

I said, *'What?'*

'Between us we've managed to observe the house for about ten minutes. They could be working in shifts. They might be armed to the teeth.'

'So what do we do?'

Joe grinned and said, 'Zuuullllluuuuuuu . . .'

'Joe, this isn't—'

'Never underestimate the element of surprise.'

There were three steps up to the door. He took them in one stride and swung his boot and the door shot backwards. As he stepped into the hall, he raised his gun and clasped it in two hands, looking right into the lounge but keeping the sights trained on the stairs. He started up them. I moved in behind him. There were commemorative plates and antiques on shelves on one side. The carpet was thick underfoot and would have masked our progress if we hadn't just smashed the door in.

We arrived on the first-floor landing. No movement, no resistance.

Joe scanned the short hall to his right and brought the gun back on to the next flight of stairs.

He took the steps two at a time.

By the time I got to the top, he was at the foot of a third set, clearly leading up to the roof space. These were uncarpeted, narrower, clearly of more recent construction. They ended at a white door, closed. He began to move up, one at a time, cautiously, gun extended.

I whispered: 'Joe, be careful.'

Joe put his free hand on a silver-coloured door handle; he took a deep breath, then moved the handle down sharply, threw the door open and stepped into the gap with the gun raised and ready. He stood there, unmoving. There was no sound from within.

At least until he said, 'Fuck.'

'*Joe?*' Heart in my mouth.

He said, 'Your Christine?'

I stood at the bottom of the steps.

Dread.

'Yes, Joe?'

'She wouldn't be about eighty and have hearing aids the size of ear trumpets?'

'No, Joe.'

'Then I think we've just rescued Peter Quinn's mother.'

'*Joe?*'

'On the plus side, she's still fast asleep.'

I moved up beside him. There was an unmade bed directly in front of me. To the side, an armchair with an old woman asleep in it. She had a blanket across her knees with a *Grazia* on top of it, and there was a portable TV with *Loose Women* on pause. Her hearing aids really were the size of ear trumpets.

Joe said, 'Let's just . . . back away . . . no harm done . . .'

We backed away.

Right out on to Violet Street.

37

Joe said it was nothing to be embarrassed about. I said it was quite a lot to be embarrassed about. He said based on the available evidence and the fact that a young girl's life was at stake, it was the right call to make. I said that evidence amounted to a copy of *Grazia* and some Tesco own-brand coconut body butter and we'd called the wrong number. He said nothing ventured, nothing gained, and I had to agree. Nothing gained. Peter Quinn arrived back ten minutes later with a bulging Tesco bag. We'd closed the door after us, but the lock was buggered so the breeze had almost immediately flapped it open again. As soon as he saw it he dropped the bag and charged inside. As he disappeared from sight, his groceries began to spill across the pavement. A couple of minutes later, a police car pulled up outside and two uniformed officers hurried in.

As we drove away I said, 'Maybe he's got her stashed

300

somewhere else. Somewhere close by. Maybe that's why he keeps popping out of the house.'

But Joe was shaking his head. 'He wouldn't have called the police, he wouldn't have invited investigation. He's acting like a man who has nothing to hide. At the end of the day, Dan, we don't even know if she is in trouble, she might have just gone to ground. And what was it you said happened on the way up, when she got sick on the Pass? Maybe she got the same again, but worse, maybe she just keeled over somewhere and got covered up by the snow and they just haven't found her body yet. On the other hand, maybe she just forgot to bring her phone charger.'

He grinned at me. I shook my head.

'So now that we've solved that one, what next?'

What next, indeed.

Christine was a sideshow. I had started out looking for Billy the Bear. And then for whoever had killed his mum. And now that I had disturbed the hornets' nest, I was feeling compelled to work out what Sunny Jim's master plan was, mostly so that I could thwart it in revenge for what he had done to Sara Patterson and a little because it was the right thing to do. It would be easy enough to write off what had happened to Billy and Moira as a business dispute, an argument over who owned what because Stroke City Girls was so lucrative. Sunny Jim was now taking over that business – for sure, Jacko would very soon be out of it one way or another – but I couldn't believe that this was his ultim-ate goal. It had to be a means to an end. And that end was approaching – why else would he be pussyfooting around me? I mean, he had basically wagged a warning finger at me and guided me to the train station. He just didn't want anything to upset his plans when they were so close to fruition. Equally, I did not believe for one minute Danny Lynch's old-man act, his protestations that he was no longer involved; the swiftness with which I'd been taken to him when I'd asked for the most feared man on the Bogside, and the way he'd reacted when he'd heard about Sunny Jim and the cam-girls business was surely proof that he was still active. But I had no idea if it was simply a power struggle with Sunny Jim or whether he had his own master plan in the works.

My only connection to either of them was Michael, who came across as dim but still somehow managed to work for both at the same time as well as passing on irrelevant information to the police. It was impossible to say where his loyalties truly lay, or to know if they lay anywhere. He was related to Danny Lynch, but families are odd things. He wasn't a player, for sure, but every Great Train Robbery needed its Ronnie Biggs, a gopher to do the stuff nobody else could be bothered with, someone to open the doors, make the tea or fetch the sandwiches. But if and when Sunny Jim's master plan swung into action, Michael would be there or there-abouts. As we drove through the city, the only thing it was possible to know for sure about Michael was where he was at that exact moment in time, for in handing him back his phone in the hospital I had of course connected it to my own.

I pulled the car in to the side of the road and took out my phone to check where he was, half expecting it to come up that he was right behind me.

But he wasn't.

He was forty-five minutes away along the coast road and just entering Sunnylands Caravan Park – which was home to Harry Lime.

Forty-five minutes by Google Maps and a sedate pace, but considerably less if I stuck the foot down. The road was largely clear of snow and the traffic was light, so there was nothing to slow us. On the way I tried calling Harry, but it went straight to voicemail. I didn't leave a message as there was no telling who had his phone. There was a good chance he wasn't there at all, that he had simply collected his belongings and gotten out as quickly as he could; but I had to be sure. And why else would Michael and whoever he was with be going there? Maybe now that I was theoretically on the train home, Michael had been switched to watching Harry instead of me, or someone at the caravan park had spotted Harry and tipped off Sunny Jim. Harry could be sleeping off the drink, or taking his time sorting through his gear, blissfully unaware that he was about to have at least one visitor. If Sunnylands was indeed closed for winter, then there weren't going to be many witnesses to what was going to happen, and no one to come to his rescue if he cried for help.

Apart from us.

Joe studied the map on my phone as we drove.

He said, 'This time, let's not go rushing in like fucking eejits.'

'Okay,' I said.

It felt like an incredibly long drive. We listened to the radio. Jack Caramac was canvassing views on what, if anything, Moira Doherty's murder meant for the peace process. The usual nutters were phoning in. It was depressing. After a bit I switched to a CD. When we were a few minutes away from the park, Joe said: 'We're going to turn off the main road just along here, and the entrance is about a quarter of a mile along, and then the avenue loops back round on to the main road. So let's just do a drive-past, see what we can see.'

We turned on to Benone Avenue. It was lined on both sides with low snow-capped hedges. The fields on either side were virgin white. Up ahead I could see a big *Welcome to Sunnylands* sign and then we were passing a wide entrance with big farm gates three-quarters closed across it. A large white van was idling there while the driver spoke to a ginger-haired man in a luminous jacket and clutching a clipboard. I had a quick view of an administration building to the left, a car park with half a dozen cars in it, and then several outhouses on the right. About fifty metres further on I could just see the first of the caravans, but those beyond were mostly hidden by a shallow incline that I guessed led right down to the strand.

When we were past, Joe said, 'Well?'

'I think the guy with the clipboard is Sunny Jim's driver.'

'Awful lot of cars there if they're just after your man Lime.'

'That's what I was thinking.'

'And I've heard of organised crime, but a clipboard? For a murder?'

We'd come to the end of the avenue. I pulled back out on to the main road and then stopped at the first lay-by. I said, 'Sunny Jim's a businessman, fingers in lots of pies. Maybe he's an interest in the park, maybe Billy the Bear used his cam-girl money to buy some caravans, or even the whole park, and Sunny's inherited that too. What do you do at a caravan park in the winter? You refurbish it for the summer. That's why there's so many cars there, and vans. And if there's some annoying costume designer who refuses to accept you're the new owner, who keeps sneaking on to the grounds, you'd be within your rights to chase him off, right?'

'Right,' said Joe.

'It could all just be perfectly innocent.'

'Exactly.'

'On the other hand . . .'

'On the other hand.'

'We know, or we suspect, that Sunny is planning something, something big. He's no more into cam girls than I am; he's an unrepentant Republican who's recently benefited from the best military training in the world, even if they do say so themselves. So if he is planning something big, and there's lots of moving parts to it, he might just need to organise it away from public gaze. Where better than a deserted caravan park in the middle of nowhere in the middle of winter?'

'Deserted apart from Harry Lime,' said Joe.

38

Joe said, 'We'll wait for nightfall.'

I said, 'Nightfall? Are we in a Western?'

He laughed and said, 'A North-Western maybe.'

We had, of course, broken out the whiskey by then. It was only a quarter-bottle, which I kept in the glove compartment. Just a few wee nips to take the edge off the cold, and the nerves.

Out of nowhere Joe said, 'Have you ever eaten a badger?'

'Not recently. You?'

'Yup. One of my survival courses.'

'They served it?'

'God, no. I shot it. After I lamped it. Once they're caught in the beam, you can line up your shot perfect. Right between the eyes, one hundred metres. I was like a sniper.'

'A badger sniper.'

'Had my butcher's knives with me, of course. I don't go anywhere without them because you never know . . .'

'You never do.'

'It's an art, you know, gutting anything and preparing it.'

'Tell me about it,' I said, clearly not meaning for him to actually do so.

But he did.

'So I removed its back legs at the femur, cut it as close to the pelvis as I could. I also removed the feet at the ankle joint. There's quite a lot of fat on a badger, so I used that instead of cooking oil. You get more flavour if you cook it on the bone, but it's best to remove the bones first, then slip them back in, that way when it's cooked through you can take the bones out without ruining the look of it. I wrapped it in tin foil, set my fire, cooked it slow. Really very nice indeed. Tastes a bit like venison.'

'What does venison taste like?'

He thought about that for a moment, then said, 'A bit like badger.'

'I am a wiser man indeed,' I said, and shook my head at the sky, which was resolutely refusing to turn black.

Joe said, 'Fuck this, I'm going to take a look.'

He began to open his door.

I said, 'Hold on, I'll—'

'No. We've been over this before. They know you. I'm just a rambler. I want to see the lie of the land. I'll be five minutes.'

And he was gone. He was a law unto himself. But I knew he could handle that self. The bluster about *Bravo Two Zero* and boning badgers was exactly that. I had seen him in action before, and I knew some of his history. I had every confidence.

It was an odd feeling, sitting there alone, with the white sheen off the snow and the distant roar of waves on the strand, combined with the knowledge that something big and dangerous might be afoot. I looked up Sunnylands on the phone, read that it had more than two hundred caravans on site. About half were owned outright, others were summer rentals. It would be handy to know which one was Harry's. There was an owners' association and a contact number, but when I checked it I saw that it was the same number as for the park itself. I didn't want to tempt fate by calling them, so instead I called Human Resources at the Forum and said I was a National Insurance inspector and wanted to check what home address they had for him, and they said that for Data Protection reasons they couldn't give out that information, and I said that it was exactly for Data Protection reasons that I needed it; we debated the lunacy of Data Protection back and forth but they refused to budge, even when I threatened them with a raid that could seize every one of their computers and keep them until the twelfth of never, so I called them a shower of unco-operative fuckwits and hung up. Then I called back and asked to be put through to the costume department and I asked the woman who picked up for Harry's address because I was a friend of his but had lost track of what caravan it was and she told me to hold on a minute and came back in half that time with number 122. I thanked her and wallowed in a warm fuzzy glow of triumph, at least until Joe hammered on my window and almost induced a heart attack.

He got back in and said, 'All right. We shouldn't be too long now. I walked around the edge of the site; it's all fenced off but getting over shouldn't be a problem, it's not exactly Stalag Luft Whateverthefuck. There's a gate down below that gives direct access on to the beach, and someone manning it as well. The caravans are set out in avenues, which aren't lit particularly well, and most of the activity is between the administration block and the beach. Lots of cars, three big white vans. Be handy to know what number caravan is Harry Lime's.'

'One hundred and twenty-two,' I said. And added, 'Not just a pretty face.'

'Or even.'

I had largely forgotten about my swollen nose, so it was good to be reminded. I showed him the layout of the camp on my phone and pinpointed where Harry's caravan was. We traced a route to it, letting our fingers do the walking.

It just didn't seem to get any darker – until, not suddenly at all, it was.

Joe reached inside his coat and took out his gun and checked it. He then held it out to me and said, 'Have you fired one of these before?'

'Not as I recall.'

'Well take it, just in case.'

'What're you going to do?'

'I have another.'

He showed me it. It appeared bigger. He also showed me a butcher's knife. It was curved. I asked why it was curved and he said it was a skinning knife. I said that was good to know and hopefully we would run into some badgers. He said maybe not.

We were about a quarter of a mile away from the park entrance. We drove a little closer, with the lights off. We didn't really need them. The moon was up and reflecting off the snow. I locked up the car and we started walking. We pushed through a gap in a hedge. There was a pristine field glistening ahead of us, then a wooden fence and the caravans beyond. We crouched, we observed as best we could, and then made a dash across the field. Joe was surprisingly nimble for a big guy. He beat me to the fence by half a dozen metres. We both knelt by it, catching our breath. When we looked back, our trail across the field was clearly visible.

'What we . . . should really have done,' Joe said, gulping in air, 'was . . . like . . . attach branches of fern . . . to the back of our shoes . . . so they'd . . . brush away our tracks . . . as we crossed . . .'

'Next time,' I said.

We turned and peered through the slats in the fence. There wasn't much to see beyond the backs of darkened caravans. We gave each other the nod and climbed over and hurried a few metres across to the closest. We moved along its side, then peered out at the road in front: thick with snow but with one set of tyre grooves straight down the middle. Nothing moving. The corner of the administration building was just visible off to the left. The car park appeared about as full as it had before. We darted across the road and into the next row of caravans. The road meandered in and out of the various avenues, with the whole site sloping gently down towards the sea. As we drew closer, we could hear the waves crashing on to the beach.

We'd been doing the run, crouch, breathe routine for about five minutes when Joe pointed ahead and said, 'Should be just down there on the left.'

As I looked towards it, a movement off to my left caught my attention. Two figures just coming around the bend in the road. Joe had been about to set off across it, but I just managed to grab hold of his sleeve and pull him back. I nodded in their direction. Joe saw them too, and we very slowly backed up, then lay down flat on the snow behind the caravan.

They were two youngish-looking men in black windcheaters, scarves and gloves. One was carrying a flashlight, which was ranging across the fronts of the caravans on either side of the road; the other guy had some kind of a rifle over his shoulder, but seemed more concerned with getting the cigarette in his mouth lit than spotting intruders. As I looked out, I could see our footprints clearly leading right to where we were. The flashlight scoped across our caravan. The guy with the gun swore. He stopped, flicking at his lighter. 'Too fucking windy,' he said. The fella with the flashlight came up to him, and they huddled around the lighter. Our footprints now led out from either side of them. I felt Joe tense against me. His hand moved towards his jacket pocket. Mine moved to mine.

I had a pistol in my pocket, and I was afraid to use it.

But I didn't think Joe would need much encouragement to shoot them – or skin them alive.

The guy with the torch stepped off the road and on to the snowy bank in front of us. He came right up to the caravan. We could see his feet, but not what he was doing, at least until a low cloud of piss steam began to rise. His mate laughed and said something about yellow snow. The guy with the torch zipped up and trudged back. Then they continued on up the hill in the direction of the administration building.

Beside me Joe showed me the knife and whispered, 'I would have had the cock off him.'

I gave him the thumbs-up.

We moved out again.

A guard on the front gate, a guard on the back, guards patrolling within, patrolling a caravan park in the middle of nowhere. Vans and cars, clipboards, flashlights, and guns over shoulders. Something, something was happening.

We came to number 122. It was a big model, set in permanent foundations. It was dark inside, like all of the others. The only difference was that the lock was broken, probably from when Harry Lime had been chased out last time, and the door was open, though just by a couple of inches.

As we approached, the crunch of our feet on the snow sounded unbearably loud now that we needed it to be bearably quiet. Joe put his hand up and pushed the door fully open. Then he stepped up into the caravan. He stood, listening, *feeling*, maybe. I entered behind him – just as Harry Lime stepped out of the darkness and into a shaft of moonlight with a gun raised towards us and hissing: 'One more step, I'll blow your fucking heads off.'

39

'Harry, it's me . . .'

'Who the fuck is me?'

'Dan. Dan Starkey. It's okay. We're here to help.'

'Who the fuck is we?'

'Me and Joe, Joe's a friend.'

'He's not my friend. You're not even my friend!'

'Yes I am, Harry, yes I am. We've come to rescue you.'

'Who says I need fucking rescued?'

'Harry, keep it down, please – just take it easy. We're going to step into the light so you can see us properly . . . swear to God we're here to help . . . See . . . it's just me . . .'

Harry kept the gun on us, while Joe had slipped his behind his back. Harry looked dishevelled and a bit mad-eyed.

'C'mon, Harry, put it down . . . we both know it's

only effective right up close, so the only thing that'll happen if you do pull the trigger is there'll be a loud bang and everyone else out there will come running to see what's going on, and then we're all doomed.'

'It's a different gun,' said Harry. 'It's Billy's.'

'Harry, we're all on the same side.'

'And what side is that?'

'The side of the good and the just.'

Harry snorted. Joe snorted. We all snorted.

It wasn't pleasant, but it was an icebreaker.

I heard Harry let out a sigh.

He said, 'You fucking eejits. Come in here, there's a light in the bathroom, no windows.'

He moved to one side, pulled a sliding door back, and ushered us into the bathroom. He stepped in after us, closed the door and flicked a switch. We blinked in the light. Harry looked ragged. His gun did indeed look different to the one he'd pulled on me back in the theatre. He set it down on a small sink and put his hands to his face and shook his head.

He said, 'I've been trapped in here for fucking ever. I've been surviving on tins of fucking John West salmon. Do you have *any* idea what's going on out there?'

'Not yet,' I said.

It was a small bathroom, with just enough room for the three of us – Harry leaning against the sink, Joe standing under the shower and me sitting on the toilet. Although it was sealed like a space capsule, we spoke quietly.

Harry shook his head. 'I was stupid, should have

just gotten out of town. But there was stuff I wanted. Needed. Silly, sentimental stuff. So I came back. I've done it in winter before, lots of times, I know there's someone lives in the main building up there – security guard or manager, whatever – and they don't encourage it, so usually I just hop over the fence and sneak down here. So I did that, and it was all fine and so lovely and peaceful I just thought I'd spend the night. But then when I go to leave in the morning, there's a guy standing guard on the gates and even then I just thought well maybe someone's been caravan rustling or something and they're just taking precautions, so I was just about to saunter up when I sees your man driving in . . .'

'Sunny Jim,' I said.

'Aye, he's bloody hard to miss . . . and it was only by the skin of my teeth that he didn't see me, I was just able to duck back in behind one of the vans . . . and next thing you know there's actual proper guards with guns on the gates, and working the perimeter and walking all around inside, and there's vans and trucks coming in, and seeing as how they wanted to kill me last time, I thought it was better to keep my head down and wait for them to go away, except they haven't, and if anything, there's more of them.'

'You've no idea what he's up to?'

'Yes I do. He's up to no good.'

'As in . . .?'

'That's all I know, or care. I just want out, I want a ride to Belfast and then I'm on the first flight out. And not coming back.' He nodded at Joe. 'Are you a private detective too?'

'No, I'm a butcher.'

Harry's eyes flitted to me, and back to Joe.

'You serious?'

'Absolutely.'

'But what're you . . .?'

'Every man needs a hobby,' said Joe.

Harry thought about that for a bit, and then: 'Did youse really come to rescue me?'

'Amongst other things,' I said.

'That's so epic, now that I think about it. I've never been rescued before. Should we go, then?'

I looked at Joe. Joe looked at me.

I said, 'We need to poke around for a bit. If you're happier waiting in the car, then . . .' I held up the keys. He snapped them out of my hand. 'So I guess you're happier doing that. But that's okay. Just follow our tracks, will lead you straight there.'

'Follow . . . I'm not a big-game hunter . . .'

'If we're not back in twenty minutes,' said Joe, 'wait another ten. If we're not back in half an hour, drive up and down outside in case we come charging out. If there's no sign of us at all, call the cops, call the ambulance, call the Samaritans, call anyone.'

'Do youse not think you'd be better walking me to the car? What happens if I get lost, or ambushed?'

Joe said, 'You'll be fine.'

'Probably,' I added.

*　　*　　*

We switched the light off, then quietly slid the bathroom door back open and moved to the entrance. We checked that the coast was clear, pointed out our tracks and were about to send Harry on his way when Joe caught his arm and said, 'Do you know how to use that thing?' and nodded down at his gun. 'Point it and pull the trigger,' said Harry. 'Squeeze it,' said Joe, 'don't pull.' 'That's not what Billy used to say,' said Harry, and we all giggled in the moonlight. 'Now go,' said Joe, and gave him a gentle push. Harry gave us the thumbs-up and went on his way.

As soon as he'd disappeared across the road, Joe turned and re-entered the caravan. I followed him in. He was opening and closing drawers and feeling around inside them. I asked what he was doing. He said, 'Just a minute . . .' then smiled and held up a pair of binoculars. 'Was pretty sure, the views around here . . .' He pulled the strap over his head and led us back outside. 'Let's just find a little high ground . . .'

He looked about him, then nodded to our left and started off. About a hundred metres further along, he stopped beside another caravan and said, 'Right, give us a hand.' He thumbed towards the vehicle's roof. I moved beside him, knitted my hands together and he stepped up. He was a big man and I staggered under his weight, but just as I was about to give way, he managed to get a firm hold of the edge of the bicycle rack on top and pull himself up. Then he turned, reached down and took hold of my hand; he hauled me up with really very little effort at all.

We lay flat on the roof, side by side. We had a good view of the administration building, the car park and the outhouses, about two hundred metres away to our left, and then turning we could see the lower set of gates, with the wide strand and waves beyond. Joe raised the binoculars and studied ahead of us first, roving back and forth and occasionally letting out barely audible *mmm-hmm*s. Then he rolled over on to his back and raised his neck to allow him to observe the caravans behind us and the sweep down to the sea. He *mmmm-hmmm*ed some more before handing over the glasses and saying, 'Can't say I'm any the wiser. See what you think.'

I decided to do it the other way round, lying on my back first. The binoculars were pretty powerful. Three guards were now manning the lower gate, which remained closed. There were two white vans sitting on the park side; as I watched, a third arrived and lined up beside them. I could see from their exhaust fumes that all three engines were running, but their headlights were off. I ranged back across the park and saw another van meandering along the avenues towards the lower gate. I turned over and focused in on the administration building, which was fully lit with people clearly visible within, maybe half a dozen of them. The vans having moved to the back gates, the car park now contained just three cars, one of which was Sunny Jim's blue Jag. Michael was leaning against it, smoking a cigarette and occasionally passing it to Patrick beside him. I knew Michael had been working for both Danny Lynch and Sunny Jim, but was a little surprised to find that Patrick clearly was too. It was all very incestuous.

Joe said, 'Well?'

I said, 'It's about the strand. I don't know much about the north-west, but I know a lot of these bigger beaches you can drive on them. They're lining up their vans to go somewhere, somewhere along the sand, and they're jumpy enough about it to have guards front and back. But where exactly are they going, and why?'

Joe took the glasses back and examined the beach and beyond.

'There's the lights of some houses at the end of the beach, then there's the lough, then isn't that Greencastle on the other side of the water? That's Donegal, right?'

'Right.'

'So it's in the Republic, so technically another country. Right? What if they're smuggling something across – fuel, or cigarettes, something there's tax on they're trying to avoid . . .?'

'It goes on, sure – but wouldn't you need bigger vans? Tankers if it's fuel? And there isn't really a physical border any more, and there's a hundred barely marked roads they could use – this way they'd need boats to get across the lough. Seems like a lot of trouble to go to for fags or diesel.'

'What about illegal immigrants? They're smuggled into the Republic, then use the lough as a kind of back door into the UK?'

'Again – why use the beach? Easier and quicker by

road. And none of it fits in with what we already know about Sunny – something big, something spectacular. Smuggling in a ton of Chinese waiters isn't exactly striking a blow against the Empire.'

Joe lowered the glasses. 'We need to get closer,' he said.

'I'm not sure that's a—'

'And when I say we, I mean me. You wait here and I'll just—'

'Joe – I appreciate the thought, but I brought you up here to protect me, not to disappear off on solo missions. If anyone's going, I should . . .'

'Dan, listen to me – if you go down there with me, then we double the chances of us getting caught. If you go down by yourself, then I'm failing in my duty to protect you. The best way I can look after you is for me to go down and you stay safe here.'

I was looking at him, trying to work out the flaw in his argument.

After a while, it came to me.

'But you don't even know what you're looking for.'

'And you do?'

'Of course I do. I'm looking for a desk with a big folder on it marked *Diabolical Plan*.'

'Exactly. Dan, they won't see me. Guaranteed.'

I sighed. He handed me the binoculars.

I said, 'Well – be careful.'

'I always am. I'll be five minutes.'

He gave me a wink – and then simply rolled over the side of the van. By the time I pulled myself to the edge, he was nothing more than a set of footprints in the snow.

Five minutes passed.

Then ten.

And then a shot rang out.

I flattened myself completely on the caravan roof and cautiously raised the binoculars again. It was hard to tell where it had come from. Figures began to emerge from the main building, coming down the steps, shouting indistinctly, pointing across the car park. I moved the glasses towards a small group just coming from behind one of the outhouses. With a sudden lurch in my stomach I saw Harry Lime being dragged along between two men. They got him to the middle of the car park and then threw him down. I ranged back to the main building in time to see Sunny Jim crossing towards him. Michael was part of a group of half a dozen following behind. Harry was on his knees with his head bowed as Sunny Jim stopped in front of him. One of his captors handed Sunny what looked like a red plastic folder, which I vaguely recognised. Sunny Jim opened it up and studied the contents. Then he faced the outhouses and yelled:

'Starkey!'

I realised the folder was from my car, that it contained the log book and my insurance details.

'Starkey!' He turned to face towards the caravans. 'I know you're out there! Get down here now!'

I got flatter.

'Starkey! I'm going to count down from ten! If you don't show yourself, I'm going to put a bullet in your pal's brain! And you know I will! Ten!'

Given the scale of what he was planning, even if I didn't yet know exactly what it was, I knew that giving myself up would not mean that he would spare me. He had already threatened to shoot me if I showed my face again. Now, at the moment of his big moment, I knew he wouldn't allow anyone to interfere with it, not Harry, not me.

'Five!'

He had neglected to shout out nine or eight or seven or even six.

He was not a patient man.

A voice from below said, 'Hey.'

I peered over the edge, hoping, even expecting to see Joe, Joe with his own master plan, Joe ready to whisk me away, Joe about to absolve me of responsibility for what was going to happen to Harry Lime.

But no.

It was broken-jawed Patrick with a rifle aimed at me, and some other guy with a handgun.

If he had needed a word with an extra syllable or two, Patrick might not have been able to manage it. But the 'Hey' and a wave of his rifle was enough to inspire me to stand up. Enough for his mate to shout across that they had me and were bringing me in. I lowered myself over the edge, and hung there for a moment, and then dropped with a grunt and slipped on to my back and winded myself; none of Joe's stealth or dignity, just a middle-aged man with middle-aged-man knees, floundering in the snow. Before I got up, Patrick's companion knelt on my stomach while he searched me; he took my gun. I got to my feet and Patrick immediately rammed the butt of his rifle into my back and I staggered forward.

'Kefh walkin', wankhor,' he hissed.

'That's easy for you to say,' I said, and immediately regretted it as he struck me again, same place, twice as sore.

We crossed the car park.

Sunny Jim, floodlit by the moon, watched me all the way; as I drew closer, I saw that his burn appeared darker than before, while the jaundice I'd noticed in his eyes seemed to have spread to the normal half of his face. As I finally stopped before him, he threw my driving documents down.

He said, 'I thought you were getting the train.'

I said, 'Remembered I had my car.'

'Do you also remember what I said I'd do if I saw you again?'

'Vaguely.'

He shook his head. 'You should have gotten out while you could.'

I said, 'Harry – you okay?'

Harry's head came up. I could see now that his lips were bloody and swollen and one eye was starting to close over. He said, 'I didn't tell them anything . . .'

'That's because there's nothing to tell,' I said. I nodded at Sunny Jim. 'So what now? I don't suppose there's any point in asking you to let him go? I mean, I'm the one poking around trying to find out what's going on; Harry just needed a bit of assistance to get away. He hasn't done anything wrong.'

'Very noble, Starkey, but *really*?' He turned to Harry. 'Is that right? Are you as innocent as this driven snow?'

Harry averted his eyes.

Sunny Jim laughed.

I said, 'What?'

'You mean you don't know his little secret? Harry, why don't you tell your wee mate all about it?'

Harry concentrated on the snow.

'A little shy, are we? Do you want me to tell him?'

I said, 'Harry?'

He wouldn't look up.

'Oh yes,' said Sunny Jim. 'You running your arse off looking for Billy the Bear, and Harry here knows exactly where he is, don't you, bum-chum?'

I said, 'Harry, what's he talking about?'

Harry still wouldn't look up. At least until Sunny Jim clicked his fingers at one of his gang and was handed a pistol; he moved across to Harry and crouched beside him. He placed the barrel under Harry's chin and gently moved his head up.

'C'mon, Harry, tell everyone what you did. Tell us how you didn't like Billy consorting with the likes of us, how you didn't like him helping his old friends, how you didn't even go to see him in prison, how you promised him a big dirty weekend up here with you when he got out and instead of that you fucking beat him to death. And nearly fucked my plans up in the process. Are you not going to tell him *any* of that?'

Harry looked up, finally.

'Please . . .'

Sunny Jim pulled the trigger.

Shot him through the throat, up through his mouth and out the back of his head. Everyone jumped back. Three behind him got sprayed. My knees buckled me down into the snow. As Harry slumped, Sunny Jim stood over him and hissed down, 'And that's for giving me the fucking runaround for weeks instead of taking your fucking punishment like a man.'

He pivoted, gun in hand, and barked, 'So what about you?'

I looked at Harry, his eyes open, on his back. Red snow.

I said, 'I'd be just as happy with community service or probation or . . .'

If it sounds pathetic, it was.

The gang behind were wiping at themselves and laughing.

Sunny Jim was facing me, not deliberately but somehow magically framed by the entirety of the full moon now as it began to wane, a two-faced super-villain with his blood-spattered gang.

'Oh no, Starkey,' he crowed, 'no chance of that at all. I have a much better idea for you. *Much* better.'

40

'Hey Starkey – Starkey, I was reading about you, Googled you, you used to be a journalist, you ever do sports? You ever get like a VIP seat? Ringside seats to the boxing or something like that?'

Sunny Jim was waving me across the flat roof of the two-storey administration building. My hands were Scotch-taped behind me. Half a dozen of his cronies were standing around him, facing the sea. It was quiet, it was intense. You could feel the excitement. Patrick and his chum pushed me towards them. Patrick would probably have liked to propel me right over the edge.

'Sure,' I said.

'Well we haven't got any actual seats,' he said as I was finally stopped just short of flight, 'but you are about to see something money can't buy.' His brow furrowed as he looked at me, and then he suddenly reached out and I tensed for a blow, but instead he took hold of the binoculars I'd entirely forgotten about and whipped them away. 'How thoughtful,' he said, and slung them around his own neck. He took a phone out of his pocket, pressed a button and raised it to his ear. 'Okay,' he said, 'let's get the party started.'

Everyone was now looking down the slight incline across the roofs of the caravans towards the beach and the sea beyond. The three white vans began to move through the far gates, while keeping their main lights switched off so that only the red glow of their rear lights was visible as they swept away across the sand towards the houses at the far end of Benone Strand.

One of Sunny's men muttered, 'Come on, ye boys.'

The others picked up on it, repeating it, and then clapping their hands together and whooping as the red lights raced away.

I said, 'Unless they've made joyriding an Olympic sport, I don't know what you're all getting so excited about.'

Sunny Jim glanced at his watch. 'Well,' he said, 'you're about to find out.'

And *instantly*, from the houses at the end of the beach, a sudden flash of light, followed a millisecond later by a violent *boom*, then another flash, another *boom*, a third, a fourth . . . the guys around me clapping and cheering and Sunny Jim just standing there nodding as the sound rumbled across the beach towards us.

And still the vans were racing on towards what had to be devastation, towards the fierce glow of multiple fires, where people *had* to be dead.

I said, 'What the fuck have you done? Blown up some houses? To prove fucking what?'

Sunny Jim let out a sudden *Ha!* 'Houses, Starkey? Are you kidding me? This is the biggest fucking prison break in history!'

I stood there, mouth hanging open, staggered both by my own stupidity – I'd looked at the prison on the map earlier and then somehow managed to blank it out – and by Sunny Jim's audacity. A prison break. The night sky was lit up by flames and floodlights, by the moon and the stars, by a distant roar that was more than fire, and more than the crashing waves; it was the roar of men, men escaping, fleeing, stampeding through the breached walls of Her Majesty's Prison Magilligan, hundreds and hundreds of them charging across the beach, into the sand dunes, across the snowy fields to lose themselves in the murk of Binevenagh Forest, stopping cars, throwing themselves into waiting vehicles, seizing motorbikes and bikes and horses and for all I knew fucking space hoppers. It was an ants' nest kicked over and the cracks were swallowing them up. And the white vans waiting to cherry-pick the worst of them before racing back towards us.

Then I was being taken back across the roof and down the stairs; everyone else was moving too, but unhurried, methodical, sticking to a plan. As we arrived on the ground floor, I saw Michael and another guy splashing petrol over the furniture and up the walls. The front doors were open. One of the white vans came roaring up, crushed full of prisoners, guys on the roof, guys hanging out the back doors, and they were yelling and hollering and beating on the sides. Sunny Jim stood in the doorway and raised his hands to them as they sped past and they responded with a cheer and a chant of his name. Patrick caught hold of my arm and pulled me towards a room at the back. We followed a snail-trail of blood to get there. As he pushed me through the door, I saw Harry Lime's body lying dumped on the floor. Patrick forced me down on to a chair, and, having already Scotch-taped my hands, proceeded to further tape them to the chair and then did the same for my feet. Michael came in and splashed this room too. Splashed Harry. Splashed me. He gave me a wink, then hurried out and away.

Sunny Jim appeared in the doorway.

He said, 'What's my name?'

I said, 'Jim Owen. Sergeant Jim Owen.'

'Aka . . .?'

'Sunny Jim, though frankly I think it's impolite to—'

'Shut up. I'm nicknamed after a brand of firelighters, am I not? Appropriate then that I light this one, don't you think?'

He shook a box of Swan Vestas at me; my death rattle.

I said, 'What is the point of this?'

'Of them finding your body, and *his*, charred in the ruins? Everyone will pin the blame for the prison on youse, of course!'

'They'll never believe that in a million years!'

'Of course they won't, Starkey. But it will sow

331

confusion for a while, and after they realise it wasn't either of you, they'll still allow it to be believed, because it'll be convenient to have a scapegoat so that they can keep saying it was some lunatics who won't be allowed to derail the peace process. But they'll have gotten the message. We're back, and we're not going away.'

He took out a match and struck it.

As it flamed up, he opened the top of the box a fraction and jammed it in. Then he skimmed the matchbox across the wooden floor. As it hit the far wall, the whole box ignited, and a moment later the wall went up.

From the front door someone called for him to hurry up, they were leaving.

But Sunny Jim remained in the doorway, a smile on his hideous face.

He said, 'For a few moments, Starkey, you're going to know what it feels like to be me.'

'What, a fucking nutter?'

He laughed. 'That's it, Starkey. That's it.'

I laughed right back at him.

Sunny Jim said, 'Why the fuck are you laughing?'

'Have you never heard the expression, he who laughs last laughs longest?'

'No,' said Sunny Jim and turned out of the room.

All four walls were now burning, and it was spreading across the floor towards me. I pulled at the tape, at the chair, I tried kicking my legs, but Patrick had done a good job. I could just about see through the thickening smoke Sunny Jim crossing the reception area and then moving swiftly down the steps to his waiting Jag.

Michael was holding the back door open for him. Sunny Jim climbed in. Michael closed the door and then hurried around to the passenger door and got in. A moment later the Jag zoomed away. The only sounds then were the crackling of the flames all around me and, in the far distance, sirens from the breached Magilligan prison.

I didn't want to die, but I particularly didn't want to die Scotch-taped to a chair and melting. It was already getting hard to breathe. Pieces of the ceiling were falling around me.

I had been in moments-from-death situations before. I had tried then to edit my panicked final thoughts down so that when it came there would be something lovely to go out on, images of Trish usually, of her laughing and smiling and preferably with no clothes on, of us in a bar getting merrily pissed and then stumbling home with a Chinese, the Clash on the record player, dancing around with LP covers on our heads to 'White Riot'; of John Wayne and James Stewart and Iwo Jima and Harvey, of De Niro talking to me, of Cuban Pacino and a mountain of coke, of Georgie Best lobbing Pat Jennings and the rest of Spurs . . . except that those were memories or fantasies summoned because death was about to be instant, usually a shot to the head. But this would be different, this would be long and lingering and slow. The best I could do would be to open my mouth and invite the smoke in so that at least I would not be conscious for the worst of it. But I couldn't do it. I would keep my eyes open and struggle on, because even if they hated me, I had people out there who I loved or quite liked, people I had sworn eternal love to, or for whom I had sworn to take revenge. Patricia. Bobby. Lol. Little Dan. Sara lying battered and unconscious.

I would not succumb to—

Behind me the window cracked and shattered from the heat.

I closed my eyes and prepared my words of last resort.

A prayer to a saint to make it quick.

I said them.

Out loud.

Words nobody would ever hear or know.

When I opened my eyes, Christine was standing there.

And I thought: *Jesus H. Christ, I'm losing it now.*

I closed them again.

And opened.

And it wasn't Christine, it was a mad fucking butcher.

Joe was using his skinning knife to slice the Scotch tape.

He was saying, 'Who the fuck is St Jude?'

And I was saying, 'The patron saint of lost causes.'

He was saying, 'Sounds like Fenian shite to me.'

And I was saying, 'You'd be surprised.'

41

We sat in Sara's room in the hotel and watched the coverage on Sky News. Twin beds. One each. We also hit the whiskey. Joe wouldn't stop laughing about how I'd looked yomping across the field to my car. 'A black and white minstrel on the run from a slave plantation,' he said as he hot-wired it like the expert he appeared to be. I'd showered the smoke off me, but I couldn't do much about the depression that had settled. Joe was happy because he'd done what he'd been asked to do: he had watched my back and saved my life. It didn't seem to matter much to him that Sunny Jim had carried out his master plan, that he had breached the walls of Magilligan prison in five different places, blown holes in the accommodation blocks, set off smoke bombs and fireworks to confuse everyone. I was beliquored up, and scowling at the breathless, exhaustive and fact-light coverage on the telly. It was still the early hours, so most of it was

335

pointless speculation and panic-stoking. They were quoting mysterious inside sources as saying that more than three hundred out of the over five hundred inmates had taken advantage of the breaches to escape; of those, more than half were thought to have been quickly recaptured, but that still meant that around one hundred and fifty were still on the run. The police and the Northern Ireland Prison Service were struggling to cope. There was talk of the army being called in. People were told to stay behind locked doors, to not answer to strangers. And then they would contradict that by saying that inmates assigned to medium-to-minimum-security prisons like Magilligan generally posed a low risk to public safety. Talking heads said it wasn't the crimes of the inmates that was the concern, but the sheer volume of escaped prisoners.

After a while we were pretty drunk.

Joe said, 'I don't know what you're so pissed off about.'

I said, 'Billy the Bear is dead, Harry Lime is dead, Sara's still lying unconscious and Sunny Jim has carried out his spectacular and will probably get away with it; he'll have his headlines, the whole world will be talking about it. And I've to slope back off to Belfast with my tail between my legs.'

'But a couple of free nights in a nice hotel, hard to beat.'

'There's that,' I said.

'You're alive, Trish and the kids aren't in their traditional danger.'

'There's that also.'

'And if you think about it, how spectacular is spectacular?'

'Spectacular enough.'

'Well that's a matter of opinion. Once the smoke clears, literally, what has he achieved?'

'Oh I don't know, the biggest prison break in history?'

'Dan – *Dan*. I've done time. Hard time. Magilligan is a couple of metal bars short of being an open prison. Like they said, it's medium to minimum security. That means if you put your mind to it you can more or less walk out of there. The people they put in places like Magilligan – they pose the least risk to public safety. They're dodgy accountants, shoplifters, drunks and useless burglars. It's not like Sunny Jim has unleashed the most dangerous terrorists this side of an al-Qaeda coffee morning. He's released a tidal wave of white-collar criminals stapling their way to freedom. Half of them didn't take their chance, and the rest have probably just got caught up in the rush and wish they were back inside already. They'll be freezing their bollocks off out there.'

'That may be, but he still has his spectacular, his statement. By the time we drag ourselves out of here in the morning, the whole world will know about it.'

'But will it, really? It'll be a three-minute wonder, Dan, believe me.'

I lay back on the bed, still watching the coverage, but gradually drifting away. I was exhausted, and the adrenalin that came with being burned alive and then rescued by super-butcher had finally worn off. I was angry at myself for not preventing Sunny Jim from carrying out his master plan, because although I had no particular skill set, I had always been adept at somehow managing to put a spanner in the works. But not this time. This time Sunny Jim had laughed last.

I slept. I dreamed I was lying in Trish's arms. She was stroking my head and saying that everything would be okay. That Sara would be fine and that at least some of what Joe had said was right. Sunny Jim had wanted to strike a blow against the Empire, and was of a generation inspired by the Twin Towers, by the Mumbai massacre, by carnage and outrage in Bali, in Kenya, and viewed like that, the bombing of Magilligan and the freeing of so many low-level prisoners had to be seen as anticlimactic, as nothing more than a fleabite on the Empire's arse.

I woke. I tossed. I turned.

Joe was snoring for Ulster.

The TV was on but the sound was muted.

I read the news scrolling across the bottom of the screen. Prisoners were still being rounded up. I was thinking about the white vans on the beach, and how Sunny must have either underestimated the numbers that would break out, or he'd provided them specifically to pick up certain favoured individuals. I knew that among the convicted prisoners were a number of inmates being held on bail awaiting trial; if they were terrorism suspects, they might ultimately expect to serve their time in a higher-security establishment closer to Belfast, and this might be a last chance to break them out. But there had been no particular outcry about dangerous prisoners being on the loose. Perhaps that would come in the morning. Or perhaps Sunny Jim had just been providing the vans on a first come first served basis, or was providing transport only for those who came from his own neck of the woods, from the Bogside.

I got up and stared out at the Peace Bridge. The few flowers that had been placed there to mark the spot where Moira Doherty had been shot were gone now, blown away or stolen. I didn't know for sure if Sunny Jim had killed her or had her killed, but it did not seem unreasonable to assume that she had become part of the cam-girls business through Billy, and then had a falling-out with Sunny Jim either over the ownership of Billy's share, or perhaps because she had discovered that he intended to use the money raised by the site to fund his spectacular strike against the British Empire. Maybe Billy had deliberately been sent into prison by Sunny Jim to set up the breakout from the inside and confessed it to his mum while under the influence of crush. Perhaps Billy had had a larger part to play in the breakout, or even in Sunny's organisation, which was why Sunny had reacted so extremely to Harry Lime killing him.

Yes, maybe now, in the growing cold light of day, it all did make some kind of sense and I was feeling bad about it only because of Sunny Jim's smug conviction that he would get away with it because too many important people were too afraid of upsetting the apple cart.

I was still standing there when Joe sat up, sending a cascade of minibar bottles to the floor, and said, 'So is that us? Back to Belfast?'

'Aye,' I said, 'more or less. I've a couple of people to see if you want to hang around for a lift, or you can get the train, whatever suits.'

'No rush then,' said Joe. 'Sure it's not often I get a relaxing break.'

He lay back and closed his eyes.

No hint of a smile.

Trish phoned. She said, 'I've been watching the news, I see what's happening up there. Is it all your fault?'

'Not this time,' I said.

'But you had something to do with it. It has your name written all over it.'

'You think?'

'I know. How's Joe doing? Am I full of good ideas or am I full of good ideas?'

'You're full of good ideas. And he saved my life. He dived through a window into a burning building and dragged me out.'

'I think you'll find it's *dove*, he *dove* through a window into a burning building, et cetera, et cetera.'

'And then he carried me off, like on the wings of a *dove*?'

'Hmmmm. We'll agree to differ. You coming home?'

'Yep. Not that I have a home.'

'You coming back in this general direction?'

'Shortly.'

'How's your other true love doing?'

'Still in a coma last time I checked, thanks.'

'That's a Smiths song, isn't it. "Girlfriend in a—"'

'I have no time for the Smiths, or for you, for that matter.'

'Oh don't. You know I don't mean it. How is she really?'

'Like I say. But I'll stop off and see her before I bring Joe back.'

'And are you going to get him for it, this guy who had her beaten up, this . . . Chicken George, is it?'

'Sunny Jim. And no, it doesn't look like I am.'

'That doesn't sound like you. Usually you get there in the end.'

'Well this one isn't so neat and tidy.'

'What about your other girl, your barely legal girl?'

'Trish, she's—'

'Christine, have you found her?'

'No, not yet.'

'And is that likely, if you're coming home?'

'No. I don't know if she's really in any trouble. She's probably fine.'

'So you're giving up.'

'There's nothing to give up on.'

'Well, never mind. I'm sure there are other, easier cases waiting for you when you get home. Back.'

'Trish . . .'

'Gotta run, your grandchild is wailing and his parents have hangovers. See you later.' She hung up.

From the bed, Joe, hands clasped behind his head,

said, 'I didn't hear any of that, but it still sounded like wifey was giving you a hard time.'

'Wifey always gives me a hard time,' I said, 'and she's not my wife.'

'Sounds like she is. You should stand up for yourself.'

'I'll bear that in mind.'

'See that you do. Now, I'm starving. Let's get us something to eat then hit the road.'

'Sounds like a plan,' I said.

'But just give me a minute while I dove into the shower.' He gave me a wink and rolled out of bed.

'Oh fuck off,' I said after him.

Although not so loudly that there was any risk of him hearing.

42

Sara was awake. Or more accurately, she was conscious. She was still drugged up and her face was swollen and her lips were dry as crisps. Her eyes were open, but only just. I held water to her lips and she blinked her thanks. The nurse said they were bringing her slowly out of an induced coma, and that we shouldn't expect miracles. I said I was well in with the Messiah, so bloody right I was expecting miracles. A gurgle came from Sara. She was probably trying to get me to shut up, but I took it as a positive sign. I showed her the bag I'd brought from her hotel room: her laptop, her make-up, her changes of clothes, her lingerie with *Dan Starkey was here* written on the labels. Getting a smile out of her was hard.

I held her hand. It was cold, and felt brittle.

She gave me a little squeeze, and I got quite emotional.

Joe was sitting in the corridor outside. He'd worked

with Sara before, again at my request, but he said he didn't really do hospitals, or sick people, and that if she wasn't up to discussing philosophy or taking part in an arm wrestle, he'd prefer to wait until she was.

After ten minutes of hand-holding and blinking and telling her that she was going to be okay, I was starting to see his point. Luckily this coincided with a knock on the door and a man in a smart grey suit and with short dark hair and an intense demeanour came in and asked me if I was a relative, and I said it depended who was asking, which he did not appear to find very funny. He repeated the question and I threw it right back at him. He said he worked for the *Belfast Telegraph* and was looking after both Sara's and the newspaper's interests. He said he was trying to track down someone called Dan Starkey who'd apparently been masquerading as a *Telegraph* reporter and charging a room and sundry expenses to the newspaper's account at the City Hotel. I said that it was outrageous that someone could take advantage of the mortally injured like that and that I was her cousin Tim from Broughshane and I planned to be with her until the very end. 'Although I'm just popping out for a coffee now, if you want one?' He looked aghast and said he hadn't realised it was that serious and I looked sad and said, 'Oh yes.' He nodded at Sara for quite a while, but I could almost hear the cogs turning in his head. I said, 'Is that a yes or no for the coffee then?' He said, vaguely, 'No . . . no . . .' and I moved to the door. I was halfway out when he said, 'Excuse me . . . Tim? You wouldn't happen to have any ID on you, would you? You just can't be too careful these days.'

'Absolutely,' I said, patting my jacket, 'there's a lot of loopers on the loose out there. Damn it – I've left my wallet in the car. Tell you what, I'll nip out and get it, be back in five with that coffee.'

'I don't want a . . .'

But I was already moving down the corridor.

Joe was sitting on a plastic chair about ten metres along. I said, 'Joe,' out of the corner of my mouth, 'Joe – if the guy in the doorway tries to follow me, distract him while I get away. See you at the car in five.'

I kept walking.

The *Telegraph* man shouted after me, 'Ahm – excuse me, sir? If you could just hold on a min—'

But I was through the swing doors and away.

Joe joined me in the car five minutes later. He got into the passenger seat and buckled himself in. He said, 'Never met an accountant I didn't want to punch.'

'Was he an accountant?' I asked.

'No idea,' said Joe, 'but I wasn't taking any chances.'

'You actually punched him?'

'Of course I didn't. I'm not a nutcase. We collided in the corridor and he came off bratwurst.' He smiled. 'Butcher's joke.'

'Fair enough,' I said, and started the engine.

I had not much enjoyed Londonderry, and I wasn't quite done with it yet.

The rain was coming down hard when we left the hospital, sheets of it blowing and swirling, much as it had been when we arrived. The snow had turned to sludge and the sludge to ice water, which was flowing freely along the gutters and pooling at dips in the road. As we skirted the Foyle, it looked swollen and brown and menacing. St Comgall's soon appeared through the curtain of rain, with cars parked all around and worshippers emerging from the church with coats pulled up over their heads or battling to keep their umbrellas from blowing inside out. There was a deep-looking lake of water around the gates, with drivers nervously inching forward through it; a queue of vehicles was waiting to exit.

'Completely forgot it was Sunday,' I said to Joe as I took the water at speed, causing it to spray up over the departing congregation.

'Nice one,' said Joe.

I parked. I said, 'I just want to say goodbye to Rev. McCutcheon. Why don't you come with me?'

'Is he going to attack you, or convert you?'

'No, but I wouldn't mind your take on him.'

'Really?'

Joe beamed. He got out of the car and joined me as we hurried across the car park and up the steps into the church. Rev. McCutcheon was standing inside the front doors, shaking hands and exchanging small talk with his parishioners and directing those who wanted to join him for coffee and sandwiches towards the community hall next door; there were young girls and boys in New Seeker uniforms holding umbrellas waiting to escort them across. He spotted me, and his brow furrowed. He looked at Joe. He bade farewell to the elderly couple he was talking to and came across. He put his hand out and I clasped it; he patted it like I was one of his flock.

'Mr Starkey,' he said, 'I didn't really expect to see you again. And . . .?'

He put his hand out to Joe. Joe kept his hand where it was.

'Joe,' said Joe.

The Rev. kept his hand out for just a moment longer before moving it up to push through his receding hair.

'Joe's my partner in solving crime,' I volunteered.

Joe kept with the serious demeanour.

'Well?' Rev. McCutcheon asked. 'Any news?'

'Nope,' I said. 'What about you, hear anything? Has God been on the phone? Concerned parent and all that.'

'No, Mr Starkey. And I don't think that's very funny. You shouldn't be making light of the situation, especially considering the abuse I have had to endure because of your actions.'

'Abuse?'

'Abuse. And threats. Peter Quinn came to see me last night. He was ripping. Thinks I sent a couple of heavies round to threaten him.'

'I wouldn't know anything about that,' I said.

'He has security cameras all over his house. Two men broke his door down and threatened his mother.'

'Wasn't us,' I said.

'And we definitely didn't threaten his mother,' said Joe. 'We didn't even wake her up.'

I looked at him. Rev. McCutcheon looked at him.

I said, 'You sent us there, Rev.'

'I didn't tell you to . . .!' He glanced at the last stragglers leaving the church, and lowered his voice. 'I didn't think you would . . .'

'A young girl is missing,' I said.

'That doesn't give you the right to—'

'Yes it does,' I said. 'But you can relax – I'm back to Belfast. The more I think about it, the more I'm convinced she may already have gone in that direction. Forty days in the wilderness, or three in Londonderry, it probably amounts to the same thing; I think she's had her crisis, and now she's going back home.'

Rev. McCutcheon clasped his hands together. 'Do you know – I think you might be right, Mr Starkey. The Lord moves in mysterious ways, and I'm sure Christine does as well. Will you be joining us in the parish hall for tea and sandwiches?'

'No,' I said.

I gave him a nod and turned away. Joe, after a moment's hesitation, came with me. We stepped out into the rain and wind.

Rev. McCutcheon called after us: 'You know, it's never too late to convert!'

We ignored him and kept walking, down the steps and into the car park.

'So, what'd you make of him?' I asked as we splashed across to the car.

'Wouldn't trust him as far as—' Joe began.

But he was interrupted by someone shouting out the Reverend's name. There was an old woman rushing towards us, and then past us. She shouted his name, again, and again; the wind got under her Sunday bonnet and blew it off and she didn't even pause.

'Rev. McCutcheon, come quickly!'

Rev. McCutcheon appeared in the doorway.

'Mrs Wiley, what is it?'

'Rev. McCutcheon! Your house!'

He looked towards his parish house. We looked too. It just looked like an old house in the rain.

'Mrs Wiley, what . . .?'

'The basement!' She was at the church steps now. She had her hand to her chest and was struggling to catch her breath. 'I was just . . . walking past . . . the water's flooding in! The drain's overflowing and it's . . . like a river!'

The Reverend's face looked . . . astonishing. As if someone had pulled out the support beams and all of his features had collapsed.

He staggered down the steps.

He said, 'I must . . . we must . . .'

He began to hurry across the car park, but quickly lost his footing on some unwashed black ice and went sprawling.

We ran up as he regained his feet.

'Please . . .' he said, his face ashen, 'the basement . . . we must . . .'

Joe said, 'Not much you can do about a flood. Call the Department of the—'

'No . . . you don't under—'

He broke through us and continued towards the house. A small group of his parishioners were standing looking helplessly at the water flooding through a fence and down some steps to what must have been a patch of garden just below street level but which was now totally submerged. There was a window with wire across it, but the flood water had already smashed through it and was pouring through into the basement.

The Reverend was fumbling in his jacket for his keys, saying, 'Oh my Lord, oh my Lord.' He found them, but there were at least a dozen keys on the ring and he couldn't find the right one. He said, 'I have to get in . . .'

Joe said, 'Anything valuable down there, it's gone . . .'

The Reverend's eyes widened. They met mine, and I knew, I knew.

'Joe,' I said, 'she's down there. Christine's down there.'

Joe's mouth dropped open a little, then he gave a short nod. He stepped forward, grabbed a handful of the Reverend's jacket and jerked him back with so much force that he went head over heels on to the tarmac. Joe moved up to the door, gave it one mighty kick and it flew open. As he charged into the house the Reverend rolled over and got to his feet. As I followed Joe into the house, the Reverend began to back away.

Joe was already at a door halfway along a dark wood-panelled hall that had a bolt across it and a padlock. He took out his gun and cracked at the lock with the handle. It didn't make any impression at all. He whacked it three more times. Nothing. He turned the gun round and lined up his shot. He squeezed the trigger. Bang. The lock was hanging off, my ears were ringing, and there was a hole in the wall behind me, about an inch to the left of my left ear, where the bullet had ricocheted off the lock and embedded itself.

We both looked at it. Joe laughed. 'That was close!'

My heart was thumping out of my chest.

My ear lobe was singed.

Joe pulled the door open.

There was a light switch to his left, then stairs leading down: I could see the top three but the rest were under water.

Joe said, 'Fuck.'

'She's down there!'

Joe said fuck again.

I squeezed into the doorway beside him.

Joe said fuck again.

'What? She's down there, I know she is . . .'

'If she's down there, she's dead.'

'No, we need to . . .'

Joe looked at the water, dark, freezing, still rising.

'I can't swim,' he said.

'Joe . . .'

'I can't fucking swim!'

I took off my jacket.

351

I said, 'Pick up a brick in your pyjamas.'

Joe said, 'What?'

'That's what you had to do, Bronze medal in primary school.' I kicked off my shoes. 'Dive underwater in your pyjamas and pick up a rubber brick. Like I was ever, ever going to need that skill.'

I moved on to the second step.

Joe said, 'Are you mental? If she's down there, she's dead, and so will you be if you go after her.'

'Didn't you hear me, Joe? I have a bronze medal. They don't just give those out to anyone.'

And I plunged into the water.

43

It wasn't *anything* like diving for a bronze medal.

At school, or, more accurately, at the local swimming pool, the water was warm, there were lifeguards on standby to hook you out if you got into difficulties, and there wasn't seven kinds of shit floating in it. At school there was just one kind of shit floating in it, and he was always fucking doing it. He was a liability. They had to close the whole complex down and get the industrial cleaners in and he swore he wouldn't do it again, but sure as hell a few weeks would pass and he would have another crap in the shallow end. This was nothing like that. It went beyond being a bit cold, slightly uncomfortable. Cold in the past was chipping ice off a windscreen with bare hands, a brain freeze from Harp Ice on a warm day, making the shower a quick one because the immersion hadn't properly heated the water.

This was *cold*.

Cold so you can't feel your legs.

Or you *can* feel them because they're being stabbed repeatedly.

Like the ice bath equivalent of total war.

I was barely submerged before something heavy slammed into my head. My eyes were open and stinging from the dirt; it was a book, and by fuck if it wasn't one of those massive illustrated Bibles, like the devil himself was warning me off. I was stunned, and almost let the breath out of my lungs, but I recovered, I swam on, deeper, down the steps, along a short corridor, pushing crap out of my face the whole way, more books, lamps, empty bottles clunking into my forehead, my feet snagging on curtains and rugs and Venetian blinds all caught up in the washing machine swirl of the flood waters surging around looking for an exit. My chest was straining, already desperate to turn around, get back to fresh air. I didn't know that she was down there; or if she was, if she was a prisoner, if she was dead already, because the water was too high, too furious. If she had been capable of escape, she would have escaped.

I was into the basement, pulling myself along by fixed bookshelves, peering into the murk. There was a heavy oak-looking desk still sitting defiantly on the floor; nearly everything else had floated up. My chest was bursting. Panic set in. The water was flowing in through the broken window, but there was no way to get out through it for air, the force was too great. I had to get all the way along the corridor and back up the steps for another breath. It was already too late. She was dead, and I would be dead too if I left it any longer. Hard luck. Good try. Think of Trish. Think of the grandkid. Think of Sara. Why was I even thinking of Sara? An acquaintance, barely a friend, she'd been battered round the head, she probably wouldn't even be as pretty any more, and then I was wondering if I'd ever thought she was pretty or just never acknowledged it, and that maybe when she did wake up properly she wouldn't remember me, or remember who she was, and I could tell her all sorts of crap, like we were engaged or had been having sex every day and the sooner we got back to that the better, and then I realised that actually I was dying because there was no air left in me and I turned and began to swim back to the corridor knowing full well that there wasn't enough in my lungs to get me all the way along it, but then I saw something, something just above me, a sliver of light, and my brain was saying, don't go towards the light, don't go along that tunnel, that's the end, that's the *very* end, but I couldn't help it because there was nowhere else to go, and the light meant relief, the end to the bursting pains in my heart, so I rose towards it and reached out and I wondered if it would burn if I touched it, just another few inches, but then my foot was caught on something and I pulled at it, pulled and pulled and my chest exploding, fucking computer cables, and I had to claw at it and tear at it and my brain bursting out of my ears and my eyeballs rolling down

my cheeks, but then it was free and the light was the
end I needed and I reached out for it . . . and my fingers
broke free, and a moment later my head came up into
air, and I gasped and spat and heaved and thanked God
for some kind of an air pocket and also for what was
floating there in front of me, a bed like an air bed
bobbing in a holiday swimming pool and with Christine
lying on it, lying on it pale but not blue, asleep but not
dead, Christine, Christine, Christine . . .

I swam to it. I shook her. Her breathing was too deep,
too steady; nobody could sleep through this tumult so I
knew that he had sedated her and that by pure fortune
or chance or God's shining light she had risen with the
flood water, blissfully unaware. I could see now that
there were restraints, some kind of wire around her
wrists securing her to the hollow frame of the bed. I
started to untie her, but my fingers were so numb with
the cold it was like trying to thread a needle wearing
oven gloves. All the while the water was rising, and the
air pocket was diminishing, and the knowledge of it
wasn't helping. I got the nearside hand free and it flopped
down into the water. The shock of it forced a groan from
her, but her eyes remained closed. I made the mistake
of putting weight on the side of the bed so that I could
reach across to her other hand, instead of ducking under
and coming up on the other side; and the next thing I
knew the bed had up-ended, and Christine was on top
of me and wide awake at the sudden freeze and thrashing
around in a mad panic while still half tethered to the
bed. I was trying to keep hold of her while struggling to

free her other hand; I forced her back to the surface and into the shrinking air pocket, where there was now barely room for our two heads. Her eyes were mad and she was fighting, fighting against me, jabbing, butting, biting, and still I tore at the wire. It cut into her and she screamed and she had me by the hair and was dragging me under and there was nothing I could do but grab her by the throat and force her up until her head was pressing against the ceiling and her eyes bulged out as she fought for breath and I screamed her name at her and that I was trying to save her fucking life. Some kind of focus came into those blue eyes, if not clarity or understanding, then she just relaxed against me and I thought she was slipping back into unconsciousness and so I shook her hard, yelling at her that I needed her to stay awake.

I finally managed to pull the wire away from her skin and work at it underwater until it was up into a loop through which I could squeeze her wrist; she was free then and clinging to me, but there was only a couple of inches between the water and the ceiling now. I was kicking for both of us. I clasped her face and made her look at me and told her she needed to take a massive breath and hold it, that we would have to swim a long way, and she nodded and I counted to three, then we took our breaths and dropped under and began our journey.

It was probably an imaginary conversation, caused by lack of oxygen and brain freeze. I turned to her amidst the debris and said, 'God may be omnipotent, but he's not very good at untying chicken wire.' And she said, 'Yes he is. He sent you.' And I said, 'Right. You could apply that to everything that happens in this world.' She said, 'Exactly. That's how he's omnipotent.' And I was in the middle of saying bollocks to that when my head broke into the air, and Joe was standing up to his waist on the steps and behind him the crushed, terrified faces of the New Seekers. And though my ears were frozen and full of sewage, I could read his lips. He was saying: 'I thought you were . . .' and I was coughing and spluttering and he was saying, 'Was there no sign of . . .' when Christine erupted out of the turmoil and Joe grabbed her and dragged her out and up the steps and I was shouting, 'Don't worry about me!' I got out and after them but I only managed a couple of steps before my legs buckled and I was flopping backwards into the flood when two New Seekers grabbed me and dragged me back.

I was much too old for this.

The elders of the church were gathered with us in the kitchen. Christine and I were at a table, sipping coffee, clad in blankets while our clothes whirred around in a tumble dryer; the elders weren't that old, and they had bug eyes because Christine – CHRISTINE! – was sitting drinking Nescafé and being funny and charming and charismatic, all the things you'd generally expect of a clued-in, savvy teenage Messiah. I was just achy and sore to my bones, but also sore because neither

Christine nor the elders would countenance phoning the police so they could go after Reverend McCutcheon. Joe, leaning against the sink, drinking milk from a plastic container, was no help either. He said he'd never called the police in his life and he wasn't about to now. I protested that McCutcheon had kidnapped a young girl, held her hostage, drugged her and who knows what else and he couldn't be allowed to get away with that, and Christine said he really hadn't done anything, that he had just wanted to talk, to know the answers to the big questions, and when she couldn't or wouldn't provide them he had insisted on her staying, and so she had stayed, and next thing she knew she was asleep probably because he'd put something in her drink. But he wasn't malicious, he just had a thirst for knowledge, and was ambitious, though he had a strange way of showing it. It was the way we treated paedophiles in the seventies – oh, they're just a bit funny, they don't mean any harm – and I was getting in a rage about it. Joe told me to relax and enjoy being a hero, and I said I wasn't a hero and everyone disagreed with me. 'A saint, maybe,' I said, and nodded at Christine, 'and you have it in your power to make me one.' Joe said, 'If you're a saint, I'm Greavsie,' and we smiled, partly at the joke, but mostly at the knowledge that nobody else in the room had a clue what we were talking about, and by at least twenty years.

They wanted her to stay.

They wanted to make it up to her.

They wanted her to preach in their church, which was her church, and bless them and lead them to the Promised Land.

But she wanted a Pot Noodle and to hit the road.

She told them not to worry, that she loved Derry and loved their church, and she would come back, that there was much work to be done but they were strong enough to do it; God had tested them and they had come through stronger than ever. In short, she told them exactly what they wanted to hear, while at the same time moving towards the exit.

We walked out to the car. The rain had stopped, the water was finally beginning to drain away. I was three quarters of a saint or two thirds of a hero, but I didn't much feel like either, I just felt like getting out of Londonderry.

I said this to Joe and he asked me why I kept calling it Londonderry.

'Because that's what it's called,' I said.

Joe said, 'You fucking header, and you wonder why other people don't move on? I'm as Prod and loyal as they come and I've been calling it Derry for years.'

I said, 'Then you can't be that Prod or loyal.'

He gave me a long look and then said, 'You just like winding people up, don't you?'

'That's my job,' I said.

44

We drove out of Derry. Joe beside me, his bag of weapons in the boot. Christine was in the back. We were leaving the madness of the Maiden City behind and heading for home. The police were running around like headless chickens looking for escaped convicts. They weren't helped by the fact that they didn't even seem to know exactly who they were looking for. There were checkpoints everywhere; we were waved through them all. I looked at Christine in the mirror and said, 'You're doing that Obi-Wan Kenobi mind thing with the stormtroopers, aren't you?' And she said, 'What?'

Maybe we were just lucky.

Home was an hour and a half away. Even though I didn't see that much of Patricia, knowing she was there, close at hand, made Belfast worth living in. I had no blood connection to Bobby or Lol or little Dan, but I was sure that familiarity would breed content. For the umpteenth time in my life someone had tried to kill me – *Sunny Jim, burning building*; I had been beaten up – *Harry Lime, gay costume designer* – and I had almost drowned – *basement dungeon, icy flood*. I was tired, just tired. I didn't even fancy a drink. I had been experiencing a mild hangover since 1979 and I was tired of that too. I had never made a serious effort to give it up, and *would not* be told, but now maybe it was time. Hanging around in bars in middle age was not cool, and drinking alone at home was worse. Maybe I could be a better, nicer person. Reconnect properly with Trish. Or maybe there was even an outside chance of making it with poor, battered Sara Patterson. Perhaps abstinence would make the heart grow fonder. Joe asked me what I was smiling at, and I said that my ice bath had cleared my head, that I was seeing things properly for the first time in weeks, maybe months or years.

'Endorphins,' said Joe. 'They'll disappear soon enough.'

'Brilliant,' I said.

We passed by Claudy, and then entered Dungiven. I stopped at a garage to fill up and Joe got out to get coffee. He asked Christine if she wanted anything and she just shook her head. She had been chirpy enough on the first part of our journey home, but in the past five minutes she'd fallen silent. Now that I looked at her properly, I saw how pale and sweaty she looked; she'd been held captive, and drugged, and forced to swim through filthy icy water, so I shouldn't really have been surprised that she was succumbing to something; but something else pinged at me too, that this was how she had been last time we were on the Glenshane Pass. Now it was just a couple of miles ahead of us.

I asked her if she was okay, and she nodded.

'Just a bit cold.'

I followed Joe into the shop and got her a hot chocolate.

She sipped it in the back and as we set off again I cranked the heat up.

We began to rise up on to the Pass. Here the snow, which had by now largely been washed away from Derry and much of the surrounding countryside, remained thick, and hung ominously over the road in deep banks. The cloud was lying low and grey and damp. I could see the High Chaparral up ahead with its red neon sign, and half a dozen cars parked for lunch, and the road beyond it winding in and out as the Pass rose to its highest point, which was lost in the mist.

As we were approaching the bar I said, 'Do you fancy stopping for lunch, just for old times' sake?' and glanced back at Christine, but she didn't seem to hear me. She was clutching her stomach and there was sweat rolling down her brow.

I said, 'Shit.'

Joe said, 'Bollocks,' but not because of Christine. He was looking in his side mirror. He turned and we both stared out of the back window at the police car with its flashing lights coming up behind us. I slowed down, hoping it would pass us on the way to something important, but instead it drew right up and gave us the full beams and we both swore again and I pulled the car into the side of the road just past the entrance to the High Chaparral.

We sat there, waiting.

I glanced at Joe and said, 'The guns in the boot? I don't suppose you have a firearms licence or anything as civilised as that?'

'Course not,' said Joe.

The police car sat behind us, full beams on, lights flashing, but no movement.

I said, 'What are they waiting for?'

'Checking the number plates,' said Joe.

'Why would they do that?'

'Maybe you were speeding.'

'I wasn't speeding.'

'Maybe you thought you weren't but you actually were.'

'What're we going to do?'

'We're going to stay calm. And besides . . .'

He opened his jacket and angled the inside pocket towards me. I could see the handle of his skinning knife.

'Oh for fuck sake,' I said.

Behind us, the doors opened. I watched in the mirror as two police officers climbed out. One came up to my window. The other stayed at the back and slightly to the right, giving him a good view of both sides of the car. He had his pistol drawn.

The officer on my side tapped my window and then moved back several feet. He said, 'Sir, would you step out of the vehicle.'

I said, 'What seems to be the problem?'

He said, 'Step out of the vehicle.'

I glanced at Joe and he gave me the nod. I glanced at Christine and was going to tell her to buck up her act and get the Jedi thing working, but her eyes were closed.

I got out. He asked to see my driving licence and I handed it over. He asked me if I was the owner of the vehicle and I said I was. He asked if I had the log book and insurance with me, as required by law, and I said, 'Ah – I see what you're worried about.'

It had come to me that they were on the lookout for my car because they would have established that the prison break was launched from the caravan site and my driving documents would have been found lying in the car park, thus linking me to the escape.

I said, 'I can explain.'

Before he could agree to that, the passenger door opened and Joe got out. He came round and stood beside me. Both cops watched him like hawks.

The cop in front of us asked Joe for his ID.

Joe said he didn't routinely carry it.

They asked for his name and address and he gave both. It was a different name and an address I'd never heard of, though he gave it with conviction, right down to the postcode.

The closest cop said, 'And who's in the back?'

'My daughter,' I said, and not for the first time.

'Could you ask her to step out of the vehicle as well?'

'She's really not feeling very well.'

'Nevertheless.'

I turned and looked at Christine. Her eyes were open now. I indicated for her to join us. Her door opened, but instead of climbing out and standing beside us, she tumbled out, landed on her knees and began to throw up.

The cop in front looked confused.

'What's wrong with her?' the other demanded.

'Carsick,' I said, and started to move to help her, but he hissed, 'Just stay where you are!'

I put my hands up and said, 'Anything you say.'

The first officer moved beside Christine and crouched down. 'You all right, love?' he asked.

Christine retched again. He put a hand on her back and rubbed at it. He said, 'I don't think she's carsick.' He helped her up and into the back of the car. She sat with the door open, her legs hanging out and her white face resting on the seat.

The cop stepped away from her and said, 'Would you mind opening the boot?'

I glanced at Joe.

The second cop said, 'You can either do it now, or in a couple of minutes when our colleagues get here.'

Joe nodded at me.

I took the keys out of the ignition and moved to the back of the car. I put the key in and was just turning it when the first cop said, 'Stop. I'll take it from here. Now back up.'

I moved back.

I looked at Joe. He was moving slightly, pressure first

on one foot, then the other, like he was getting ready to attack. He could handle himself; I also knew he wasn't particularly fond of cops and had a skinning knife in his jacket.

Somewhere above us there was a rumbling, like approaching thunder.

The first cop, looking in the boot, said, 'So what's this?'

I just wanted to go home. I sighed. I might not be going home for months.

I said, 'What does it look like?'

He said, 'It looks like – is it a bed? No, a cot. Ah, right. IKEA. Those are right bastards to put together.'

I said, 'Tell me about it.'

The second cop said, 'Check what else there is.'

Whatever way Joe had organised it, the IKEA box was taking up almost the entire space. It was lying open with the different lengths of bar spilling out. Their weight and their dispersion meant that they would all have to be lifted out before the rest of the boot could be searched.

The first cop said, 'I'll need a hand.'

The rumbling sound was growing louder, and I thought, great, I'm going to get another drenching, but then I saw that Joe was looking up the Pass. I looked that way too, up to the highest visible point, where the sound seemed to be coming from, and as I did, a green truck with a canvas cover emerged with a diesel roar from the mist. A moment later another appeared behind it, then another, and another, until there was a long string of them negotiating the curves of the descent. Not for the first time, the army was coming to the relief of Derry, though this time it wasn't to end a siege but to help an over-whelmed police force with the mopping-up of escaped prisoners.

'Brits are back,' I said. 'Wonder if they'll stay as long as they did last time.'

The second cop gave me a frosty look and moved to the boot. He put one hand on the IKEA box and indicated for his comrade to do the same at the other end while keeping his gun trained on us. Though mostly on Joe. There was something about him.

The four-tonners were advancing towards us. A round dozen. Maybe a couple of hundred soldiers to hunt down mostly minimum-security prisoners freezing their bollocks off in the wilds of the north-west.

The surlier cop was finding it difficult to shift the cot using just the one hand.

He shouted across to me, 'Hey – you. Take this end.'

He stepped away from the boot.

I gave him a shrug and moved up. I said, 'While we're here, maybe we could put it together.'

The other cop just looked at me.

I took hold of the cot and helped him lift it out.

Joe's bag was sitting there.

The surly cop said, 'Hey, what the hell are you doing?'

I looked to Joe, who was just standing there.

And then I realised it wasn't him, or me.

Christine was out of the vehicle again.

But she wasn't being sick; she had stepped out on

to the road, and now she was walking, very deliberately, towards the oncoming trucks.

I shouted after her.

But she kept on.

The cops were yelling too.

She picked up speed.

The little sick girl was running full pelt at the four-tonners speeding down the hill straight towards her.

And then she stopped.

And spread her arms.

And waited to be hit.

The first truck slammed on its brakes and there was a screech, and I put a hand up to blot it out, because I'd seen a lot of death and I didn't want to see this one.

There was a crash, loud, metal corrupting, yells and shouts.

But when I moved my hand, Christine was still standing there, and the first truck was inches from her thin little crucifix body, but the second had piled into the back of it, and the third into the back of the second. Soldiers were jumping down and shouting out and gathering round. The cops had forgotten themselves and were moving towards the girl and the crashed trucks and the soldiers.

And Joe was beside me saying, 'No time like the present.'

He reached into the boot, grabbed the bag and was just about to throw it as far as he could when I said, 'No.'

'What the fuck?'

'Wait,' I said.

There was something Christine was saying, even though she didn't know she was saying it.

She had been sick on the way to Derry, on the way back. Same place, no reason, no warnings, just violently ill.

Here. By the High Chaparral.

And something had moved her to it.

And I didn't give a damn if it was ley lines, God moving in mysterious ways, or she was snorting crush, there were alarm bells ringing. Something had forced her out of the car, something had caused her to step in front of those trucks.

I was staring at her, with the soldiers now surrounding her, not knowing what to do.

The army trucks, backed up.

The police stopping halfway there, realising they'd each started running to help her thinking the other would stand guard on their suspects.

The army, usually confined to barracks, brought in to help quell Sunny Jim's prison break.

Sunny Jim's master plan.

From a medium-security prison.

Accountants and drunks and street-corner dealers.

Or a spectacular strike against the British Army.

What had Danny Lynch said – that Sunny Jim joined the army and got the best training in the world?

A dozen trucks, hundreds of soldiers on an exposed road, the most direct route to the north-west. A military target, no civilians at risk.

What did Sunny Jim have first-hand experience of?
Roadside bombs.

I stared along the road towards the convoy. And then
back along it as far as the High Chaparral. And as my
eyes roved across, I saw something I could only have
seen from this position, once I was past the bar: the
back end of a blue Jaguar car peeking out.

A bar.

A restaurant.

A command post.

'Jesus Christ, Joe, they've booby-trapped the fucking
road!'

'They . . .'

There was no way of knowing if Christine, somehow
forewarned, had stopped them short or if even now
they were on the verge of extinction.

'They're in the bar, Joe, the bar! Sunny Jim!'

Joe stared at the bar. He looked back at the army
and the police. Then he said, 'Fucking hell.'

He opened his bag. He took out his gun. He took out
another. He held it out to me.

I am useless.

But I took it.

Joe was smiling.

Fucking smiling.

He said, 'So what's the plan?'

'This,' I said.

I raised the pistol.

I pointed it at the convoy.

And I started shooting.

Joe said, 'What the . . .?'

The soldiers began to scatter. Those who hadn't already jumped from their vehicles now threw themselves out and dived for the sparse undergrowth away from the exposed road. One of them grabbed Christine and carried her under his arm.

'And now,' I said, 'we run like fucking fuck.'

'Where?'

Joe ducked down as a bullet whizzed past him and cracked into my car.

'There!' I said, already moving, already charging towards the High Chaparral.

There was just something, some crackpot notion that came to me, that if we ran in that direction, the soldiers would get up and follow us and somehow stop Sunny and his gang doing what I knew they were going to do. I somehow didn't consider that Sunny and his men might shoot us down before we got anywhere near them.

Joe caught me within a few strides.

Then we were both running full pelt towards the High Chaparral with bullets now cracking and yipping around us from both sides.

But we kept on straight, not even dodging and weaving.

We charged through the gates and:

KABOOM!

A massive explosion somewhere behind us knocked us flying.

I was still in the air when . . .

KABOOM!
KABOOM!
KABOOM!

. . . three more massive detonations rocked the Pass.

I landed in a heap still twenty metres short of the bar. I just had a glimpse of it, with all its windows shattered, before debris began to rain down on us. Rocks and stones and dirt and plants and twisted pieces of metal. We lay there with our hands over our heads and our faces pressed into the gravel until the rain began to lighten.

'You okay?' but I sounded like someone else, someone far away.

'I don't fucking know!' and he sounded the same.

I rolled over, let out my latest groan and peered through the smoke and dust. The road we had just run along was as decimated as a First World War battlefield. The first two trucks were shredded – but the others were largely untouched. Some of the soldiers were just beginning to rise from their positions, but then someone shouted out: 'Keep down! Keep down!'

I rolled back over. Figures were now emerging from a side door of the High Chaparral and hurrying across the car park.

They did not look much like diners caught up in a terrorist attack.

They wore balaclavas and carried pistols and rifles.

It seemed like there were a lot of them.

Sunny Jim's blue Jag was the first off the mark.

Of course it was. He would make the fastest getaway because he could, because he was in a different league.

And there was only one way out, and it was along the gravelled track before us and through the open gates behind us.

Sunny Jim in his blue Jag with three other cars behind, with gunmen hanging out of the windows yipping and hollering at the carnage they thought they had caused. Hardly even aware that we were lying there in front of them.

At least until Joe sat up, like he was on a picnic and had decided on some fun after a lazy doze, and started cracking off bullets at the speeding Jag.

And because I was bored, and am easily led, I sat up too and fired off what I had left.

I probably didn't hit anything.

But Joe did.

He took the driver out with his first shot, and the Jag just came to a dead stop, the driver's foot jammed down on the brake. The car behind crashed into the back and the one behind crashed into that one, and so the sweet sound of another concertina was added to the crackle of gunfire and the over-revving of engines. Bullets were erupting all around us and I could no longer tell if they were coming from behind or in front. I just lay back flat like I was dead because I was quite sure that I soon would be. I had no bullets left anyway. I had done my little bit to avert a massacre and that wasn't such a bad way to go out of things, a saint and hero twice in one day when I'd been such a loser for most of the other ones.

But of course, I could not stay dead.
I had to know what was going on.
I moved my head up, just an inch, just to see.
And *whump*.

45

It was dark, completely dark. I was lying on something soft, something musty and scratchy and catty, and from feeling around and being a world-renowned expert in lounging, I judged it to be a sofa. I touched my face, the swollen nose. When my fingers reached my forehead, I winced. Blood there, sticky, a cut, a graze. Foreheads bleed a lot. Even a little nick. If there was a bullet in there I probably wouldn't be alive. And I did feel alive. Remarkably alive. The rest of me was aching, but no more so than usual. I stretched my hand out and it connected with something cold, which fell over and hit a wooden floor and gave a plastic glug. I felt around until I got hold of it – a bottle. I released the top and raised it to my clogged nose and sniffed at it. It didn't smell of anything in particular, so I took the tiniest mouthful. Then I drained it. It was water. Probably.

The light went on. I shielded my eyes and said, 'Is it time for work?'

'Fuck up. They want you downstairs.'

When my eyes cleared sufficiently, I saw that it was the guy who'd been with Patrick when they'd discovered me on top of the caravan. Only his head and shoulders were visible. I was in a converted, windowless roof space. I presumed he was standing on steps. Either that or he was levitating. I said, 'Where am I?'

'Safe house,' he growled.

'Safe for me?'

'Yeah, right.'

I sat up, and wished I hadn't. I clutched at my head and groaned.

He told me to hurry up.

I looked at him. I also looked at the square panel he had pushed up to allow him access, and at the lagged water tank on the other side of it. I realised that all I needed to do was go over and kick him in the teeth, force the panel closed and stand on it and they would then be unable to get at me. I would have plenty of water to drink. I could hold out for days. I could also make a hole in the roof, knock out a couple of slates and yell for help. And then I thought that they could certainly shoot me through the panel, or smoke or burn me out, and that if I was a prisoner in the Bogside and hollered for help out of a hole in the roof they would probably shout back, 'You've made your bed so you can lie in it'; mostly I was coming to the realisation that I wasn't thinking straight because of blood loss and terror. In certain quarters I was considered a saint and a hero, but it was so subjective; since I had screwed up their massacre, my captors probably wouldn't feel that way. I didn't know how I'd ended up in someone's roof space; why they had taken the time and trouble to load me into a car and spirit me away from what was literally a battlefield when they could much more easily have finished the job where I lay.

But I was going to find out.

I did a kind of stagger-shuffle across to the opening and reversed on to a set of ladders. The guy had already descended. When I got to the bottom I was escorted along a poorly lit hall and then down two flights of stairs. It was an old house, with damp spots on the ceiling and the wallpaper peeling away from the very top of the walls. There was a window on the first-floor landing that gave me a view out across a large overgrown garden, neighbouring houses that were probably more than a shout away, and the Foyle beyond. I wasn't in the Bogside. I was in the Waterside. Smart idea to have your safe house in what was, ostensibly, enemy territory.

I was walked along a passageway, and past an open kitchen door through which I could see what looked like an old Victorian range, antique plates displayed on shelves, and a long wooden table around which a family appeared to be enjoying a meal. They didn't look up. I was taken through a stone-floored utility room and out of a back door. It was night-time, stars out, the air crisp and cold. I crossed a yard strewn with discarded fridges and cookers and bikes and masonry towards a long white-walled shed with a rusting corrugated-iron roof. We entered through a side door. It was a workshop full of drills and hammers and angle grinders and tools I would never have any use for or understanding of. There was a chair in the middle of the concrete floor. The chair was for me. I sat in it and nodded around the interior and said, 'I never really got DIY. Why do it yourself when you can get someone else to do it for you, and properly. My wife's very good that way. You married?'

My escort just looked at me.

I said, 'I'm Dan. You are?' When he said nothing, I said, 'I'll call you Liam. Everyone needs a name.'

There were footsteps across the yard.

I said, 'Liam, I want you to know I don't blame you for any of this. Unless, of course, it gets violent again, in which case I hold you totally responsible.'

He shook his head at me.

Patrick and Michael appeared in the doorway. Sunny Jim followed them in. He was smiling. It was not a good look. Of course, he was starting from a disadvantaged position. He said, 'Starkey, the spanner in my works.'

He stood to one side, and then nodded at Danny Lynch as he entered the workshop. Danny in a smart suit that would not have looked out of place at an undertaker's, Danny who had been pulling the strings all along.

I said, 'My lucky day. Hansel *and* Gretel.'

'Starkey,' said Danny, 'you always were a pain in the hole.'

I looked from one to the other and said, 'Has *no one* got a kind word for me?'

'And always the joker. Well – I'll give you a kind word. Curious. You're certainly that.' He turned to Sunny. 'Remind me, James – what did curiosity do?'

Sunny Jim said, 'I'm not here for fucking parlour games, Danny. Let's just get this done.' Danny gave the slightest of shrugs. Sunny came up close. 'You're probably wondering why you're here at all, Starkey.'

'Nope, not curious at all.'

'I'm going to ask you some questions. You're going to die. A swift bullet to the head; or sometime in the next twenty-four hours, long and slow and not very pleasant. It will depend on the quality of your answers. I believe my friend Patrick has a score to settle with you.'

I looked at Patrick, with his tragic face. There were a lot of them about, not least my own. He just might enjoy working on me. As if to confirm this, he strolled across to one of the work benches and began to peruse the hammers.

I said, 'I think I'll go for the long, slow death. That way there's always a chance of the cavalry coming over the horizon.'

'There's no chance of that,' said Danny.

'In that case, I'll bend over backwards to help.'

Patrick came forward with a hammer.

He hit my knee.

I went, 'Fuck! For fuck sake, you haven't even asked me any questions yet!' and cradled it.

'We're not fucking messing,' said Sunny. He turned to Michael and said, 'Hold him.'

Michael moved behind me, put his hands on my shoulders and took a firm grip.

'Okay, Starkey,' said Sunny, 'it's quite simple really. How did you know the army trucks were going to be there, on the Pass, at that particular time?'

'I didn't.'

Patrick hit my other knee. My body automatically tried to bend forward to protect it, but Michael held me in place. I let out a yell. It was quite high-pitched.

'Let's try that again.'

I cried out, 'I'm trying to tell you the fucking truth! Look, if you want me to make something up, I can – but we were just driving home and we got stopped by the cops. If we hadn't been stopped by the cops we would have been away past the army trucks and wouldn't have known a thing about it.'

Sunny nodded at Patrick, and he whacked my left knee again.

I said, 'Fucking fucking fuck the Pope.'

'Let's try it again. You stopped outside the bar. You told the police what was happening and you sent the girl forward to stop the trucks. Then you led the soldiers to us.'

'No, that's not how it happened—'

Patrick whacked me again.

He wasn't even asked to.

This time he hit my arm.

I yelled.

I'm not a brave man. I would have given up Anne Frank if the Nazis had switched one bar off on a three-bar electric heater. I believe in honesty, and love, and beauty, and sex, and Liverpool, and the Clash, but above all I believe in self-preservation.

'Starkey,' said Danny, 'just tell us, you'll save yourself a lot of pain.'

'I am . . .'

'Then who betrayed us?' Sunny roared. 'Which fucker sold us out?'

I should have guessed that this was his main concern, that something we had stumbled upon, or been guided to by fate or Christine, was actually a result of dissension in his ranks, that a trusted aide had betrayed him. Sunny's moment of triumph had been snatched away from him and he was looking to blame someone from within.

I glanced back at poor thick Michael. I could easily have fingered him, back when I thought Danny and Sunny were on different sides, but not now that they were working together.

'Okay . . .' I said, rubbing at my arm, 'enough . . . Jesus . . . look . . . it's not a national secret. I just thought you knew this already.'

'Knew what?'

'Harry Lime. It was Harry Lime.'

'What're you talking about? The fruit?'

'He told me all about it. Billy the Bear told him.'

'Billy didn't know!'

Sunny Jim stepped up closer. He put his hand out

and took the hammer off Patrick and raised it. 'Now tell me the fucking truth . . .!'

'Wait . . . wait! Look . . . Billy mightn't have known it all, but he knew enough. You sent him into prison to set up the escape; maybe he worked it out from there, or someone squealed to him. All I know is Harry knew about it, and he told me . . .'

'And why would he tell you? Why wouldn't he go to the police?'

'Because he wanted to be a hero and bring you down himself! Maybe he saw one too many plays, wanted to star in one, but that's why we were at the caravan park, he led us there . . .'

'So if you knew about the break, and you know about the army, why didn't you do anything about it, Starkey?'

'I don't know!'

Sunny swung with the hammer, arm right back for extra force, but just as it was beginning its downward trajectory, it was stopped suddenly by Danny Lynch reaching out and catching his hand.

'What the fu—'

'Enough,' said Danny.

'You don't tell me what . . .!' Sunny yelled, wrenching the hammer free.

'In this case I do.'

They stood, face to burned face, eye to jaundiced eye.

'Listen, James,' said Danny, 'I'm not in the torture business, and frankly, with everything going on, we're running out of time for it. Besides, I think he's telling the truth.'

'He's not fucking—'

'Listen to me. Billy knew enough. And I know exactly why Starkey didn't go to the police. Harry Lime wasn't the only drama queen around – I know Starkey of old, and he's always wanted to be the big man in the big picture. He wanted to save the day, he's the one wanted to be the big hero. But actually he's as chicken as they come. When it came to standing up, walking through a minefield and stopping those trucks, he couldn't do it. He sent a little girl to do it instead. He's a piece of shit. So let's not waste any more time on him, just finish it off and let's get the hell out of here.'

They hadn't broken eye contact throughout. Danny Lynch was the first to look away. He opened his jacket, slipped a hand in and produced a gun. He handed it to Sunny.

'Fuck this,' said Sunny, dropping the hammer and taking hold of the pistol. He turned his mad horror face to me.

I said, 'It's customary to let a man have a final cigarette, or compose a message to his loved—'

'Fuck up,' said Sunny Jim. He raised the gun to my face, and pulled the trigger.

It clicked.

Just clicked.

He pulled it again and again and again.

Then he looked at Danny and said, 'What the fuck?'

Danny said, 'Sorry, my mistake. Michael, would you do the honours?'

Michael took a gun out of his coat. He checked that it was loaded. Then he raised it and shot Sunny Jim through the eye.

Sunny looked a little surprised.

As Sunny was falling, Michael switched to Patrick and put a bullet in his throat. Patrick stumbled off to the side, collapsed on top of one of the work benches and began to bleed out over the tools.

Patrick looked somewhat astonished himself.

Michael was behind me still. I was waiting to feel the gun at the back of my head.

Danny Lynch, the unruffled undertaker, stood before me.

He said, 'I do like it when a plan comes together.'

I glanced very briefly at Michael. He was putting the gun away.

I said, 'I don't want to be presumptuous, but am I off the hook here?'

'Oh aye,' said Danny.

Michael moved round and stood beside him. Danny peered down at Sunny, clearly dead on the ground. He reached down and removed his own gun from Sunny's hand and put it back in his jacket. He smiled at me and said, 'I never have it loaded. I'm actually quite quick to anger and it's far too easy to kill someone when you've the means. I much prefer to talk it out.' He saw my eyes flit to Sunny. 'There are always exceptions,' he added.

I shook my head. 'I don't really know what's happened here.'

'Starkey, when you make a cocktail, you want to shake it really hard, but you don't want to break the shaker.'

'That's much clearer,' I said.

'Well, let's just fall back on a cliché, then. Keep your friends close, but your enemies closer. In case you don't know, that's from Sun *Tzu*, as opposed to Sun*ny*. *The Art of War*. Know it?'

'Sure. It's on my bedside table.'

'Starkey . . .' He let out an exasperated sigh. 'My point is, Sun Tzu and Sunny were both masters of war. Which is all well and good when you are at war. But we're at peace.'

'But the prison break, and the army . . .'

'Well, sometimes when you're at peace people forget there's a potential for war. So they have to be reminded. The prison was one part of it, and what *might* have happened with the army was another. The roadside bombs were never supposed to go off; it was only meant to be a show of strength. But Sunny insisted on going his own way. He would have loved a massacre, but it would have been counterproductive. He was a liability.'

I nodded at dead Patrick and said, 'You killed your nephew.'

'Cousin,' said Danny, 'about six times removed. On that basis most of Derry's related to me. I'll get over it.'

'And he was your mate,' I said to Michael.

'Not really,' said Michael. 'He was a bit annoying. And slow on the uptake.'

'Right,' I said. 'And what about the guy I was with? Joe. Is he dead?'

Danny looked at Michael. 'Is that the guy who . . .?'

'That's him,' said Michael, 'the fuckin' head-the-ball I was telling you about. He was shooting away at us, then he ran out of bullets and just charged at us. He took about six of our guys out and was banging away at the rest of them when we got outta there, skin of our teeth. Nah, he's not dead. I heard the cops took him away, and it took a right bunch of them to do it too.'

Well that would have made Joe happy, I thought.

Good old butcher Joe, who'd saved my life.

'Starkey?' said Danny. 'One thing. How *did* you know about the bombs? Because I'm pretty sure Billy only knew about the prison, and I'm not sure that his bum chum even knew about that, let alone the army thing.'

'Is this some kind of trick question, where I tell you the truth and then you kill me?'

'No.'

'You would say that.' He was about to respond, but I cut him off. 'But actually, it doesn't matter, because you can still shoot me, whatever I say. So the truth is that I didn't know about it. The cops must have been on the lookout for my car, and they just happened to pull me over on the Pass.'

Michael nodded beside Danny. 'The cops were there for about an hour before they arrived,' he said, 'and Sunny was going to send us out to kill them, but then it all kicked off anyway.'

'But what about this girl?' Danny asked. 'The one who stopped the trucks. Who told her to do that? How did she know to stop them short of the danger zone if you didn't tell her? More importantly, who the fuck is she working for that she had access to that kind of detailed information?'

'God knows,' I replied, 'but I think we should all be on our toes.'

The bodies, they said, would be disposed of.

We passed through the house again and the family still didn't look up. They were well trained, or terrified, or both.

Outside the house there was a red Volvo waiting for us. The curator of the Irish Republican Archive was sitting behind the wheel. As I got in, he asked me how it was going and I said it was going okay. As we pulled out, Danny Lynch asked where he could drop me and I had to think about that. My car had been caught up in the events at the Pass and I was sure the cops were all over it. The police had Joe the Butcher and probably would for sometime. And I hadn't a clue about Christine. Danny Lynch would not have let me live, or let me go, if he thought I had anything that could connect him to either the prison break or the bombs on the Pass. The best thing would probably be to walk into the police station and ask after my car. To act dumb.

I knew there would be exhaustive questioning to come, but for now I was just exhausted, and battered, and bloody, and I wanted to go home. I checked the time, and it was too late to catch a train. But there were night buses that would have me in Belfast in a couple of hours. As we drove along, I realised that I had no car, and no phone or wallet – and I'd no desire to go back to the safe house to look for them and no desire to prolong my association with Danny Lynch and his comrades. So I asked the curator to drop me at the hospital. It was only a couple of minutes away. When we pulled into the car park, Michael got out and opened the back door for me. I said to him, 'With all this going on, I hope you haven't missed your paper round.' He didn't realise it was a rhetorical question and only stopped his explanation of how he hadn't when I turned away from him and bent to Danny Lynch's window. I tapped on it and it came down. He said, 'Starkey?' I said, 'Sara Patterson. The reporter. Was that done on your orders?'

'Nope. That was Sunny throwing his weight around again.'

I nodded and turned away.

'Starkey?' I stopped and looked back. 'What would you have done if I'd said yes, it was me?'

'I'd have hunted you down.'

And, funny, I was able to say it with a straight face.

And he was able to hear it without bursting into laughter.

Maybe we both knew that far from being luckless, I always managed to walk or limp away. That not only was I insatiably curious, I was also like a dog with a bone. That the bad guy usually lost.

I walked into the hospital.

A nurse took one look at the cut on my head, the blood on my clothes and the state of my swollen face and tried to direct me to the casualty department. But I just kept going until I came to Sara's room. I looked through the glass panel in the door. Her light was on and she was sitting up in bed watching television. It had been about twelve hours since I'd left her, barely conscious and still wired up. The improvement was remarkable. The wires were off and the monitors gone and she was drinking from a can of Coke. I opened the door and stepped in. She looked at me.

I nodded.

She nodded.

I pulled out the chair meant for visitors and positioned it so that I also had a view of the screen.

She said, 'I saw your pal earlier.'

I said, 'I don't have any pals.'

'Joe the Butcher. Bandage on his head, arm in a sling, and a lot to say about the price of mince and the sexuality of his armed guard.'

'That's Joe,' I said. I nodded at the TV. 'Anything good?'

'Movie,' she said. 'And no.'

We watched some of it.

After a bit she said, 'Man from the *Telegraph* was here too.'

'Yes, I met him earlier. Nice chap.'

'He had three cracked ribs. He was in agony.'

'Nothing to do with me,' I said.

'He seemed to think you'd scammed a room off us.'

'He did seem very suspicious,' I said.

'And you told the doctor you were my fiancé.'

'He must have misheard,' I said, 'though I am open to offers.'

There was a commercial break.

She said, 'You look like shit.'

'You're no oil painting yourself.'

She said, 'What are you even doing here?'

'I was wondering if I could borrow a tenner,' I said. 'For the bus home.'

She said, 'What the hell can you get for a tenner these days, Starkey?'

I rested my head back against the chair. It was good to know that there wasn't someone behind it with a roll of sticky tape or a gun. It was nice to relax and enjoy the mugginess of a private room in a National Health hospital, and to feel safe, and to know that Sara was recovering beside me, that Joe was okay, Christine hadn't drowned and that Trish and Bobby and Lol and little Dan were all alive and well and getting on with their small, uneventful lives, and I came to an instant decision: that that was exactly the kind of small, uneventful existence that would make me very happy indeed. I was going to get out of this game, because it wasn't a game, it was hell and I was done with it.

I smiled at Sara and said, 'Do you want to shift over so I can put my head down?'

She smiled back and said, 'Absolutely not, you bloody chancer.'